HIGH STEEL

JACK C. HALDEMAN II
AND
JACK DANN

TOR®

A TOM DOHERTY ASSOCIATES BOOK
NEW YORK

This is a work of fiction. All the characters and events portrayed in this book are fictitious, and any resemblance to real people or events is purely coincidental.

HIGH STEEL

Cover art by Tim Jacobus

A Tor Book
Published by Tom Doherty Associates, Inc.
175 Fifth Avenue
New York, N.Y. 10010

Tor® is a registered trademark of Tom Doherty Associates, Inc.

ISBN: 0-812-51433-5
Library of Congress Catalog Card Number: 93-17044

First edition: July 1993
First mass market edition: June 1994

Printed in the United States of America

0 9 8 7 6 5 4 3 2 1

Praise for *High Steel*
by Jack C. Haldeman II & Jack Dann

"Put your money down and take home *High Steel*, a novel of science fiction that lingers in the mind as only the best such writing does. . . . One hell of a read."

—Harry Crews, author of *Body*

"An occasion and a triumph!"

—Barry N. Malzberg

"A remarkable success. What makes [*High Steel*] so intriguing, I think, is the authors' concentration on narrative. . . . The book is a predator, like a cat with blazing eyes, gorging on the good meat of genre: Dick, William Gibson, Greg Bear (for transcendental AI-shamanism shticks here very succinctly conveyed), Joe Haldeman, many others. There are aliens, and Jupiter, and FTL, and Einstein the AI god, and New England School of Ethical Romance sehnsucht *à la* Richard Grant and Co, and the kitchen sink. And it spins high and dry and off the end of the last word. It is most highly recommended."

—John Clute, *Interzone*

The authors would like to thank the following people whose support, aid, and inspiration were invaluable:

Richard Alverson, Harry Crews, Patrick Delahunt, Edward L. Ferman, Dannie Gordon, Joe W. Haldeman, Vol Haldeman, Merrilee Heifetz, Trina King, Louise Kleba, Barry N. Malzberg, Kim Mohan, William Nabors, Jeanne Van Buren Dann, Karen and Bob Van Kleeck, Albert White, Sheila Williams.

They are sending me a voice,
From there, where the sun goes.

Our Grandfather is sending me a voice
From there, where the sun goes down.

I hear them talk, they come to me.
I hear them talk, they call to me.

I hear our Grandfather's voice
He is the winged One.

He lives there, where the Giant lives,
He is sending me a voice.

—Sweat lodge song

HIGH STEEL

Data Burst ID = 1105033HBD

From: CEH [Farside Station]
To: John Stranger [SOC 187735-NN-000]
Location: Trans-United Reservation D5-South Dakota-116

Date: 4 Apr 2177
Time: 1:46 P.M. GMT

Subject: Draft Notification

Note: An immediate reply to this transmission is mandatory by law. Refer to Trans-United Directive 2045 E, Section 12, also known as Tribal Treaty Sundown.

++++++++++ start personal copy ++++++++++

Dear John Stranger,

Greetings from the Trans-United Space Engineering Corporation.

Congratulations upon being selected by T.U.S.E. for orientation and training on Station Central. To serve is an honor.

You will report to your terminal induction building on 7 April, 2177 at 6:00 P.M. local time.

Do not bring toilet articles or a change of clothes. Everything you need will be provided.

Welcome aboard, from your Trans-United Draft Council.

Your presence is required by law and tribal treaty.

++++++++++ end personal copy ++++++++++

Reference: USCC Directive 27AI—Indigenous People Act.

Print locations: Remote 2, Local 7.

Key: SOC 1877335-NN-00

The old man walked beside John Stranger, staring down at the rocky trail. It was not a time to talk. His face was leather, as wrinkled as the earth. His lips were chapped and parched, as if they had never touched water. Years beyond counting had marked him, molded him. Now he was ageless, timeless.

The stark landscape stretched out below them: muddy columns carved by wind, deep ravines, vertical dikes, fluted ridges. It was desolate country. But it was their country. The way down would be difficult, but Broken-finger could climb almost as well as John. He often boasted that the Great Spirit would not make him weak and sick before taking him "south"—the direction of death. He had always been strong. He was an Indian, not a *wasicun*, not a white man. He would take his strength with him to the outer-world of the dead.

Broken-finger was a medicine man. Since John Stranger had been a child, the old man had taught him, trained him. That would all change.

They climbed down a sharp basalt cliff face, carefully searching out toeholds and handholds. Their progress was slow, the sun baked them unmercifully. But they were used to it; it was part of their lives. When they reached a rocky shelf about halfway down the cliff face, they paused to rest.

"Here," Broken-finger said, handing John a thermos of bitter water. "We can wait while you regain your strength."

John felt dizzy again. Had it really been four days since he had climbed alone into the vision pit? Time had blurred, scattered like sand before the wind.

"You had a good vision," Broken-finger said. It was not a question, but a statement. He knew. It required no answer.

John blinked, focused his eyes. The spirit-veils were fluttering before him, shaking up the yellow grass and rocks and hills below like rising heat. He could see his village in the distance, nestled between an expansive rise and the gently rounded hills beyond. It had been his home since birth. Seventeen years had passed. It seemed like more.

The village was comprised of fifty silvery hutches set in a great circle, in the Indian way. Broken-finger used to say that a square could not have much power. But a circle is a natural power; it is the design of the world and the universe. The square is the house and riser of the *wasicun*, the squared-off, divided-up, vertical white man.

"Everyone down there is waiting for you," Broken-finger said, as if reading John's thoughts. "A good sweat lodge has been prepared to sear your lungs and lighten your heart. Then there will be a celebration."

"Why a celebration?" John asked as he watched a spotted eagle soaring in circles against the sharp blue sky. It was brother to the eagle in his vision. Perhaps the spirit-man was watching.

"The village is making you a good-time because you must make a difficult decision. Pray your vision will help you."

"What has happened?" John stoppered the thermos, passed it back to the old man.

"We received news from the *wasicun* corporation yesterday." He paused, saddened, and stared straight ahead. "They claim their rights on you."

John Stranger felt a chill crawl down his back. He stood up and walked to the edge of the shelf; there he raised his hands and offered a prayer. He looked for the spotted eagle and, as if in a vision, imagined that it was flying away from him like an arrow through the clouds.

"We must go now," he said to Broken-finger, but he felt afraid and alone, as if he were back in the vision pit. He felt hollowed-out inside, as isolated as a city-dweller. They climbed down toward the village together; but John was alone, with the afterimages of his vision and the dark smoke of his thoughts and fears.

Below him, the village caught the sun and seemed to be bathed in light.

With an easy fluid motion John unsnapped the end of his tether and moved to the next position on the huge beam. His feet automatically found the hold-tight indentations at the adjacent work station. For a brief moment his body hung free of any support. He was weightless and enjoyed the feeling of freedom. This was one of the few pleasures up here to his liking. The Earth hung above his head: a mottled globe, half darkness, half light. The cross-strut he needed floated slowly toward him. Anna was right behind it. Of all the damn luck: Anna. Anybody else. He shifted the joiner to his right hand and attached the proper nipple. There were twenty other floaters out on this shift; they could have sent someone else. The chatter on the intercom bothered him. He tongued down the gain.

"Bellman to Catpaw Five." The direct communication cut through the static and low-tone babble. Mike Elliot was bellman; John was Catpaw Five. The bellman directed the placing of the beams, the floaters did the work.

"Five here," slurred John. Mike was a stickler for rules and regulations. From the deck he could afford to be. It was different outside.

"Strut alpha omega seven-one-four on its way."

"I have eyes," said John.

"Acknowledge transmission, Catpaw Five." Always by the book.

"Transmission acknowledged. Visual confirmation of alpha omega seven-one-four has been achieved. Satisfied?"

"This transmission is being monitored, Catpaw Five."

"They're all monitored, so what's the difference? Fire me."

"I wish I could."

"I wish you would." Damn uppity bellman. They were all the same. "And while you're at it, why did you send Grass-Like-Light? She has second shift today."

"She goes by Anna, floater, and I put her out because I wanted to."

"You put her out because she's a royal pain in my—"

"You're on report, John."

"Stuff it."

"Firing on five. Mark."

The seconds ticked down in his head. It was automatic—and he had already forgotten Mike. At the count of zero, three low-grade sparklers fired. Aluminum trioxide, mined on the Moon. These one-time rockets were cheap and dirty, but all they needed. The boron filament beam, its apparent movement stopped, hovered a meter to his left. Sloppy.

"You missed," John said.

"You're still on report."

John shook his head, reached out with the grapple and pulled the near end toward the join. Mike was always excited, always putting floaters on report. It didn't mean a thing. People were cheap, but the ability to walk high steel wasn't common. They could hire and fire ten bellmen before they would touch a floater. Anyone could work the calculations, but walking the steel was a rare talent. There was no way he could ignore Anna.

"Down," he said, activating the local channel.

Anna fixed a firing ring around the far end of the beam and slowly worked it into position. She drifted easily, lazily. The beam slid gracefully into plumb.

"That's got it," he said. "Thanks," he added as an afterthought.

".You're welcome," she said in a dry voice. Without another word, she hit her body thrusters and moved away from him to her next position.

John ignored the snub and went to work with the joiner. Five of the color-coded joints were within easy reach; he didn't even have to move from the hold-tights. Some ground-based jockey had probably figured it all out before the plans were shipped up and the beams forged in space. As usual, they had blown the obvious cross-joins. He had to unhook for those, swing his body around to the other side. What looked easy on paper was often a different matter in space. His helmet lamp created a glare in his eyes as it reflected off the beam. The blind-side joins were the worst: no support. He clipped his joiner back on his belt and took a breather.

The tube that connected the globes of the barbell was taking shape. He'd been on the job for almost a month, from the very beginning. The tube looked like a skeleton now, but soon the outer skin would be worked into place and this job would be finished. After that, it was on to the

next assignment. He could see several other floaters working on the tube: anonymous white-suited figures in the
distance.

"That's got it, shift one," came the bellman's voice over
the intercom. "Come on in."

John waited for the transport, really nothing more than
a raft drifting by. It had been an uneventful shift; most of
them were. They were ahead of schedule. That, too, was
normal. Damn Anna, anyway. Damn Mike for slipping her
on his shift. He knew how much that bothered him. John
was used to his regular crew, knew their habits and eccentricities by heart. He didn't need other people. He didn't
need Anna.

When the transport drifted by, he reached out and
hooked himself on by the grapple. It was showy, but he
didn't care. He looked to see if Anna noticed. She didn't
seem to.

It didn't matter, he told himself.

"The skids are arriving right on schedule," Anna said,
pointing at the nearest port. Outside, the small craft blinked
and glittered against the darkness. John Stranger didn't
look; he made a point of not turning his head. It was loud
in the wardroom, too many people packed into too small a
place. After the riggers left, they would put up partitions,
make it comfortable for the small number of people who
would man the manufacturing station. Now they were
packed in like fish in a tin. Riggers got little respect and
fewer comforts. She leaned toward him across the small
table, and it made him uncomfortable, although it didn't
mean anything. Everyone leaned forward while resting in
zero-g. It was reflex. A pencil floated past her face.

"So go have a good time," John said. The independent
whores, male and female, always arrived just before the
topping-off party. They were direct competition to the
T.U.S.E.-supplied whores, who were more expensive but

classier. It was almost time for the party. The job was almost finished. Soon the flag would be secured. Then would come the release, the time for the crew to become as blind and as drunk for as long as possible at the bosses' expense.

"What I do is my business," Anna said. "As it happens, I plan to have a good time. That is still permitted."

John twisted his foot compulsively into the hold-tight grid on the floor. "You've turned white enough. Go ahead and have a good time with the *wasicun.*"

"I'm not white," she said defensively, pulling away from him. Only the hold-tights prevented her from floating to the ceiling. "You're a hypocrite," she said bitterly. "You're no more Indian than the rest of your friends." She waved her arm at the others in the room. "Some medicine man. Are *these* your people?"

John's face burned with anger and embarrassment. "Yes," he said. He was to have been a *wichasha wakan,* a holy man, a healer. Clearly half the riggers—the floaters— were his own, his own blood. They were Indian, yet they weren't. They had turned away from their heritage, forgotten the way of the Sacred Pipe. They had jumped at the chance of reward and a way out of the restrictive life of the ever-dwindling reservations. He could not understand, nor could he forgive. He had been taken away from his people, while most of them had left to become white men. A few, it was true, had been drafted. Anna was one.

She grinned at John, as if she could see right into him. "Spend the night with me," she said, baiting him. "Or aren't you man enough?"

"Our ways are not the same."

"Up here we are all the same," she said. "We are no longer in the woods, we are no longer dirtwalkers." She unlocked her cleats from the grid. Before pushing off she said, "John Stranger, I don't think you could even do it with a *wasicun.*"

John winced. Perhaps he had studied the ways of the

People too long and didn't know enough about the world. But the People were the world!

The lights flashed twice, a signal. Fred Ransome, one of the bosses, walked through the wardroom shouting, "All right, riggers. Play time's over. Now move. Get yourselves back into the dark."

John rose, cleared his head. He was pulling a double shift, like most of the other floaters. He didn't mind the work, just the people he worked for. While he was working, he could forget—forget that he was outside the sacred circle, forget Anna's face and her words.

He would not take Anna, nor any of the whores. He was a *wichasha wakan*, a medicine man, even here. He was. *He was!* They could not take that away from him, no matter where they moved him, no matter what they made him do.

But in his heart, he was not so sure.

The shifts seemed to blur, one melting into another, as constant and predictable as the stars. Somehow immense loads of planking moved into place. Endless floating mountains of beams were connected into struts and decking. Slowly the skeleton grew, took shape. The two massive globes at opposing ends of the station were each large enough to house a fair-sized city. They dwarfed the tube that connected them, even though the tube itself was over fifty meters in diameter. Pipes, endless mazes of twisted wires, and interlocking tunnels ran through the length of the tubes. Waldos walked down large tracks where the men would not be able to stand the gravity. In the middle of the connecting tube was a smaller globe, ringed with ports. It would hold the personnel manning the station.

Now the silvery covering was in place, and what had once looked as light as a delicate mobile seemed to gain in mass as strut after strut was overlaid with the metallic skin.

Like predators circling a great whale, the tiny skids and larger Trans-United ships floated, patient as the coming and going of the seasons. Even from where he stood at the aft end of the barbell, John could make out the details of the jury-rigged skids, odd pieces of junk bought or stolen, thrown together almost casually. The skids were dangerous, the reason for the high mortality rate of the freebooters. But they were free; free to die, work, or skiff off toward the asteroids, there to mine and get by until caught.

The freebooters were the people who had slipped through the otherwise smoothly running cogs of life in space. They belonged to no nation-state, no corporation, no colony. They came and went as they pleased, selling services and paying for what they needed, stealing if they could not pay. They were rarely bothered by the officials—in this area, the Trans-United Patrol—as long as they maintained a low profile. Over a hundred thousand people lived and worked in space, and the freebooters were an insignificant percentage. They moved easily, usually unseen, from the richest condo to the roughest manufacturing complex. If they made waves, they were dealt with, usually by dumping them out into space. Without a suit.

The skids held pleasures of a coarse and vulgar nature. The Trans-United corporation men on site made much use of them, the illegality of the situation adding greatly to the excitement. The freebooters were one of the darker sides of life in space.

But their lives were free.

The rest of the crew caught up with John. He clipped himself to Sam Woquini and they started to crab their way across the silvery skin of this dormant creature they had helped create. They worked as one, easily, as they had for the last year, without giving danger a thought, for their interdependence was mutual.

The Boss had ordered this final walk-through. As usual, he had wanted it done immediately. Everything had to be rushed. They had finished three weeks ahead of schedule and still the Boss hadn't let up. John tried not to let it bother him; it was just the city-dweller mentality, the *wasicun* way of life. They had yet to learn patience, to learn how to flow easily with the life-forces.

All across the station the floaters drifted, making their final visual check. It was largely unnecessary, but protocol required it. They were dwarfed by the gargantuan structure they had given birth to, small specks against their grandiose creation.

John let his mind wander as he and Sam made their lazy way across the surface. He recognized the small signs of his own work as well as those of others. It was strangely comforting. There was pride involved here, satisfaction at a job well done. That was one of the few rewards of his situation. It could almost make up for the static he caught from the Bosses—Trans-United Brass—clowns, every one of them. It could never make up for the time they'd stolen from him, the years lost, away from the ways of his people. He felt the bitterness rise. He felt cheated.

The geodesic had docked and the party had been in full swing for over an hour. John had no intention of going. He sat with Sam on a large skid that had been used to haul material around during the construction of the station. Since the job was, for all practical purposes, finished, the skid had been moved well away from the station. A large collection of equipment hung in space around them, ready to be moved to the next job.

"Stranger and Woquini, get your respective butts over here. Time to make an appearance." Mike Elliot's voice came through scratchy and loud on the voicebox inside John's helmet. Elliot, the bellman, always seemed to be shouting. He knew the floaters kept their volume controls at the lowest setting.

"We're not going to make an appearance," said John. *Wasicun* always have to make noise, he thought. Only Sam knows how to be quiet.

"You're coming, and right now!" shouted Elliot. "There's brass over here that wants to meet you. If you no-show, it's an automatic extension at my option. You know the rules. Right now I'm of a mind to tack a few years on. Might teach you a lesson."

That was always the kicker. They had draftees by the short hairs and could extend their tour for nearly any reason at all. When the corporations had worked out the conscription agreement with the government, they had held all the power, all the cards. Most of the land, too.

"I can make things hard for your friend." Elliot was getting frantic. His voice cracked. Must be getting a lot of pressure. John would have stalled on general principles, but there was Sam.

"Don't do it on my account," Sam said. "How hard can they make it for me? I've got a contract."

John knew about contracts; they were no better than the treaties of the past. They could be bent, broken, twisted in a thousand ways. He shook his head.

"We'd better go," he said. He looked at the Earth below him. The horizon seemed to be made of rainbows. It shifted as he watched. An erupting volcano traced a lazy finger of smoke. He'd been watching it for a month. A storm, one of the great ones, twisted and flickered in the ocean. All this beauty, and he had to go into a crowded geodesic and make small talk with the Trans-United brass, fat cats who had never been alone a moment in their lives and were driven to turn Earth and space into frogskin dollars.

There was a small cycle tethered to a docking adapter on the skid. John moved toward it. "Give me a hand," he said to Sam, and they swung the cobbled-up cycle into position.

The cycle was the usual floater variety, simple, made out of parts lying around. It was just a collection of spare struts joined together and a tiny thruster that powered it with bursts of nitrogen. Several other cycles of similar design were scattered around the construction site. Floaters used them to get wherever they were going and left them there for the next person.

John gripped one of the struts and aimed the thruster. "Hop on," he said to Sam.

"No, thanks," Sam said. "I'm going the fun way."

Sam grabbed a whipper and swung it over his head, catching it on the edge of the skid with a perfect motion that was a combination of long practice and an innate skill that could never be taught. He let it pull his body up in an arc and let loose of the whipper at the precise moment that would allow his angular momentum to carry him to the geodesic docked at one of the swollen ends of the manufacturing station. His body spun end over end with a beautiful symmetrical motion. He let out a loud whoop that rattled John's voice-box even with the volume turned all the way down. John smiled at his friend, then laughed. Sometimes Sam did crazy things just for the fun of it. On the reservation he would have become an upside-down man, a joker, the holy trickster. Up here he had respect: he was very large and good with his hands, sometimes with his fists. Sam's whoop rose and fell. It was full of joy, the joy of living.

"Clear all channels," shouted Elliot. "What is that? Who's in trouble? Stranger, is Woquini okay? It sounds like he's dying."

"He's not dying," said John. "He's living." He doubted Elliot would know the difference. He squeezed the thruster and headed for the geodesic.

The Trans-United geodesic globe was actually a pleasure station brought in for the topping-off party. It was expensive, but the corporation could well afford it. There were enough gambling, sex, and cheap thrills available to satisfy all but the most jaded palates.

Sleds, flitters, skids, and cycles clustered all around the end of the barbell-shaped station and the docked geodesic. Parties like this brought the whores and hucksters out in force, along with the independents looking for work, hoping to sign on with someone. Independents were always looking for work; existence was precarious without corporate patronage. There were even private cabs—small energy-squandering vehicles—bearing the insignia of other corporations. They had come to check out the competition, look over the terrain, make connections, wheel and deal.

Off in the distance solar collectors hung in silent, glittering beauty for kilometers and kilometers. To John, they were a beadgame in space, mirrors for Earth. They were beautiful, they were useful. They were in balance. The image of a bird in flight, somehow frozen, came to John. It was perfect: harmony and balance. How could such things be made by the *wasicun?* All this for the frogskin.

John and Sam arrived simultaneously at the entrance to the geodesic. Sam's trajectory, which would have given a computer a headache, was perfect. They had both known it would be. They unsuited and allowed themselves to be dragged into the party.

The topping-off party was a tradition that went back hundreds of years, its origin lost in legend and fable. At completion of work on a project—be it bridge, barn, or skyscraper—a flag, or sometimes a tree, was placed on the highest part of the structure. It was a christening of sorts and accompanied by a party, nearly always at the company's expense. If the owners declined to supply the whiskey for the party, the flag was replaced by a broom, expressing the workers' displeasure and embarrassing the company.

Like much of man's life on Earth, this tradition was carried into space. It was never planned, it just happened. It gave the men roots, a sense of place. For the same reason, the person who directed the placing of the beams was called a bellman, though bells hadn't been used as a signal in hundreds of years.

It was loud in the geodesic, much too loud for John. A

mixture of floaters and corporation brass milled around, along with a scattering of other hangers-on, independents, and whores. The corporation brass were easy to spot by their obvious inability to handle zero-g. He picked out the floaters, equally obvious by their advanced stages of intoxication. They were a mixed ethnic bag: Scandinavians, Germans, Irish, Scots, Hispanics, the ever-present English. Most of them, however, were his own people, in blood if not in thought. As usual, they were making fools of themselves before the white man. He fought a rush of hatred, not only for the *wasicun*, but for his own people as well.

He was immediately ashamed, for in his heart he felt he was no different than the others. He found his oblivion in his work, his dreams, his love of the immensities of space. They found their oblivion in booze, sex, and drugs. He was a freak, the outcast, not they.

The only other person he had met up here who came close to holding to the ways of the People was Sam. But Sam had chosen space; he had not been drafted. He seemed to have struck a balance between the old life and the new. In a way, John envied him.

He sometimes thought he saw some of the signs of the old life in Anna, though they were deeply buried. He got the feeling that she had turned her back on her past. John was a constant reminder of those times to her. Perhaps, he thought, that was why they never got along. . . .

A young woman drifted over to John, offered him a nipple of scrag. He politely refused—it would be a double bind if he was high and anything happened. Most of the floaters could handle it, but he knew he couldn't. He would be leaving the party as soon as possible.

A well-dressed man in his late sixties was holding court with a man about half his age. The younger man was a dirtwalker by all appearances. He stood perfectly still, as if one wrong move would send him floating away forever. His legs were tense, his feet jammed firmly in the hold-tights on the floor grid. His knees were locked. It would take a collision with a skimmer running full-bore to dislodge him. Uncomfortable as he looked, he was hanging on every word.

"In essence, we are smack in the middle of the greatest industrial park ever envisioned—" the older man said.

John shook his head, pushed away. Soon the old man would be talking about the high moral road of financial return, the ethics of the profit motive, and how space—by definition—couldn't be polluted. He'd heard it all a thousand times and was sick to death of it. If he allowed them to drag him into their conversation, he'd certainly say something wrong and get into trouble.

There was new gossip from the Belt, chatter about business interests on the Moon, but mostly talk centered around the station they'd just finished. Everyone seemed to think it was a marvelous feat of engineering. When set into rotation, the station would produce a graduated gravity source, with a maximum of fifty g's at the rounded ends. It could never have been achieved on Earth. What would eventually be manufactured there was a mystery to John: more square cities, for all he knew or cared. It was a job, plain and simple. He was pleased that the floaters' end had worked out well; beyond that he had very little interest.

Two of the Trans-United brass separated from a crowd and kicked over toward him. There was no easy way to escape. He braced himself.

"So you're John Stranger," said one of them. "I hear you're one of our best men up here."

"Do you know me?" he asked, making an attempt to be civil.

The man smiled and tapped his ear, indicating that he wore a computer plug. He turned to his companion.

"Mr. Stranger here is an American Indian, as many of our floaters are. They work well on the beams, seem to have no fear at all. We recruit and draft heavily from the tribes. They seem to have a, ah . . . natural ability. It's in the blood. Wouldn't you say that was true, Mr. Stranger?" He took a sniffer from his pocket, inhaled deeply. Some sort of drug, a stimulant, most likely.

Another sweeping generalization.

John swallowed his anger. It would serve no purpose to start trouble with the brass. He'd spend the rest of his life in servitude that way.

"Some say that," said John, instantly sorry he'd compromised himself. A cowardly action. "I'd better get back into the dark," he added, moving away. The man caught his arm.

"Can't leave now," he said. "This party's for you, for all of you. Can't thank you enough. You men and women are the real backbone of our operation."

The thought turned John's stomach. "I really have to be going," he said. If he didn't get out, he was going to do something foolish. He almost didn't care.

"We're having a spin party later in the living quarters on the station when they start the rotation. Just be a few of us. Ought to be pretty spectacular. If you're free, consider yourself invited."

"I'll keep it in mind," John said, backing away. No way he'd show up at something like that.

As he left the two men, he caught a glimpse of Anna across the room. She was talking with a young man, a pretty whore. She met his stare arrogantly, as if they were two opposing forces, two incompatible states of mind. She turned her attention back to the boy.

John was depressed. There were things about Anna that he felt drawn to, others that forced him away. It was a complex feeling. It was unsettling.

He had to get out of the geodesic, back into the dark, into space. He felt closed in, trapped. It was almost a claustrophobic feeling, a vague sense of uneasiness that brushed his heart, the pit of his stomach. He had never felt those things before, not even in the sweat lodge. All he knew was that he had to get out of there.

He found Sam and together they left the party, suited up. It wasn't until they left the geodesic that the pressure lifted from John. It had been all out of proportion to the situation.

He was still angry with himself because he hadn't stood up to the Trans-United bureaucrat. The sense that he had betrayed something important weighed heavily upon him, yet on another level he felt there had been no choice. It was a bitter feeling. He was no better than the others.

He was a hypocrite.

2

It was the first time John had been inside the computer bubble, the mobile command center for this operation. He wouldn't be there now if Sam hadn't talked him into it. Sam was a friend of Carl Hegyer, who was running the board. The bubble hung well away from the station; they had a panoramic view. Sam had thought John might like to watch the spin from there. He admitted it was better than being with the brass in the center of the station, or watching it with the drunken revelers in the geodesic.

Spin was imparted to the station by an extremely simple and cheap method. The surface of the station was covered with thousands of small, one-shot aluminum-trioxide rockets. The crew called them sparklers. They were dirty, but that didn't matter in space. What mattered was that they were cheap, composed of elements easily mined at the lunar complexes.

Through the programmed computer, Carl Hegyer could select the number and order of rocket firings. They would fire only a few at first, to get the station moving. Slowly they would increase the rotation by firing more and more rockets until the desired rate of spin was achieved. The point they were aiming for was that which would produce a fifty-g force at the rounded ends of the station. That would still leave the majority of rockets in reserve. The immediate area had been cleared in preparation for the firing. The geodesic party, still in full swing, had been unlocked from the station and moved a short distance away. Most of the brass and dirtwalkers were in the swollen living quarters in the middle of the station.

The digital mounted next to the CRT screen on Carl's console ticked down. A signal flare soared across the darkness like an orange comet. The two-minute warning.

Carl broke the silence in the bubble. "All this will probably seem pretty anticlimactic," he said. "I'm not much more than the guy that pushes the plunger. It starts slow. Not much to see at first."

He was right. When the digital ran down to zero, John had difficulty even seeing the rockets fire. Carl pointed to a few scattered dots on the station's image on the CRT screen. "Those are the rockets firing," he said. "We ought to be seeing something soon."

John looked out the large, curved port at the station. There were more rockets firing now, sending out white sparks like small magnesium flares. As he watched, one edge of the station occulted a star. It was moving. Still slow, but the movement was perceptible.

Although John had worked on several projects since his training, this was the first time he had seen his handiwork put into motion. It impressed him, moved him, touched something deep in his heart.

For this was *wasicun*, the work of the white man. Yet somehow, as the ponderous station gradually picked up speed with its trail of metallic sparks, it seemed more like the work of the People.

There was symmetry here, balance, purpose. There were circles linked with the circle of the Earth. For a moment he forgot about the dirtwalkers on the station, the brawling party in the geodesic, the drunks and whores. Here was purpose, direction, in a fluid way. Relationships were being expressed that he could only guess at, not yet hold.

"It's beautiful," Sam said softly.

John could only nod. Carl was busy at the console, fingers flying over the keyboard. Once in a while he would touch the CRT with a lightpen, triggering an individual rocket passed over.

It was going faster now, as fast as John had ever seen anything swing in space. He knew the station needed fifty g's at the ends, zero-g at the center. It was necessary for the centrifugation and sedimentation of the material they were manufacturing. That seemed like a lot of g-forces, but the station was large, strong. It would handle it.

John saw it first, looking through the port. Carl saw it an instant later, through the computer. An unevenness, a ripple spread through the pattern of the firing rockets. Suddenly the board went wild, every telltale in the room went from green to red. Outside the port, the universe was lit with a blinding white flash.

"Jesus Christ," cried Carl, frozen. "No!" A whole bank of rockets along one arm had fired at once. Not one rocket, not ten; but hundreds of them.

The station swung in a ballet of death, caught in an ungainly pirouette by the uneven forces. The wrenching stresses pulled at the station in a way that could never have been anticipated. The metal twisted, buckled, finally reached the breaking point and sheared. Before their horrified eyes, the station broke apart, one end of the barbell ripping away. It headed inexorably for the geodesic, a precise arc of destruction. The rest of the station, out of control, cartwheeled wildly away.

Time froze. John was held by fear, the old fear taught to him by Leonard Broken-finger. It was the fear of one who can see with his heart, who can sense the spirits in the sweat lodge and in the vision pit. As bits of steel, aluminum, and boron silvered through space, catching the sun in their terrible dance, John became a *wichasha wakan*. He saw through the eyes of his people; he was in the center of the circle.

Those aboard the geodesic must have tried to get out of the way. Yet it happened too fast; they had no chance. John's people were in there; his spirit reached for them.

The terrible fear, the crawling fear broke through his heart. "Oh Wakan Tanka, Great Mystery, all those people, don't let them die. . . ." John felt the wings of Wakinyan-tanka, the great thunderbird. They were made out of the essence of darkness; they were as cold as ice, yet they burned his skin.

The geodesic was struck dead center. It burst apart as metal and people were torn and tossed in a thousand different directions. Steel struts and beams careened end over end, but the tumbling limbs and bodies of the dead seemed to be propelled by what looked like red gas: blood.

He heard himself screaming, and he remembered: *Wakinyan-tanka eats his young, for they make him many; yet he is still one. He has a huge beak filled with jagged teeth, yet he has no head. He has wings, yet he has no shape.*

From somewhere distant, Sam yelled: "Do something, Carl, do something."

From somewhere else, came Carl's voice: "I can't."

And Sam: "Save the others."

Carl: "I can't stop it. Calculations are too complex. I can't."

John felt the cold breaking of death, the death of all, Indian and *wasicun* alike. He broke, and was made whole. He pulled Carl from the chair, sat down in front of the computer console. Sam yelled, Carl screamed. These were disruptive forces, he blocked them out, ran his fingers lightly over the keyboard.

He touched a button and a single rocket fired on the wildly careening remains of the station. He touched another button and a rocket fired someplace else on the skin of the station. There was a rhythm, a balance. Action and reaction, all parts of the whole.

Gently he felt his way into the heart of the computer. He did things, things happened. Forces were moved, stresses transposed from one place to another. It was all a matter of balance, of achieving a point of equilibrium. The computer was a prayer and he was in the pit again, close to the spirits that flicked in the dark and the thunder-beings that carried the fear. His fingers danced over the keyboard. He felt, rather than saw, the forces he was manipulating. It was internal, not external: he was part and parcel of the things he did. He grabbed the lightpen and stroked the image of the runaway station on the screen. Under his fingers more rockets burst into life, counterbalancing the undesired motion. With the sureness of an ancient hand painting a Hopi jar, he sought out the proper forms, the pattern. The station slowed.

The fear, the ancient fear carried by prayer, was breaking him. It gave him the emptiness the *wasicun* built, transforming it into a wisdom. He frowned, added a few last strokes with the lightpen, tapped a few more buttons. The station stopped, motion arrested.

John slumped forward, drained of energy. He shook himself, looked around, half expecting to see the rolling desert, the towering mesas. Instead he saw Sam and Carl, though he didn't recognize them at first.

They stared at him with amazement, with fear, unable and unwilling to move, to break the spell. They could not comprehend what they had just seen.

John looked at them and understood that, and more. Much more. He stood.

"We'd better go," he said. "Some of them may still be alive."

They followed him. They would have followed him anywhere.

* * *

It was cold on the mesa top; the sky was just beginning to lighten. The smoky dawn blurred the sharp pinpoints of stars and once again returned shape and substance to the world.

Leonard Broken-finger crouched on his haunches before the yawning opening of the vision pit. He held a leather bag that had belonged to his great-grandfather. But the bones and stones and roots and relics it contained were his own medicine.

The medicine the spirits had given him in a dream.

The young man in the vision pit made stirring noises. His name was Jonas Goodbird. He was tall and gangly— taller than anyone on the reservation. He was not handsome, yet the women said he had a way about him. Jonas never seemed to lack for a woman.

"You've been here four days," said Broken-finger. "Your vision quest is over. I hope *Wakan Tanka* has helped you."

"I'm still alive," said Jonas in a quavering, unbelieving voice.

"Of course you are; though by all appearances, not by much." He made a gurgling sound deep in his throat, which was his way of laughing. As long as anyone in the tribe could remember, the medicine man had not smiled. Stories were told that his lips would break like pottery; and children still made a game of trying to get old Broken-finger to laugh and break his lips. They had never succeeded.

Jonas was getting ready to leave the vision pit. It would take a few minutes for him to gather his wits. Broken-finger left him to this and walked to the edge of the mesa. He faced east. He was like a gnarled tree, already shaped by the wind.

The dry, cracked gullies stretched out below him, faded brown and red in the morning mist. And once again Broken-finger felt that this would be a good time to die. He was tired, yet strong. But it was not his time . . . not yet. He looked longingly at the towering rock formations below him. Those were the shapes of time.

They did not have to bear the weight of flesh and spirit.

He thought of others he had walked down from the vision pit. There had been many. Some blurred into the darkness of deep memory, some stood out like figures carved out of light. He thought of John Stranger, gone now three winters, taken by the *wasicun*. He was special; the spirits clung to him like fire to good hard wood.

The sun broke the horizon.

He raised his arms to the heavens and stood that way for endless moments. He stared at the rising sun as if he were at sundance.

He felt the cold brush of wings.

Wakinyan-tanka. . . .

He has wings, yet has no shape.

There were terrible things happening.

There were beautiful things happening.

It was a time of changes, a shifting of the order.

And he felt the presence of the thunder-beings. An overwhelming sadness seemed to engulf him. He felt empty, as if his organs and sinew had been turned into air, into dust, into sunlight. He held his arms high, for they were without weight. A tear made a shiny trail down his dry, wrinkled cheek, as if squeezed out of his squinting, blinded eyes.

Yet he smiled for the first time in fifty years.

The presence of the ancient spirit creatures was a sign. He would live a little longer. His people would survive a little longer.

His lips cracked and blood ran down his chin, dribbling onto his brown yet frail chest.

And he thought of John Stranger.

* * *

They arrived at the ruined station before the rescue vehicles. From the outside it looked to be the disaster that it was. One end had been torn away, leaving a twisted mass of beams, wires and pipes. John led Sam and Carl to the living quarters in what had once been the middle of the station. It appeared intact, but had been under considerable stress. What g-forces it had been subjected to could only be guessed at.

It was pitch-black inside. The air was stale but breathable. He could hear low moans. Moans meant life. John flipped back his visor and turned on his lantern.

His lamp stabbed through the blackness. Bodies floated in horrible, contorted shapes. Here and there an arm waved, a leg moved. Twisted wreckage was everywhere.

John, Sam, and Carl worked together quietly, with purpose. They separated the living from the dead, did whatever they could for those who hung in between. Some they lost, some they saved. John drifted to the floor grid. It was twisted and buckled; people were trapped there. He worked at freeing them.

A soft voice called his name. A hand touched his shoulder. Anna.

"I thought you were dead," he said. "Dead with the others on the geodesic."

"I . . . I came here. It was . . ." Her voice trailed off.

Suddenly the chamber was filled with light as the rescue crew entered. They were efficient and noisy, barking orders everywhere. They took over. A part of John relaxed. In the bright light, Anna looked terrible. The side of her face was purple with bruises, her left arm hung at an odd angle. She was staring intently at him.

"You've changed," she said, slowly reaching out with her other hand to stroke the side of his face. There was awe in her voice, tinged with fear.

"I am what I always have been," John said, knowing even as he spoke that it wasn't so.

A long road lay ahead. He had but taken the first step.

Data Burst ID = 2587966LRF

From: BJN
To: Study Crew, Stranger Project
Location: Trans-United Billet Ozma
Access Classification: Level Three Confidential
Password: REDMAN.1755.XYX
Reference File: SOC 187735-NN-000
Date: 2 Nov 2180
Time: 9:14 A.M. GMT

++++++++++ start personal copy ++++++++++

The stochastic analysis of the subject, John Stranger, has been completed and is as follows:

The subject has an extraordinary intuitive ability to make correct choices in structured and free-form double blind situations (reference Krebb-Healer and Thompson protocols). Trials = 100. Success rate = 100%.

As to kinesthetic awareness, the subject was flawless in both the Cameron and Shaller tests. Trials = 100. Success rate = 100%.

No subject has ever achieved these numbers before. The probability that this is due to chance approaches zero.

CONCLUSION: The subject intuitively makes correct decisions in apparently ambiguous situations. The subject has high awareness of his surroundings and the relationships between objects in his environment.

NOTE: The subject is uncooperative.

WEAKNESSES: Tribal loyalty.

CLOSE RELATIONS:

Leonard Broken-finger   SOC 15782-NN-863
Anna Grass-Like-Light   SOC 16364-NN-347
Sam Woquini   SOC 13827-NN-676

**** EXPLOIT WITH EXTREME CARE ****

This subject is potentially dangerous.
This subject is potentially useful.

RECOMMENDATION:

Observation, manipulation, and tight control.

++++++++++ end of personal copy ++++++++++

Print locations: Remote 27, Local 5.

3

Data Burst ID = 1654435LKR

From: FKD [Module 7]
To: SLH [Module 32]

Date: 3 Jan 2181
Time: 7:34 A.M. GMT

Subject: John Stranger [SOC 187735-NN-000]
Status: Permanent draftee (involuntary)
Time remaining on contract: Indefinite.
Work level: Bellman, Near-earth orbital construc-
tion.

PRIVATE MODE: No diskcopy.   No file.   No key.
Hardcopy (ID required) only.

++++++++++ start personal copy ++++++++++

Stan:

This is just for your information. Leighton has
tagged this guy (John Stranger) for observation.
He's heading a team of floaters that will be in your
sector and I thought you ought to know that they'll
be watching him closely. That means they'll be
watching you, too. Don't fuck this one up.

I'm not sure why the old man has taken such an interest in him, but they've got him nailed but good. I
guess he's some sort of a trouble-maker.

All his records are flagged, so burn this hardcopy
after you read it. Hope to see you the next time I get
out that way. Things are about the same here, busy as
usual. Same old shit. Take care, and watch your ass on
this one.

Frank

++++++++++ end of personal copy ++++++++++

Print location: Remote 32 [node 6]

Key: NO KEY: PRIVATE COMMUNICATION.
WIPE/DISK HARDCOPY ONLY

++++++++++ addendum ++++++++++

FILE NOTE: The above was intercepted on Net 53, on 3
Jan 2181 at 7:34:15 A.M.

ACTION:
Frank Dexter terminated with prejudice.
Stan Hawkins transferred to asteroid mining complex
53-YT.
Key: SOC 1877335-NN-00

John Stranger drifted in the blazing star-filled night as he
watched his crew crawl over the surface of the satellite like
a handful of ants on a silver, spiny barbell. They were almost finished, and it looked like they'd be about forty hours
ahead of schedule. This one had been simple: replace a few
solar cells and attend to a module that had deteriorated
because of an acid leak. He wished they could all be so easy,
but it never worked out that way. Each gravy run was in-

variably followed by a ball-buster. It would probably be a furnace or the remoras next. Soon his easy-going crew would be raw with tension, including Sam Woquini, who bragged that any duty was just *sleeptime* for him.

"Hey, Bellman," called a voice through the static. It was Mike Elliot, John's immediate superior.

"Yeah, you got him," John said.

"Shift channel," ordered Elliot, using his rank to grind John whenever the occasion presented itself.

Damn, John thought, tonguing to confidential. It had to be trouble.

"I've got some new orders for you, Stranger," Elliot said. "You're on your way to sector omega-ten."

"No fucking way," John said. "My crew has earned the right to some safe duty. And I know goddamn well that omega-ten's all watchdogs, most of them sentries. Cluster bombs, for Christ's sake. I'm not completely crazy. Send some other unit."

"You're available and it's you they're sending," Elliot said. He always sounded condescending when he was enjoying himself. "The orders have already been cut."

"Put me on report if you want, I'm not doing it. I'll be fucked if I'm taking my people in there without a weapons team."

"The papers were signed by Director Leighton himself," Elliot said in a sickeningly smooth voice. He knew he had John by the balls; Leighton was the one man you couldn't buck. John could imagine Elliot's baby-face, looking serious, as if he wasn't really getting a charge out of this.

"When does this duty start?"

"Right now. Gather up your crew. We've assigned you some extra people. And you'll need a briefing with Murphy."

"If they're not weapons people, I don't want them. New people just get in the way."

"You work with who I tell you to work with, Stranger."
Elliot broke the connection with a loud snap.

John opened a channel to Sam Woquini. "Did you get
that?"

"I couldn't resist tapping in," Sam said. "I already got
Anna, so don't worry. Look, we've slept our way through
all the other missions and we're still here to tell the tale, so
don't worry about it. I'm getting the sled now. Be there in
a few minutes."

John watched his friend, who was a distant white speck
blinking in and out of the darkness, move toward the sled.
Everything out here was either deep black or blinding
white, except the distant stars, which shone steadily. Some
of the pinpoints of light appeared ruddy, others were blue-
white or copper. The heavens were like massive fireworks
caught in stop-motion.

All around John small satellites with huge fans of solar
cells hung in orbit. In the distance were the L–3 and L–5
habitats surrounded by factories and labs, and the ever-
present debris that seemed to gather around them.

John bit his lip as he watched Sam pick up the rest of the
crew. His people weren't rested enough to work the watchdogs, not yet. They needed more time. Omega-ten was a
crowded and complicated sector, a real bitch.

Too many things could go wrong.

Ray Murphy was feeding numbers into the computer as
John watched the greenish hologram flicker into life. It was
a three-dimensional representation of the omega-ten sector, with color-coded points of light identifying the various
objects in orbit within the area. It was too crowded, there
were too many points of light, too much debris. Red bands
crisscrossed the sphere, indicating microwave transmission
pathways to be avoided at all costs. There were too many
red bands. There was too much of everything except empty
space.

"This is what omega-ten will look like when you enter," Ray said. "We're clearing vector seven-five for your approach pattern." He tapped in a few more numbers, and a yellow beam appeared, running diagonally through the hologram.

"Give me real time," John asked without looking up.

Ray made some adjustments, and the points of light began to move. It was a complicated picture, orbits swinging in every direction. A watchdog's orbit constantly changed to lessen the chance of someone destroying it. Debris and space junk drifted through the sector, each piece watched as closely as the satellites, for in the wrong place it could be just as deadly. To the uninitiated, the hologram was mass confusion; to John Stranger it was a delicately balanced system, a ballet of vectors in space; a balance felt rather than seen, in a way he could not describe.

But something was wrong, a pinpoint of light moving against the flow.

"There it is," John said. "That's the one."

Ray nodded. "Watchdog 26–BCC. Sentry-class watchdog. Cluster bomb. We're having trouble keeping control. In fact, we may be losing it entirely. There's a good chance it's already snatched."

John felt wired, nervous. He didn't like this at all. A sentry-class watchdog with cluster bombs was the worst of a bad lot. A snatched one was a nightmare. There was absolutely no telling what it might do.

The original watchdogs had been sent up as spy satellites to monitor ground activities and serve as early-warning systems. The move to armed sentry-class *peacekeeping* machines was swift and quiet in the years following the two-hour period in which ninety percent of Iraq was pounded into rubble in retaliation for a chemical warfare attack that killed every living thing within twenty miles of Tel Aviv.

Ironically, the rain of death came from what had been

thought to be a weather satellite. It had been constructed and launched for Israel by Macro Technologies.

When countries went into space to protect their borders, they turned to the corporations that had experience in space. Organizations such as GTE, Macro, ComSat, and Trans-United had been building satellites for years. The corporations already had the hardware, the research teams, and their own launch vehicles. This arrangement allowed them to become as wealthy and powerful as nation states.

But before the nation states could react, the delicate balance of world power had shifted. Shifted completely, irretrievably.

A new age had dawned.

Nations could no longer be certain who controlled their satellites. Even the smallest corporations had the ability to wipe out entire countries or the ground bases of competitors.

Now corporations and nation states alike participated in a covert but deadly war. . . .

Snatching was the gaining of control of someone else's satellite. It involved deciphering the codes that controlled the satellite and overriding the original programs with your own.

Sentry-class watchdogs, because of the weapons they carried, were prime candidates for a snatch. Even though satellite technology was extremely sophisticated, watchdogs were snatched more often than anyone was willing to admit. It was often an inside job. People like Ray were watched closely to protect them from being kidnapped and to keep them from selling out. Trust was a rare commodity among those who dealt with the doomsday machines.

"We may have lost it last week," Ray said. "I just don't know. It follows some commands, but not others. It may be a malfunction, or it may be something else."

"Yes," John said, feeling cold and nervous. "It may be something else, all right. Give me a look inside the watchdog."

As he looked into the holo, at the images of circuitry and machinery, he felt that he was already in the omega-ten sector, carefully dancing with death.

Leonard Broken-finger stood on the edge of a deep ravine in the center of the reservation. The ground was striated umber and rust; it was dry and lifeless, as dry as the still air that seemed to suck the very moisture out of him. His face was wrinkled and the color of pipestone; his body looked as desiccated as the land. But he was as strong as the distant rock towers that the ancients had thought were the whitened bones of a great, primeval monster. He was as implacable as the stones underfoot.

He watched two young boys stalking a rabbit in the dusty, dry rush below him. They carried sticks with charred, pointed ends. Broken-finger knew them well, and he felt a profound sadness well up inside him. Soon, they would be taken away by the corporations, drafted into service to work behind desks or in space. And when the boys returned—if they ever returned at all—they would behave like strangers.

So very few had had the old talents, the medicine spirit, and they were all but gone now. Gray Fox and Afraid-of-Bears had died working in space for *wasicun;* their bodies were never even returned for proper burial. Broken-finger imagined that their souls floated in the sky like ghostly stars. They could have brought strength and resolution to their people, but they never had the chance.

Russell Inkanish had felt the spirit early; he was barely eight years old. Broken-finger had devoted himself to him, but it wasn't enough. The corporation drafted him when he was eighteen; he came back four years later, a narcodrine junkie who wandered the desert like the other spirits that could sometimes be seen flickering and ghosting through the deadlands on moonlit nights.

John Stranger had been the strongest. He had seen the spirits as light in the vision pit. He had screamed in the sweat lodge when the heat blistered his back. He could have been a *wichasha wakan,* a medicine man. But he, too, had been taken too soon. There were times when Broken-finger could still feel John's presence. He had been gone a long time. Broken-finger had the strong intuition that the corporation was using John for a different purpose than any of the others; they were testing him, as he himself had done many times in the past. John had never failed Broken-finger. He had many things in front of him . . . if he could survive.

Broken-finger stood as still as stone. He stared at the sun, but didn't burn with the terrible heat that poured down upon him. Tired of chasing the rabbit, the boys had returned to the village. Broken-finger noticed nothing, yet missed nothing.

He was thinking of John Stranger.

John was in the center of the circle, which was broken. Broken-finger could see the circle in the blinding whiteness of the sun. Images played in the white fire. He saw fire falling from the sky, killing hundreds; and John's hand was on the firebolts. How could that be?

And Broken-finger felt the coldness of living corpses beneath him, as if the very stuff he was standing on were made of human bone and sinew. As if the dead were below him. Yet they were not dead. They were now spirit.

He felt a vague brushing and thought of Anna Grass-Like-Light. Something dangerous and strong and sad was working inside her. She was with John. There were others, too. He could feel their presence as pain. He could see them burning, as he stared into the sun.

Many would soon die.

Broken-finger shivered and blinked. Now the sun was far to the west. He tried to move, and felt the familiar brush of cold wings. The vision that was given to him at his first vision quest many years ago returned once more. He shook with the vision, seeing it once again, for it was as real as the ground upon which he stood. He cried in joy and terror as he faced its beauty and power. He saw the creature of myth and dreams, the greatest of thunder-beings, the being that can be seen but not comprehended. He saw his own dream of it, a dream which changed with his every thought and prayer.

Wakinyan-tanka eats his own young, for they make him many; yet he is one. He has a huge beak filled with jagged teeth, yet he has no head. He has wings, yet has no shape.

Broken-finger prayed for John and the others.

He blinked again and it was dark. The day was gone, as if absorbed into John's burning eyes. The sky was filled with stars. Perhaps John and his people were one of those floating points of light. Broken-finger gazed east, toward the village. He wanted the company and comfort of his family, but instead he walked toward the flashing neon of the corporation-owned commissary.

John Stranger sat by himself in a videotect booth in the orbiting pleasure-dome, but he was not hooked in. He didn't need to lose himself in the videos, which were simulated experiences, mostly sexual. He just wanted to be alone. He left the booth on transparency, but turned off the outside noise. All he could hear was faint thunder. Broken-finger used to say it was the thunder-beings whispering to him. It was more likely the result of an old ear infection he had had when he was a child.

He looked out through the transparency at the rows of iron bandits and telefac booths on the casino floor. There were also telefac games, where winners received a jolt of electric pleasure and losers had their nights spoiled with bone-crushing migraines; and there were traditional gaming tables, such as roulette, chuck-a-luck, craps, hazard, liar's dice, vingt-et-un, and slide.

On this floor the crowd was mostly floaters, although corporate executives and their consorts drifted through, slumming. The more expensive and more deadly pleasures were upstairs, where the organ gambling and deformation games were being played. But they were closed to floaters. What the first level provided, though, were house whores—natural men and women; birdmen with implanted genitalia and feathers the color of rainbows; geishas; androgynes; drag queens and kings; children; machines promising clean, cold sex, although their exposed organs were fleshy; and all manner of genetically engineered mooncalves.

It was obvious that the providers didn't believe that a floater could think about anything above the groin. Perhaps they were right, John thought. He saw Shorthair take a drink from a robot that had the logo of the Trans-United Corporation emblazoned on its chest. Inside the sweep of the *T* and the *U* someone had painted a poorly executed fist with an extended middle finger. Shorthair had his arm around a naked woman whose skin was bleached zinc white. Thick artificial strands of glossy black hair curled around her head, moving like snakes, as if they had a life of their own. She looked pubescent.

John watched them disappear into the crowd. A fight started in the area of the iron bandits, and the M.P.'s took their time before breaking it up.

The reservation seemed an eternity away. It was no wonder that so many of John's people became, in effect, white men. It was easy to do; they were far from anything that could be called home. They were white man's tools, living in a white man's universe. John could not blame those who became lost in the frogskin world. In fact, he felt as lost as they did.

Anna Grass-Like-Light found John's booth and stood in front of it, staring in. Her eyes looked glazed and unfocused and she was trembling. John had the sudden and disquieting thought that insects were moving beneath her skin, causing her subtle yet grotesque facial expressions. She had done too many narcodrines. Anna pounded on the transparent walls, and John came out of the booth and took her to a table where they sat across from each other. She ordered a drink from a mobile vendor, then spilled part of it when she set her glass down onto the table.

"Having fun in there?" she asked, fumbling in her pocket for a narcodrine, a large bluish capsule. John stopped her before she could twist and break it under her nose.

"Leave it alone for a while," John said. "You're fucked up enough already. You look like a walking overdose."

"Fuck you, medicine man. We're about to get our asses blown up in a sentry and you're worried about some poppers? Maybe you don't need anything to cut through the shakes. You're so caught up in the old ways, you think you can just have a dream and we'll all be safe."

She popped the narcodrine. For an instant Anna seemed to soften, and John remembered her as she used to be planetside. He'd known her since they were children. She had a sweetness about her that had all but disappeared after she was drafted.

"What the hell are you doing here, anyway?" she asked. "You told me you had to be alone to get ready for tomorrow. You lied to me."

"I just couldn't stay in the barracks any longer," John said defensively. She had caught him. If they were going to survive tomorrow, he would have to put his thoughts right, dream about it, work out every detail. But he couldn't seem to concentrate in his room, even though it was quiet. Perhaps it was too quiet, because he hadn't been able to visualize his mnemonic of the watchdog. In a way, Anna had been right about John having a dream and making everyone safe. He certainly owed it to them to try.

"Why not?" Anna asked.

"I don't know," John said.

"So you came here to slum it up."

"I thought it would help to be nearby," John said lamely, "in case there's any trouble."

"You're a fucking liar," Anna said. A tic was working like a bug that had been lodged in a vein in her neck. "You came here for the same reason the rest of us did. You're scared out of your suit. So you thought that if you could see the rest of us behaving like assholes, you'd feel better. That would get your thoughts back into line real quick, wouldn't it?"

John couldn't answer. She knew him well and had touched a nerve. He couldn't stand to think of himself as a prig, but there it was.

"Do you want to fuck me, medicine man?" Anna asked softly, an edge of desperation and pleading in her voice, although her face seemed hard and angry as she looked at him.

It was an old challenge. Anna had played it before. But John had made a vow. He wasn't going to live his life on white man's terms, even if it meant staying celibate. He had to keep to the red path. He had to be the measure for the others.

"You're such a fucking hypocrite," Anna said. "I'll admit to being scared and lonely. But you, you've got a dead heart."

"Come on, I'll get you home."

"The fuck if you will," Anna said, and she stood up, looked around, then called over a whore whose skin was covered with fur like a bear. She leaned against him as he helped her away from John.

John wanted to go after her, but he couldn't, for the mnemonic of the watchdog began to spin in his mind like a perfectly transparent geode. Everything around him became peripheral, and his sight, which was now clear and focused, turned inward.

In that instant, John Stranger hated himself for what he had become . . . for what they had all become.

The trail was not difficult to follow, even at night. Although the moon had not yet risen, the air was clear and the panoply of stars provided all the light Broken-finger needed. He took comfort in the distant howling of wild dogs and the night sounds of owls and insects and scurrying creatures. He paused for several minutes and stared at the fluted towers and rills of a small canyon, all seen as shadows of different intensity. The darkest shadows in the twisted canyon were hard and cold, and he knew them well. Once he had come here to seek answers from his ancestors. He had stayed over a week without food or water, and although forty years had passed since then, he knew he could walk the canyon blindfolded and never miss a step. Time had become compressed for Broken-finger. He could remember what he had done years ago with the same clarity that he remembered yesterday's events.

As he crested the last ridge, he saw the commissary and started downhill. It blazed like some sort of aberration of the northern lights. The commissary was built of logs, in keeping with some of the old ways. It sat in an island of concrete surrounded by parked steam-cars and the small scoots favored by the young braves. Music drifted across the parking lot.

When Broken-finger walked through the door, he found the sounds of music and laughter and shouting deafening after the whispers of wind through stone in the desert night.

The large room was packed with young people from the reservation, and visitors. Most were dancing or sitting at tables. Too many were drunk or stoned. Along the far wall was a row of videotect caskets, which were all in use. Broken-finger could see shadowy figures moving to preprogrammed hallucinations inside each casket; and it made him shudder to think they were bloods he had known since infancy. Incongruously placed between the row of caskets was a stone fireplace. The stones were real, but the fireplace was not. A holo of flames flickered in the hearth, and the sounds of wood crackling had almost fooled Broken-finger the first time he was in the commissary. The other walls were covered with softly lit, enticing pictures of food items and general supplies. He could smell the items and hear the olfactories sigh as he passed each picture. If one wanted flour or boots or jewelry, one only had to press the picture, insert an ID-credit card, and it would be delivered, wrapped tightly in plastic, from some mysterious basement. Broken-finger had never used the machines, but he had watched many old men and women of his tribe stand in front of the wall as if they were at market. It's just another way to make us weak, he thought. Instead of growing corn, we push pictures. The machines were, in fact, about twenty years obsolete. But Broken-finger didn't know or care. He would rather walk twelve miles and buy from the one-armed man who had a blind wife—he knew many good stories.

A white man standing behind a long wooden counter looked up as Broken-finger approached him. He looked middle-aged and paunchy. Most of the whites working on the reservation were doing punishment duty. "What can I do for you, chief?" he asked, wiping the counter with his hand, obviously a compulsive habit.

"I'm not a chief," he said evenly. "I wish to place a call to John Stranger. He is a bellman for Trans-United. My name is Leonard Broken-finger. My last name is two words separated by a dash. You'll need to know that when you write it in your machine."

"ID card."

Broken-finger handed him a gray card.

"I take it he's topside, now," said the man.

"John Stranger is wherever Trans-United has sent him."

"Thanks for all your help," the man said sarcastically. He typed onto a keyboard behind the counter. "The satellite link is pretty good tonight, but it may take awhile."

Broken-finger just nodded and waited. A group of young people waved him over to their table. Then they made faces at him, told him stupid jokes, and finally Stan Walking, who was a good boy, begged him to crack a smile. "Come on," Stan said. "Let me at least win the bet. You've got to put on a happy face sometime."

"What is it you hear from your sister?" he asked Stan.

"She's all right, I guess. T-U transferred her again. Somewhere in South America. In Paraguay. Asunción, or somewhere like that."

"That's the third time this year," Broken-finger said.

"She doesn't care," Stan said. "One office is the same as the other, I guess. She signed up for another five-year hitch. Said the money's pretty good."

Broken-finger nodded.

"Your call is ready, chief," said the man behind the counter. "Take it in the back booth."

Broken-finger walked around the counter and stepped into the plastic booth, which immediately darkened. The door slid shut with a creaking noise behind him. Then slowly the image of John Stranger resolved about four feet away from him. Broken-finger had no sense of the cubicle he was in; it was as if he and John were in a large room.

"Broken-finger," John said. "It's been—"

"I bring you news of your father. He is not well." John's father had been dead for almost twenty years.

"Wait a minute," John said, and he leaned forward. For an instant, he was out of view. Then there was a buzzing noise; and when John's image returned, it seemed to shimmer. "There," he said. "I've attached a scrambler. If anybody's listening in, they'll get only static."

Broken-finger didn't seem to notice. "Your father has a high fever, and his mind is not well. He has many dreams and speaks them to me. They make no sense, but I promised him I would tell them to you."

"My father?" John asked.

"He fears the fire from the sky," Broken-finger said. "It brings death to his descendants and his people, and somehow your hand is on the fire. He sees that this is not your doing, but that you have been forced into this thing. He trusts your judgment, though. It is a silly dream, of course, but I have promised him."

"I don't understand," John said.

"He sees more. He is worried for you and those friends of yours of which you have spoken, Anna Grass-Like-Light and Sam Woquini. Red Feather is cold on his heart. There is danger for your people. He sees a village of frozen faces."

"We're all going out tomorrow," John said. "A watch-dog has somehow—"

"Your father knows nothing of watchdogs. He knows only the things I have told you. You will have to make a decision and it will be painful. Death will be all around you like steam in the sweat lodge. You must make your decision and not look back. You must not punish yourself for the thing you have done. This is what your father told to me in the heat of his fever. They are ramblings of an old man. But I have given my word to tell these things to you."

"And you, Broken-finger. Are you okay?"

"I am simply an old man who carries a message from another to you. Your father sees one more thing in his fever. He sees you leading your people."

"I do that every day. It's my job as bellman."

"Yes, John Stranger, that is your job. I must go now. Your father is not well."

"My father—"

"Take care, John Stranger," and then Broken-finger pressed the disconnect button that glowed on a faint console beside him. The image of John Stranger disappeared as the lights in the booth came on and the door creaked open.

Director Leighton's office occupied the entire top shell of O'Neill Seven. The expansive curved ceiling was over ten meters high, a conspicuous waste of space that served to intimidate those who had to do business with him in person. The ceiling and walls were opaqued, or polarized, to an unrelieved, dull metallic gray.

Leighton reviewed the tape. He had seen it five times, and each time he imagined he had found something new. He played it once again, this time without sound. Broken-finger's image appeared to float beside John Stranger's in the center of Leighton's executive office. Leighton sat behind an ancient oak desk with its antique fittings and appurtenances, which even included a leather-clad green blotter and a gold pen and pencil set. He used the pen and pencil; it was one of his few eccentricities.

The old man knew something, but what? Leighton asked himself. Broken-finger had been vague, and that bullshit about John's father hadn't fooled the spotters for a moment. They knew John's history well. That's what he paid them for.

He wondered about a leak. Could the old man have picked up on something? If so, what, and how much? Leighton watched Broken-finger's jaw move up and down on the screen. Just an old man? Maybe. Dangerous? Maybe. He stopped the tape.

In the darkness he pressed a button on the inside well of the desk with his knee.

"Who's on staff at the commissary down there?" he asked.

"Harry Stanton's the front, sir. The red team's underground."

"Send Stanton to Spain. Shift the red team to Utah and bring in a skeleton team. I don't want to take any chances. Has the science staff been moved?"

"Yessir. And I've made provisions to move the entire—"

"Just follow the emergency directive you've been given. Moving the science staff will be sufficient, thank you. I don't want it to look like a goddamn exodus."

"Anything else, Director?"

"Yes, who the fuck gave Stranger a scrambler?"

"An engineer named Taylor Westlake. It didn't work, of course."

"Eliminate him. Make it an accident. And the old man, Broken-finger . . ."

"You want the same number for him?"

Leighton pressed what looked to be a whorl on the polished surface of his desk, and the walls appeared to dissolve and become transparent. He gazed at several Trans-United ships floating near a geodesic manufacturing station. Above the geodesic and behind the junk of a jerry-rigged freebooter colony, the mirrored solar collectors hung like the wings of some fantastic rectangular bird. Leighton looked downward, relaxing as he did when he was making a decision. He had the entire room on transparency. It was as if he and his desk were weightless, suspended in space. Below him was the Earth; its hazed horizon looked like it was made of rainbows, as if it were the edge of a fragile soap bubble.

"No, I guess not," he said. "Not yet. He may be useful."

4

JOHN GOT A break, a small one to be sure, but a break none-theless. Of the three new people Elliot had assigned to him, one of them happened to be Shawn Rhodes. She was a weapons expert and had worked with watchdogs and flashers. Her experience would at least offset the other new floaters, who would only be in the way no matter how good they were. It was always difficult working with new people. Over the years his crew had grown very close. They had been through the barrel together. It didn't hurt that they were all of Indian extraction, mostly full-bloods, even though they came from different tribes and had different perceptions about the old ways.

As they approached sector omega-ten, John sat suited-up in the cargo area of the transport and talked with Shawn. The cargo area was surrounded by walls of huge boxes. Each gray metal rectangle was numbered. Shorthair said he felt like he was in a post office lobby. Sam Woquini thought they looked more like caskets.

The members of his crew either tied themselves down to the hold-tights as John did or drifted from wall to wall. They were all listening to what Shawn had to say. She spoke quietly. Her voice sounded surprisingly low for such a small woman: she was barely five foot. She was fine-featured: red hair, freckles, and a thin, firm mouth, but her eyes were as hard and penetrating as a duty soldier's.

"This sector has twelve watchdogs, ten of which we own. Basically this is a Trans-United sector, as much as any sector can belong to anybody. One of the other watchdogs belongs to Macro Tech, and the other belongs to the Swiss."

Someone guffawed. Switzerland had been completely overrun after the last firewar. Their underground bases and shelters had caved in like mines during the first detonations. The country had been looted as badly as Johannesburg. The Swiss had never regained any power. The banking industry was already settled in the Bahamas, where it was provided with safe haven by unanimous decree of the World Court of Governments and other Polities. Even Continental Cooperative had more satellites than the Swiss, and they were almost entirely a land operation.

"Besides the watchdogs, there are six flashers, two furnaces and ninety-two remoras, of which we control seventy-three. Like I said, this is a Trans-United area. Something to be thankful for."

John took little comfort in that. Remoras were killers, no matter whom they belonged to. They were programmed to protect and destroy. The small satellites hovered around the watchdogs, blasting anything that got too close. In theory, they wouldn't bother his crew as long as they stayed in the cleared sector. Ray had programmed the defensive satellites to recognize John's crew as *friend*. It wasn't much, but it was something: most space weaponry nowadays was hardwired to accept only limited external programming. The owners of the other remoras and watchdogs had been informed that John's crew was on a routine, *peaceful* maintenance mission. Supposedly, they had already programmed their satellites accordingly. Supposedly. There was always the possibility that something could go wrong, either accidentally or intentionally, and it was an even chance that someone had snatched the watchdog. Firewars had started over less. Mexico City had been cluster-bombed over a poaching claim ten years ago. In a hundred years or so it might cool off enough to rebuild.

Compared to the watchdogs and remoras, the furnaces were safe. They were just processing plants. The flashers—microwave relay stations—were a problem only if you walked into one of their invisible beams. Yet both furnaces and flashers were potential weapons. Tectonics had lost a crew to an accidental blowoff of a furnace that no one believed was an accident. If someone who knew the command sequence reprogrammed the flasher to turn a quarter of a degree, it could fry a crew or blast a city. Both of these things had happened in the past.

"There's no way we can tell exactly what's wrong until we actually go inside," Shawn continued. "It's probably just a malfunction in the guidance system, which is why they've grabbed you for the job, John. On the other hand, if it's a snatch, you'll be needing my help."

"If it's a snatch, we'll need more than help," Shorthair said as he defaced one of the numbered wall caskets with a beam marker. He was drawing little yellow flowers on the metal. He always drew those flowers on every fitting beam and column he bolted together. He never changed the design. "Divine guidance wouldn't be a bad idea."

"Thanks for the encouragement, Shorthair," John said. "I'm always open to constructive suggestions."

The voice of the transport's pilot crackled, "Five minutes to omega-ten, Mr. Stranger."

"Be right up," John said.

John and Shawn floated up the narrow passageway to the control room as the rest of the crew made a last check on their gear. From the bubble in the control room, Omega-ten looked, at first glance, to be total blackness broken only by the Earth below them. But John's trained eyes immediately picked up half a dozen remoras—small, hardly visible points of reflected light that were like the eyes of predators in some especially dark jungle night. The remoras were where they were supposed to be. Good. Now if they would only stay there.

The ship moved slowly through omega-ten, following the path Ray Murphy had worked out. As they passed the Swiss watchdog, even John smiled. It was hardly bigger than a council lodge, and the wings of its solar panels needed repair. John could sympathize with the Swiss; his own people had faced hard times for hundreds of years. He hoped the Swiss would pull through.

When the Macro Tech furnace passed in and out of view, John knew they were almost at their destination. The watchdog had already appeared on the pilot's monitor, but John stared out the bubble to see it with his own eyes. At first he could only see scattered specks of light, but then the watchdog came into view. It was a huge sphere. Dull metal. But there was something else there, too. Something deadly. "Get me Ray on the line," John told the pilot, glancing at Shawn. She had seen it too.

"Murphy here, Stranger."

"What the hell's happening?" John snapped. "There are too fucking many remoras hanging around this watchdog. They can't all be ours."

"They're not," said Ray. "Macro just sent three in there and they've got two more on the way. I don't know why. Nobody tells me anything."

"I'm scrubbing this mission," John said. "Suicide isn't in my nature."

"Can't," Ray said. "Something big's going on with the brass. I tried to pull the plug for you, but Leighton himself told me to keep you out there. Elliot's hanging right over my shoulder to make sure I keep you in line. He's here now."

"Well, fuck Elliot, and fuck Leighton, too. Macro could blast my crew any time it wanted to. I'm not going to sacrifice my people just to keep Trans-United happy."

Shawn gave him a sideways glance. No one stood up to Leighton that way.

John was seething, but his sharp-featured face masked the hatred he felt for the stupidity and venality that had taken them this far from Earth to play someone else's game.

"Stranger, you turn back now, and I'll have you and your whole goddamn crew breathing vacuum," Elliot said. "If Leighton wants it, it's big. And he's going to get it. You'd have to take the controls away from your pilot because he's not going to help you. Isn't that right, Fred?"

The pilot nodded nervously; he didn't look over at John.

"Something else Director Leighton wanted you to know before you kicked out," Elliot continued. "This is a perimeter-defense watchdog."

"I know that," John said.

"Well, what you don't know is that if Macro snatched it, the chances are that your home reservation might have been turned into a prime target area."

John felt a chill fan down his back. "Why? There's nothing worth blowing up. It's just fucking worthless land."

"Politics. Maybe Macro just doesn't like Indians. I don't know anything except what Leighton told me to tell you."

John closed his eyes, feeling sadness working its way through his raw hatred, sadness not only for his crew and the people on his reservation, but for the *wasicun*, too. They were all caught . . . trapped. He had felt this same mixture of hatred and sadness before, in the sweat lodge back on Earth.

He thought of it as a special kind of love, for hatred alone was not enough to vanquish an enemy.

"I'll get my crew," John said to the pilot in a weary and bitter voice. "Take us in."

*   *   *

They hovered about fifty meters from the watchdog on a flat, open utility sled launched from the transporter. Remoras the size of a man surrounded them, but kept their distance. The massive watchdog loomed ahead. Small portals pockmarked its sides: lasers, a last line of defense in case the remoras failed. The cluster-bomb assembly itself was larger than a house and held not only the multiple warheads, but thousands of scatter-dummies—decoys to fool anyone who tried to intercept the bomb. Directional antennae sprouted all over the watchdog's surface. They would have to be manually aligned after he finished his part of the job. It was a long and tedious process, but others would do that.

His job was simple. Go inside the death machine and fix it.

The plan was to replace the control board for the guidance system and check all the patch lines. If it was a simple malfunction, they should be able to track it down from there. If it had been snatched, however, the whole system would probably be booby-trapped. He'd either get around that or he wouldn't. It was that simple.

Shawn would go in with him.

"Sam, I want you to stay at the sled's controls," John said. "If anything happens, get the crew back to the transport immediately."

"Yes, Mr. Bellman," he said, chuckling, his voice sarcastic. He was joking, making fun of the near-legendary stupidity of most bellmen. After a pause, he said, "This job won't be nothin', you'll see. Sleeptime."

"Well, *you'd* better sleep with your eyes open," John said.

"I always do." The humor had disappeared from Sam's voice, replaced by calmness. Very little bothered him.

"Are you ready?" Shawn asked. John nodded. She drifted off the sled, and with a small burst of nitrogen from his thruster-pack, he followed. He half-expected a laser to slice through him at any second.

The watchdog looked much larger up close, and even more deadly. Its antennae twitched and turned, tracking them, along with everything else that moved in this sector. It was like a faceless medusa floating above the earth.

John and Shawn floated like divers in an ebon ocean to the only entrance into the satellite, a heavy port ringed with lasers and hold-tights. Passing into the dark side of the watchdog, John felt a brush of fear sweep past him like the shadow of a vulture. He clipped his tether to a hold-tight and tried to ignore the laser staring him in the face.

Shawn surprised John by drawing her hand back and forth across her throat; it was a universal signal in space. She wanted him to turn off his intercom so they could speak in private. He nodded and flicked the switch with his tongue. She pressed up against him. From the transport it would look as if they were working on the complicated entrance lock. She touched her helmet to his.

"There's something you should know," she said. Her voice, carrying through the metal and plastic of her helmet, was tinny and distant. "Elliot and Leighton are bullshitting you. This is a worst-possible-case sentry. There must be something down there on Earth that Trans-United wants to hide. If the shit ever hits the fan, this is the sentry that's supposed to take care of the evidence. And if I know about it, you can bet your ass that Macro knows it too."

"Thanks," John said. He understood, but that didn't make it any easier. What it meant was that if Trans-United lost a violent corporate takeover, they would burn their bridges behind them, leaving worthless land and hiding their secrets forever. His homeland was, for reasons he did not understand, one of the bridges to be burned. Literally.

And then he remembered that Leonard Broken-finger had said something about a village of frozen faces. Could that have something to do with all of this?

"We'd better move," John said.

When they switched their intercoms back on, Elliot was yelling. "Why were communications cut?"

"Can it, Elliot," John said. "We had a short, got it fixed. We can either get this job done or sit here and listen to you bitch. Which is it?"

He grumbled, then shut up.

"There, I've got it, John," Shawn said, swinging the entry port open. Feet first, she pulled herself into the small opening. John followed. They both turned on their chest and helmet lamps, which cast an intense, almost pure white light.

There was more room inside than John had expected, but he could almost feel the mass of the cluster-bombs around him. The interior of the sentry was starkly functional, full of machinery and complicated, multicolored circuitry. They were surrounded by a metal gridwork that kept them from bumping into anything they shouldn't. The grid was hinged in various places to provide access to the equipment behind it.

Shawn bent over the master control board and studied it intently. John floated behind her, watching over her shoulder.

"As nearly as I can tell, these seals are intact," she said. "They could be phonies, but I don't think so. If this egg's been snatched, it doesn't look like it was done from here. Still, could be a program snatch. . . ."

John didn't need to be told that. He felt wired, as if he was seeing everything with tunnel vision. Broken-finger had once told him when he was a child that it was the gift of danger. John turned and swung open a section of the gridwork. The attitude thruster control system seemed like a logical place to start looking for the problem. He unhooked the probe from his workbelt and scrolled down to the proper section of the trouble-shooting pad on his left wrist. Then, while Shawn worked on the board, he examined the coiled, wiry guts of the thruster controls. It wasn't hard work, but it was tedious. There were nearly fifty checkpoints to be reached in this section alone. He had to be painstakingly accurate, and there was no guarantee that the problem was in the thrusters. Carefully, he pushed a knot of wires to one side as he pressed his probe past them to the next checkpoint. The readout was good to six decimal places. He pulled out the probe, arranged the wires as they had been, and moved on.

Then Shawn changed position. After a moment she said, "Sonova*bitch!*" There was a sharp intake of breath in John's intercom. He turned and saw her sprawled against the gridwork on the other side of the room. He could see a tiny hole in her suit below her chest light. Her faceplate was frosted over.

John pushed himself off the wall toward her and slapped a quickseal over the hole. But she twisted as he applied the seal, and John saw her back. It was too late. Between her shoulder blades was a jagged hole, an exit wound, that was larger than his fist. Her suit was shredded, and the wound was a mass of flesh and shattered bone. A pink mist was pouring out of it. Dead, damn it. Booby-trapped.

Then Anna screamed.

He pushed himself toward the exit.

"Remoras!" shouted Red Feather.

John reached the port just as the first remora hit the sled. There was a soundless explosion, a blossom of flame that shattered the sled, spilling debris and his friends in all directions. Another scream: Red Feather gone.

Red Feather is cold on his heart. There is danger for your people.

Ray's voice came in loud, overriding everyone else's. It was ragged with panic. "Stranger, it's a snatch. The damn thing's been triggered. Code Blue."

John froze, and the spectacle of death hung before his eyes. His crew was scattered, injured; some were dying or dead. And more would die when the sentry activated. In a few minutes his homeland would become a hole in the desert. He pushed himself back inside the sentry.

He fears the fire from the sky. It brings death to his descendants and his people, and somehow your hand is on the fire.

Code Blue. A forty-five-second countdown. It was out of Ray's hands.

John propelled himself to the master control board, gently elbowing Shawn's corpse out of the way. He focused himself, gathered his strength, replaced his panic with a drifting calmness. He thought of the thunder-beings, the eagles without form, and he heard the thunder. He took comfort in the familiar sound as he surveyed the board in front of him. Although he had worked on a mock-up of a similar board, it had been over a year ago. He tried to remember.

And it came back to him.

First he looked for a fail-safe, but couldn't find one on this board. Damn, there was no way he could stop the countdown now.

You will have to make a decision and it will be painful. Death will be all around you like steam in the sweat lodge.

Shawn had placed a meter and a recoder over the patchpoints and had slipjacked them into the circuitry. The meter's tiny screen blinked and glowed red, indicating that the original hardwired program had been snatched. The patchpoints told him something. Besides the primary target there were five backups. But it didn't tell him where they were.

For an instant he floated there, imagining the innocent lives below. He pressed two opposing keys on the meter. It beeped when it found a patchpoint coordinate, which appeared in the read-out. He had found the newly programmed secondary target. It wasn't the reservation. He could just delete the entire program snatch, but what if Shawn had been right and the reservation was one of the hardwired Trans-United targets? Then he *would* be the instrument of destruction.

He found the third back-up target. That wasn't it either.

Then he found the primary target. It was the reservation and it was part of the jerry-rigged overlay. Leighton had been right. His homeland would be dust in a few minutes.

There was no time to waste. He deleted the snatched program and prayed that the recoder would shunt the bombs to the original hardwired targets. But what if Shawn had been right, after all? The reservation might still be one of the hardwired targets.

It was too late.

The sentry rocked violently as the clusterbombs were launched. They were committed now; a firestorm worse than Dresden was headed toward Earth.

Then everything exploded in a burst of blinding white light.

The remoras, guided by unknown hands, were closing in on the sentry and blasting it. John cartwheeled through space. The sentry had split into several large chunks surrounded by thousands of smaller pieces of debris. Everything tumbled away from the explosion.

The earth and sun spun vertiginously around him, as if in a dream of falling. The remoras were going crazy. Like a feeding frenzy among sharks, they were shooting at everything that moved. John heard the thunder loud in his ears and felt something cold brush past him—the thunder-beings.

His crew was going to die unless he did something. Using short bursts from the small spot-welder he carried strapped to his left leg, he stopped his somersaulting flight and headed back toward the others. His path was erratic as he evaded the attacking remoras. He moved without conscious thought, relying on some hidden instinct to second-guess the deadly satellites.

He had the strong intuition that Broken-finger was somehow watching him . . . guiding him.

The transporter and its crew had fled from the sector, the sled was demolished, his crew scattered. He didn't dare use any radio frequency, lest a remora home in on it.

He found Sam, and they went about the slow and dangerous task of gathering up the rest of the crew. Five were missing, five friends, five brothers and sisters. Anna chased down an oxygen tank from the destroyed sled. They linked themselves together in a long chain, and John used the tank to propel them in a snakelike dance away from the remoras. Omega-ten was a complex sector in the best of times, but now it was a churning nightmare. John held a sharp-edged picture of it in his mind as he threaded the deadly maze. Their progress was slow.

Your father sees one more thing in his fever. He sees you leading your people.

It was a long time before they were picked up.

Leighton sat at his desk and leafed through the confidential report of the sentry incident. This had been a tight one, and there was more to it than appeared in the report. Much more.

One thing was certain. A two-hundred-square-mile area southeast of White Sands was gone, vaporized. It was Macro property, and they had, as Leighton had predicted, made only a minor protest. They claimed thirty lives lost, but his contacts had put the final figure at five hundred and thirty-seven. Fifty-two employees and four hundred and eighty-five sleepers. Macro was keeping quiet because of the sleepers. Deep-sleep research was forbidden by international law. Macro claimed it was a microwave receiving station, but it had been a research installation. No matter. Now it was dust.

Ever since the radio signal that came to be known as the

Rosetta Triptych was received from the triple sun system 36 Ophiuchi, Trans-United and Macro had been involved in developing deep-sleep. Each corporation wanted to make the first contact with a technologically superior alien race. Using the Cristal-Williston Fusion Drive, which had been successfully tested, and deep-sleep, contact could be made in less than a hundred years. Not so much time in corporate terms, for corporations, unlike nation states, were used to long-range planning.

Then a minor ranking scientist working for Trans-United discovered a way to get around the neural synapse problem. One of Macro's spies got hold of the information and an undeclared corporate war began. But after a failed Trans-United deep-sleep experiment was leaked into the newsnet, the public outcry was immediate and strong. As luck would have it, one of Macro's mass graves of sleepers was also discovered by a reporter for one of the most popular sleazy yellow shows. And that immediately became hot news. Within weeks the World Court had outlawed all deep-sleep experimentation. After that, the corporations purged the rank and file of their security sections and simply moved their operations to other underground sites. Eventually the outcry died down.

The sentry ploy had been a gamble, but a carefully planned gamble. Any investigation would show that Trans-United's own property and personnel had been in danger, and that would clear the company of any suspicion. It would look like a program snatch. Leighton had banked on John Stranger's overwhelming tribal loyalty and ability to make instant decisions to pull it off. And it had worked. There would be no serious investigation.

Leighton shifted in his chair and depolarized the room. As the room lights were lowered, a thousand stars bathed the stark room in a wan milky haze. Leighton felt like an Olympian god gazing out from the heavens. He tapped his fingers on his polished desktop and tried to decide what would be the best use of the corporate asset known as John Stranger.

Held in place by restraint webbing that surrounded him like a loosely-fitting cocoon, John floated in the recovery room. Med-patches covered his arms and chest, delivering carefully measured doses of medications. Above him a monitor blinked and clicked softly with reassuring regularity. He drifted with his eyes closed and his mind troubled.

John could not stop dwelling on what he might have done differently in those last few seconds inside the sentry. He had traded the lives of strangers for the lives of his family and friends. A feeling of helpless remorse filled him as he wondered about the people he had caused to die . . . the people he had killed.

Finally he fell asleep, slowly falling through the suffocating layers of guilt and exhaustion to a spirit world cobbled out of fever dreams. He saw Broken-finger. It was afternoon. The sky was clear. There was barely any wind, and the only sound was the buzzing of flies.

Broken-finger looked into John.

You must make your decision and then not look back. You must not punish yourself for the thing you have done.

The old man spread his arms, and they turned into wings. His face melted into the terrible mask of a thunderbeing. The thunder-being rose into the air, its great wings making the sound of a bellows pumping, and John looked into the face of death.

And saw himself.

He was the thunder-being.

Taking life.

Giving life.

Turning and crying in his sleep.

5

Data Burst ID = 5348795BRT

From: DLC [Module 3, Node 26]
To: Red Level personnel only

Access Classification:
~   ***COPYPROOF***

ATTEMPT TO COPY WILL RESULT IN DESTRUCTIVE LOCKUP
ATTEMPT TO COPY WILL RESULT IN IMMEDIATE ARREST

        Password: @@1852/GHD.785LRT [code/shift
        Bravo Alpha]
        Subject: Analysis of Rosetta Triptych

++++++++++ start personal copy ++++++++++

.The Hillerman regressive analysis program was
sucessfully installed in the experimental AI construct codename Einstein, nested in the forward-
chaining logic loop. As expected, the source of the
radio signal was confirmed to be the triple star system of 36 Ophiuchi. At this time thirty-two percent
of the alien transmission remains undeciphered. The
balance consists entirely of technical data relat-
ing to the mechanics of the faster-than-light transportation system.

New information decoded by Einstein applies to the phased array subsystem and two unique alloys that apparently solve the heat-transfer problem that has been blocking the green team. This information is available on a Level One need-to-know basis.

Einstein is still working on revising the developmental scenarios. Estimates look good, but the probability is increasing that either Macro or Intertech has also broken the code. No firm information yet, but our usual friends are listening for us.

Next update in twenty-four hours.

++++++++++ end personal copy ++++++++++

Print locations: NONE

Key: NONE: WIPE ALL

++++++++++ addendum ++++++++++

CONFIDENTIAL TO DIRECTOR LEIGHTON
EYES ONLY

SUBJECT: ASSESSMENT OF DAMAGE TO WINNIPEG INSTALLATION

LOOKS LIKE A TOTAL LOSS. THE ONLY GOOD NEWS IS THAT IT WAS APPARENTLY NOT DIRECTED AT US. HOTHEADS ARE IMPLICATED. THE MAJOR TARGET SEEMED TO BE THE LOCAL ARMORY. HITTING OUR INSTALLATION WAS APPARENTLY A SIDE EFFECT, COMPOUNDED BY THE USUAL LOCAL SHOW OF EXCESSIVE FORCE. THE FREEZER WAS NOT BREACHED, BUT WE HAD TO BLOW THE SHAFT TO PREVENT DISCOVERY. I RECOMMEND A TWO-MEGATON SUITCASE TO COVER OUR TRACKS. BLAME IT

ON THE HOTHEADS. MIGHT AS WELL WRITE THE WHOLE THING
OFF. ESTIMATED ADDITIONAL LOSS OF LIFE: 27 EMPLOY-
EES, 300 CIVILIANS, PLUS, OF COURSE, THE SLEEPERS.

EINSTEIN SAYS THE WINNIPEG GOVERNMENT IS LYING. HIS
INFORMATION SHOWS THERE IS LESS THAN A 0.0715 PER-
CENT CHANCE THAT THE RECENT WAVE OF INSANITY IS A NEU-
RAL VIRUS. IS IT A FULL MOON DOWN THERE?

BY THE WAY, JOHN STRANGER IS A HARDER NUT TO CRACK
THAN I THOUGHT. THE MORE I PUSH HIM, THE MORE HE DIGS
IN. CAN YOU SPLIT UP HIS CREW? TWO FLOATERS ESPE-
CIALLY: ANNA GRASS-LIKE-LIGHT SOC 15782-NN-863 AND
SAM WOQUINI SOC 13837-NN-676. THEY'VE BEEN A CON-
STANT PAIN IN OUR COLLECTIVE ASSES, AND EINSTEIN
SAYS THEY'VE BEEN PROVIDING HIM WITH EMOTIONAL SUP-
PORT. SEEMS STRANGER HAS BEEN SUBVOCALIZING THEIR
NAMES WHEN HE'S DREAMING, ALTHOUGH WE DON'T GIVE THE
POOR BASTARD MUCH CHANCE TO SLEEP. IF YOU CAN MOVE
THEM OUT OF THE WAY, I WOULD SURE APPRECIATE IT.

LET ME KNOW ABOUT THAT SUITCASE AS SOON AS POSSIBLE.
OUR NEAREST ONE IS CURRENTLY SUBCONTRACTED IN
TORONTO, SO IT WILL TAKE A LITTLE TIME TO GET IT
THERE.

ON THE BRIGHT SIDE, I'VE GOT A SURPRISE FOR YOU. ONE
CLUE: JELLYROLL MORTON.
                              —DAMON

John Stranger twisted in his armor, an exoskeletal harness
of sensors as sensitive as flesh. He had set himself into a
wild, careening spin, and the stars flashed in trails around
him like neon in the Cimmerian darkness.

  Dan Hobart's laughter rang in his ears as John cursed in
Arabic and Hebrew, which he much preferred to the white-

bread Euro-American tongues. His own language, natural Sioux, did not contain equivalent words. He tapped the finger-switches to bring the spin under control.

"Dumb move, Stranger," Hobart said through the intercom. Hobart was a Trans-United work leader, a senior noncom. "If this had been real life, you would have lost your big red ass right there."

John took a deep breath to give his anger room to dissipate; and then he smiled at the spirits, as his old friend and teacher Broken-finger had taught him to do. Distance had no bearing on dreams, and both John and Broken-finger had the gift of the thunder-beings: the gift of dreams.

Just so did John drift in a state akin to dreaming. Now he dwelt in a psychological space where his ancestors might speak with him as easily as thoughts drifted in daydreams. In this hogan of thought, he could reach out to friends and relatives, to the living and the dead, to gain strength and peace. This was also the eternal state of the warrior, a place cleansed of hate and anger, a state of complete and perfect focus.

A ruddy sandstorm cloud raged across the heel of Africa below him. The moon was a hard, cold disk off to his left, as dirty and shadow-cracked as old cheap china. The spindles and gauzy mesh of a relay net hung above him like woven silver on a loom. And all around him the stars in their distance watched: the eyes of a thousand dwellers of the eternal night.

It *had* been a dumb move, John told himself. He had let his mind wander and dreamed about Sam Woquini and Anna Grass-Like-Light. It was a recurrent dream that always left him in cold sweat, for in that dream Anna became Corn Woman and Sam became the Sandman, tormented spirits caught in arid deadlands and corridors of ice.

Again he had dreamed of Earth.

Forty hours without sleep. It was catching up with him.

"Shall we try that maneuver again?" asked Dan.

"How about let's try some sleep?"

"There're gonna be times in the field when you won't be able to sleep, Stranger," Dan said smoothly. "And we need to know what'll happen. Now, you ready, or do you want a jolt first?"

He yawned. "Do we have to go around this again? You know I can't use that shit."

"Not can't. Won't. But eventually you're gonna have to get off your high horse and take a stimulant, Stranger. Now get yourself into position. Toni, you ready?"

"Toni's off-shift, Mr. Hobart. This is Lester. I'm set to record up here. We're tracking him now."

John looked like a fly caught in some impossibly huge metallic spider web. Thin wires and struts branched hundreds of meters in every direction from the harness that suspended him in the middle. Tiny servos controlled by his fingertip switches induced the spider web to flex and bend into any number of shapes.

It was a new device, an instant one-man work station. From within the web a person could conceivably re-form and realign one of the gossamer relay nets alone. The philosophy behind it was typical Trans-United thinking: if it worked, one man could do the work of ten. *If* it worked. So far, nobody had been able to master it. It was far too complex. It was also, as John had been told countless times, necessary for the experimental navigation system of the Mars ship they were working on. But John knew bullshit when he heard it, and this whole project smacked of it.

He switched from visual to internal, and the faceplate of his suit silvered over; his view of the Earth and Moon was replaced with a series of dancing lights. He fine-tuned the display and gently tapped a few selected thrusters. The spider web flexed and bent as it moved slowly toward the relay net. John's fingers padded softly over the various controls as one by one a series of indicator lights turned green, indicating contact between the web and the net.

"In position," said John as the last light turned green.

"Let's try zero point one three seven," said Dan. "This is a timed test. Mark time. . . . Mark. . . . Start."

Seconds started ticking off on a small display in the upper left-hand corner of John's faceplate. He managed a wry grin. Nobody had ever aligned a net within seventy percent using this clumsy device, no matter how much time they took.

John switched screens on his faceplate and tapped in the ideal configuration of 0.137. Immediately the screen became a sea of red dots. By tapping the small servo motors, he moved parts of the web against the net, moving it slightly. As sections of the net moved into position, some of the dots on his screen turned green. He was directing the interaction of a complicated balance of forces, sometimes winning, sometimes losing. The activation of a key servo would send a wave of green lights washing across the screen, gradually becoming a ripple and dying out. Sometimes the green dots turned red as a correction on one part of the net caused another part to move out of alignment.

John no longer thought in terms of individual movements, but visualized the entire screen as a sea of color. He worked intuitively, without conscious thought, eliminating the red and replacing it with green. In a few moments the screen was as green as he could make it. Any other corrections caused eddies of red to appear. He was at the limits of the spider web machine. He could do no better.

No one could do any better.

"That's it," said John. "That's all she'll do." Suddenly, he was exhausted. He slumped back into the harness.

The softly modulated voice of Einstein whispered to Dan, as if it were actually beside him. The senior noncom had not yet gotten used to his permanent implant.

Einstein: "Analysis of performance follows. Subject: John Stranger. Trial number thirty-seven. Percentage of alignment efficiency: ninety-six point three. Time: three minutes, forty-six point three nine seconds. This betters his previous time by seventy-two point six three seconds and is the highest alignment efficiency recorded by a human subject."

"Stranger, back off from the net," Dan Hobart said.

"What?"

"Back off. Half a kilometer. We're going to try it again."

TRIAL NUMBER 38.

As the bands of colors swirled like confetti in the screens before him, John Stranger heard the soughing, bellowslike sound of the thunder-beings. He felt the cold touch of wings. The formless ones. Death. He felt the presence of spirits and danger, and he fell into the deep shifting tunnel of their dreams.

But these dreams were unlike any he had ever had.

He was scourged by light more intense than the sun that had once blinded him during a sundance with Broken-finger.

He was looking into the fully-realized world of the spirits.

Yet they were not spirits. They were not from any world known to man.

He screamed as they consumed him in the fullness of their thoughts.

Director Gerard Lincoln Smith Leighton sat in the vast darkness of his office in the Bernal sphere space colony that was his fiefdom.

Here, upon what was ostensibly Trans-United property, he had built a grandiose villa to symbolize his power and status; if he could be compared to a modern day Lorenzo de' Medici, then this villa was his *Poggio a Caiano*, that architectural dream of the Renaissance humanists. Leighton's own Ivy House was built to impress heads of states, directors, CEOs, and other princes, to facilitate the constant and delicate diplomacy between governments and states and duchies and corporations and other powerful and dangerous legal entities. Leighton's villa was in fact modeled on *Poggio a Caiano*, but on a much larger scale.

It was also built to be a temporary escape from the crushing responsibilities of being a corporate prince. And for this moment, Leighton had escaped. It was as if he were floating in his cushioned chair, for he had keyed walls, floor, and ceiling to transparency, an effect provided by a hundred state-of-the-art cameras on the Bernal sphere's skin, and he was staring into the hard ice-clear beauties of near-Earth space.

He had turned the room into an eyepiece of the Trans-United orbiting telescope.

The constellations blazed around him, as if the universe were indeed the inside of a great sphere—or, as the ancients had proposed, a dark firmament punctured with millions of tiny holes through which passed those few rays of the celestial light. Around him were his factories that grew crystals and purified metals; refined here were foam steel and iron-lead alloys, which had the most interesting electrical properties. It was in these laboratories and factories that liquid-state physics had become a reality. Leighton nodded, as if affirming that all this was real, for it had been his dream.

But what gave him the most pleasure was the university that rotated in the sector beyond the labs and factories. He had devoted himself to it, and was repaid, for Leighton-Loyola University had eclipsed Oxford-Harvard as the most prestigious center of learning and scholarship. It was a world all to itself, a mirrored Stanford torus rotating in the primordial darkness, where thousands of scientists and engineers lived and did the research that would begin a new renaissance. Or so Leighton dreamed.

Beside it was the Cup and Saucer, the radio telescope that had received the enigmatic radio signal from the triple-sun system 36 Ophiuchi, which had come to be known as the Rosetta Triptych. Part of that transmission was apparently a blueprint for a faster-than-light drive, but there were still too many missing pieces of information.

And then there were the recent incidents of mass hallucinations and hysteria on Earth.

Leighton wondered, as did many others, if one were related to the other.

The confirmation of intelligent life elsewhere in the universe had several immediate effects, not the least of which was the birth of a thousand different cults, each claiming a lock on the truth. Some preached salvation, others preached doom. Many of the leaders were charismatic, hypnotic in their ranting. There was far more hysteria than logic.

For logic, Leighton turned to the scientists. He employed thousands of them, and a good number had been working on the ramifications of the alien transmission, most in the area of the faster-than-light drive. Prototypes of the drive had been built and tested. They had all failed. The logic was, well, *alien*. Some of it resisted all attempts at translation.

Most of the scientists rejected the notion that the alien race still existed. There was no time/date stamp on the transmission, and for all that anyone knew it could be thousands of years old, hundreds of thousands. The aliens and their artifacts could be dust by now.

Leighton keyed down the magnification and looked into another quadrant. A silvery spider web reached out in all directions, bending and flexing and undulating against the static backdrop of the heavens. It was part of the ship, but more than that, it was a cybernetic nervous system, a biocrystalline network linking human to machine.

He focused in on John Stranger. He was a useful tool for the corporation, but a difficult one to manipulate. He was hard to break, but he *would* be broken.

Leighton zoomed in still closer and John Stranger's features were sharp and clear through his faceplate, magnified a thousand times, floating in front of Leighton like some huge icon. Sweat stood in beads on his forehead, his eyes were closed.

Then he opened his eyes.

Leighton flinched in terror. John Stranger—overtired and overtaxed—was hallucinating, but *Leighton* was suddenly trapped in Stranger's crazed thoughts and bizarre visions.

He looked into alien worlds and screamed as his senses were overloaded by what could only be imagined as radiance.

Radiance that burned his eyes in their sockets.

Radiance that slurred his voice and fused his thoughts along the perfect yet blinding patterns of a programmed dream.

Laura Bowen's first thought was that an electrical glitch had screwed up her equipment. She checked the backup and no, what was happening was real, whatever it was.

She was sitting on a raised dais in a laboratory in one of the research hubs of Leighton-Loyola. Below her were twenty subjects in open-topped cubicles. Each of the men and women was connected to a fifty-channel physiological recorder that measured everything from blood pressure to brain waves.

The images on the bank of monitors in front of Laura danced wildly, but oddly in sync. Brain activity showed some fast theta waves coming in at 6 cycles per second, and spindle activity was increasing, up to 18 cps. It was inconceivable that all twenty subjects would slip into the same dreamlike state at the same time, but the evidence was right in front of her.

Laura tried to visualize a scenario that would cause such

a condition. Shaking her head, she sat back in her chair. She closed her eyes.

She fell into the dream.

And as she fell, the formless spirits whispered to her. She fought the dream, but she was helpless. The image of a faceless man carrying a broken lance and a shield floated in front of her for an instant and was gone, replaced by an impossibly bright light that burned everything else away. Purifying, blistering pain . . . as white and deep as God's eyes.

People were screaming, and it took Laura a moment to realize that she was one of them.

6

ANNA GRASS-LIKE-LIGHT felt awkward and clumsy and just a bit nauseated as she and Sam Woquini shouldered their way out of the crowded, filthy, graffiti-burned cable-car—part of the Rand Electromagnetic High Speed Transit System—into a chrome and glass way-station at Flagstaff, Arizona. The station looked like an uninspired, miniature version of an airily arched and cantilevered Crystal Palace. It was a nineteenth-century dream mirage, completely out of place in the deadlands of Arizona. However, the exact same design could be found in every way station under the ownership of Trans-United, for at one time, Director Leighton had developed a penchant for Joseph Paxton's Gothic designs.

Although Sam seemed totally unaffected by the shift from zero-g, Anna found every step exhausting. She had been in space too long, but then so had Sam.

But nothing bothered Sam.

"This way, Anna," he said, throwing his flight bag over his shoulder.

"Just a minute," Anna said, nodding in the direction of the rest room doors. She left her bag at Sam's feet; she had packed it light, but now she could barely carry it.

Inside the rest room, Anna pressed the clean-up pad before entering the cubicle. Gagging on the sweet smell of the remaining sterilizing gas, she leaned against the sink and pulled a narcodrine inhaler from her pocket. She inhaled a burst and felt her head clear and her strength return. Fuck it, she thought. If she had to, she'd stay high until she could get her muscles back in shape.

She closed her eyes and wished she was back in space. She needed R&R, but not down here, for Chrissakes. Everything was wrong: the air, the water, the people. It was too noisy, too dirty, and there was too much room.

But it was only for a few weeks, she told herself. Then she'd be back in orbit. Once she got out of Flagstaff, there'd be nothing but scrubby desert and a burned-out reservation. At least she wouldn't have to worry about being caught in a riot. But just being here, in this overblown Arizona village, made her anxious, for it would only take one lunatic to set off a riot. Christ, if Bangor, Maine, could be burned to the ground by crazies, any one-whore town could be dangerous to one's health.

Sam was talking to a man wearing a Trans-United security badge when she returned.

"What's happening?" she asked, picking her bag up. It was definitely lighter now.

"This is Dave Spotted Eagle," said Sam. "Our local guide."

Spotted Eagle nodded behind mirrored sunglasses. He was tall and gangly and sullen-looking, his cheeks hollow; yet there was an energy there, radiating like heat. He wore a faded black T-shirt with the short sleeves rolled over his shoulders. His arms were well muscled.

He was probably Navajo, Anna guessed, maybe twenty years old. Probably ran sheep before T-U grabbed him.

"This way, please," he said and reached for Anna's bag. She pulled it away and slipped it over her shoulder. She could fucking well manage it herself.

They threaded through the crowd, taking the glideway to the street level, where a battered, dusty, blue Ford pickup truck was double-parked, warning lights blinking and a tattered official business permit hanging from the rearview mirror. "They get this out of some museum?" · Anna asked as she and Sam tossed their bags in back.

"It works," said Spotted Eagle with a shrug. Anna and Sam climbed in, tossing a pair of work gloves, a tire iron, and a clipboard behind the seat to make room.

The truck started noisily, with a clatter of worn valves. Spotted Eagle pulled out into traffic.

"Not many roads out in the reservation," said Spotted Eagle, shifting gears and changing lanes. "These old trucks, they keep on going. Not as temperamental as the new stuff. We've got two floaters and a Lear steam bus at headquarters, but they're in the shop all the time. Sand gets into everything."

Sam was asleep before they were out of the limits of Flagstaff, his feet propped against the dash, his body jammed in against the door. Sam could sleep anywhere. She cursed him silently and fumbled in her shirt pocket for another narcodrine, which she inhaled deeply. "Does this piece of junk have air-conditioning?" Anna asked.

"Just crack the window," said Spotted Eagle with a thin smile. "Nothing like a good breeze."

"I got enough breeze as it is," said Anna, rolling up her sleeves and undoing another button on her shirt. "It's too hot and dry out here. Sucks the water out of everything."

"This is nothing," said Dave. "Wait until summer."

"With any luck I'll be long gone by then," Anna said.

Spotted Eagle smiled and squinted at her in the rearview mirror.

Anna didn't relax until they'd passed Sunset Crater. The country dropped down and opened up into a broad plain, flat and cracked and crusted like the surface of any one of a thousand asteroids, but the sun was blinding and the land seemed to be glowing white, radiating heat like the surface of a sun. In the distance were the grotesque rock formations that appeared to be as beautiful and lonely and alien as anything she had ever seen offplanet.

Soon they passed through the checkpoint and onto reservation land.

They passed through Cameron: three stores and a cluster of roadside stands, apparently thrown together with whatever sun-bleached boards were at hand. Most of the ramshackle stands had either an American or Trans-United flag flying to grab the attention of passing tourists. Some had both. Old women sat in the shade by the stands, displaying carefully arranged racks of jewelry or stacks of baskets, rugs, and trinkets. One hand-lettered sign advertised NATIVE AMERICAN HOLOGRAPHIC ARTWORK: 100% AUTHENTIC!

Anna shook her head and looked the other way. She felt angry, angry at these dollar-a-day Indians, angry at herself. At least she made more money selling out to the white man, and she didn't have to stand out in the sun all day.

North of Cameron a few widely scattered hogans were the only sign of habitation. Anna didn't know much about the Navajos, but she did know that they tended to live in family units, although often a family unit might consist of several hogans miles apart from each other. The land was not much more than hardpan, poor and worn out from years of overgrazing; it took several acres of worthless scrub to support a single sheep.

The hogans were simple affairs, squat six-sided buildings with a single door facing east, the most sacred of the four directions, the place of illumination and the morning star. The special place of the eagles—and thunder-beings. The hogans seemed to be made of anything handy; some were stone, some timber, some mud and clay. Occasionally Anna would see a cluster of two or three hogans a good distance from the road and then nothing else for miles.

Dave downshifted as they approached the road to Tuba

City. A turnoff by the intersection was littered with whiskey and beer toss-away containers. Anna smiled in recognition, recalling her own hard, fast youth. Liquor was still not allowed on the reservations, and at night the young turks probably snuck across the border, got shitfaced, and carried enough choke-dog back to get them through the night. This would be a perfect place to park and finish it off. You could see for miles in any direction; and by the time T-U or the tribal police got close, they'd be long gone. It had been harder where she grew up, in Wyoming. The border was a hundred miles away in any direction. Still, they'd managed. Kids will always find a way. She smiled, and Sam woke up.

"We almost there?" he asked, stretching and yawning.

"Not far," said Spotted Eagle.

"Look at all that green," Sam said, pointing to about an acre of corn that looked like a heat mirage.

"T-U project," said Spotted Eagle. "They've been trying for years to grow stuff out here. I guess they've got some idea of making farmers out of us. It hasn't worked, though. I figure that corn must cost about fifty frogskins an ear by the time you run all that water to it. It's so tough even the sheep won't eat it."

Anna was not impressed with Tuba City when they finally reached it. It was a small town: a few stores and restaurants, a semi-modern hotel. The tribal police headquarters was an old mobile home on cinder blocks. There was a residential area, but it was all single-story square houses, nondescript and ordinary, probably all thrown up in a month for a Trans-United project. Clouds of red dust hung over the town like a storm, roiled up by the cars and occasional horses.

The Trans-United installation was on the north side of town. The buildings were constructed of modern materials, carefully designed to look old and weathered. They were kitschy, cheaply made imitations of hogans.

Sam grunted and shook his head.

Spotted Eagle pulled into a parking slot next to one of the larger buildings. Sam and Anna followed him inside, and were hit by the rush of cool, efficient air-conditioning. A receptionist looked up from her screen and nodded cursorily to Spotted Eagle.

"He's expecting you," she said as she fed flimsies through a scanner.

A door opened and a pleasant, heavy-set man waved them into an office. He was casually dressed in slacks and a lightweight flannel shirt open at the neck; his sleeves were rolled up. His blond hair was thinning, and he had a slight overbite, which gave a belligerent cast to his face. The interior walls were covered with stunning Navajo blankets and reproductions of native sand-paintings. The outside wall was all glass, and beyond were scrubby plain, buttes, and a massive plateau that looked gray-blue because of its distance.

"Welcome to our corner of the world," the man said, breaking into an easy smile. "I'm Maxwell Bradshaw, T-U's chief cook and bottle-washer in these parts. Call me Max." He extended his hand first to Anna, then to Sam.

"You must be worn out," he said. "I imagine you've been on the go since you left orbit. How long ago was that, Anna? It's all right if I call you Anna, isn't it? We don't stand on formality out here."

Anna shrugged. "About twenty hours," she said.

"Let's get you settled in first. Get you and Sam something to eat, some rest. We can start in the morning."

"A question, Mr. Bradshaw," asked Anna. "Why us?"

"It's Max," he said. "What do you mean, Anna?"

"Look, Mr. Bradshaw," said Anna, "I don't know Navajo tribal ways from Eskimo ways. Neither one of us are Navajo. Why drag us down here when you must have a hundred more qualified people right here in Tuba City?"

"You know bureaucracies," said Bradshaw with a

shrug and a smile. "I guess I'm lucky they didn't send me a couple of deaf-mute rejects from the asteroids."

"We're them," said Sam, opening his hands and making a rude gesture.

"You two will do fine," said Bradshaw with an easy smile. "What we need here is someone who's been in space to go out and talk to these young boys and girls, get them interested in Trans-United as a career option."

"You'll draft them if they don't," said Anna.

"*I* won't," said Bradshaw. "Trans-United might. It's the company's option by legal treaty. That's their business. My business and *your* business is to pick out the best and most motivated people for the job. You see, I know a lot of these kids, maybe too well. Sometimes it's better to have an outside opinion. I've been here fifteen years and I know their families, their histories, and the way they live on the reservation. What I don't know is how they'll do in space. I've never been there, and I never will." He tapped his chest. "Weak heart," he said. "Valve trouble, rebuilt three times."

"You're missing a lot," said Sam. "Bad food, long hours, and low pay."

"I can get that right here," said Bradshaw with a laugh, "although I can't complain about the food. Dave," he said to Spotted Eagle, "why don't you show Anna and Sam to their rooms? Point out Emilio's to them. I can recommend the tostadas, but start out with the mild sauce. And whatever you do, don't bite down on any of those little green peppers."

Spotted Eagle led Anna and Sam out. As the door closed, Bradshaw walked over to his desk and pressed a button. A small screen popped out of one drawer, revealing the sharp image of a small room, one bed, and a dresser. He twisted a dial under the screen and the image shifted as the hidden camera moved, sweeping the room. Anna's room. He turned up the volume until he could hear the air-conditioner hum. Satisfied the sound was working okay, he toggled over to Sam's room and settled back into his chair.

Anna threw her bag on the bed and dug into it, scattering clothes over the spread until she came out with a bottle.

"Want some?" she asked Sam as she twisted off the cap and, coughing, took a deep swallow.

"I'll pass for now," Sam said. "I'm more inclined toward some food and some sleep."

"How about a shower first?" said Anna.

"Sounds good," Sam said. "I could use an Earthside shower. That's one thing I miss up there. Dry-sprays just don't relax you like a good shower."

"Maybe we should save water," said Anna, taking another hit off her bottle and nodding toward the bathroom. "Join me?"

"No offense," said Sam, "but I'll pass on that, too."

"Well, fuck you, Indian."

"When you and John Stranger work out your thing, then I might take a more healthy interest."

"John *Stranger!* He and I got nothing more to work out. We plug into our jobs together, and that's it."

"That's bullshit," Sam said, and he left the room.

Leighton was roused from his dream by the thrumming of the computer implant in his tooth. It intruded upon his vision of John Stranger, slowly pulled him through the layers of dream and into consciousness.

He sat straight back in his chair—appearing taller than he was, imposing—as if he were receiving a guest, and tried to remember the dream. He ran his hands through his shock of wiry gray hair; a nervous gesture.

And just as before, Leighton couldn't remember the content and substance of the dream. He only knew that he had been having recurring dreams and hallucinatory flashbacks like this for weeks. He ground his teeth in frustration.

Leighton had an eidetic memory, but he could not penetrate these dreams. He had tried dream therapy, but not even drugs had been able to break through those barriers.

Then, suddenly, an image floated up into the peripheral vision of his mind's eye.

He remembered!

John Stranger.

It was a gift . . . a revelation. Now, at last, he had a key.

Leighton could, and would, isolate this Indian bellman. He would have him tested and taken apart neuron by neuron if necessary. Leighton would uncover the source of these dreams.

But for now he needed to attend to immediate matters. His head was clear; in fact, he felt refreshed.

He tongued the implant off and said, "Yes?" although he could have subvocalized and would have been heard. He didn't bother haranguing his aide for calling him when he was in private mode.

"It looks like Macro is paying us back for burning their deep-sleep operation in White Sands," a voice said. It seemed to be coming from within Leighton's head, but that was the implant. Leighton was used to it; it was little different than thought itself.

"Get to the point," Leighton said.

"We've received new intelligence regarding the hit on the Winnipeg installation. Seems that Macro set it up. Looks like those fuckers are gearing up for a nice quiet war."

"They just got caught with their pants down," Leighton said, as he opaqued walls, floor, and ceiling. "Our security was probably better than they had anticipated. But it still grinds me that we lost all those people." He pressed his knee against the inside of his desk, which deactivated the security lock, and the door whispered open. A man in his early thirties with thinning blond hair, freckles, and a slight build quickly entered the office. He was one of Leighton's aides, and a particularly close friend, for Leighton could only trust the small group of secretaries and aides who worked closely with him and had become his counselors. They practically lived with him, at his beck and call.

This man's name was Damon Borland, and he was—as were most of the other aides—a *wunderkind*. He had advanced degrees in space law, liquid-state physics, and musicology. He also knew more about mid-twentieth-century American blues and jazz than any man alive; he composed in that tradition, and often played for Leighton. His *Sensorium Kobold Videotecta* composition was considered the major symphonic work of the decade. Leighton loved music, which was one of the many reasons he had retained Borland in his inner circle. Compliment though it was, it was also a frustration for Borland, for he should have been an independent ambassador to Macro or Brazil by this time. Leighton knew that, but he considered his own sanity more important than Borland's career, which he would take care of at the proper time.

"Suggestions?" Leighton asked.

"You might consider reprisal," Borland said. "If we leak it to their sources that we know they took out the Winnipeg shop, we'd be safe. They're not interested in escalating this into all-out war."

"I want to know if Macro has decoded any more of that alien transmission than we have. This may be the time to go in and snatch some of their people. Work up a plan and get back to me. What else do you have?"

Borland began to speak, but Leighton received a message that his mistress Antea Hetaera wished admittance. Leighton once again touched the side of his desk with his knee and the office door whispered open. He glanced at Borland, which was enough to tell him that they would continue in a few moments. Then Antea swept through the room, as if she were raw energy itself. And, in fact, she was burning with her own life energies. Although Leighton had elevated her long ago, she still considered herself a courtesan and never wore clothes, not even to the most important functions. She embodied the modern sensibility of physical beauty and displayed no obvious surgical implants or bio-ornamentation. Her face was heart-shaped and fair, dusted with freckles; her long curly hair was light brown. She was thin, as if built to be a quick sylvan creature. In an ancient age, she would have been mistaken for a preternatural creature, a naiad, siren, sylph, dryad, or any one of a dozen elemental spirits once thought to have inhabited seas and forests and the very being of things.

She did not look to be seventy years old. She did not look to be dying.

Antea had introduced an irreversible bio-organism into her system for reasons beyond Leighton's understanding. It would kill her. But for these last few months she would be as radiant as Leighton's dreams.

She kissed Leighton and held her cheek next to his for an instant. Leighton imagined that she was burning with fever, although her face did not look at all flushed. She smelled of musk and sweat, for she used no perfume; her odor always excited Leighton. "So have I interrupted something vast and important and fascinating?" she asked.

"Of course," Leighton said, smiling at her as he leaned back into the softness of his chair.

"Good. Am I not to be consulted, then, upon matters of importance?" She was being coy, but she was also being truthful, for Leighton held few secrets from her. She had never failed to provide excellent counsel, and had to be doubly guarded from Leighton's enemies because of that.

"Damon will brief you on everything that's going on *everywhere*," Leighton said with good-humored sarcasm, seemingly vitalized by her. His tone of voice changed and he said, "Damon will fill you in, and if you have any suggestions . . ."

She nodded and then asked, "Have you been in com-

munication with Fiammetta?'' She did not seem worried
about his reaction, for he had never once raised his voice to
her, although his friends and counselors often felt his high
temper.

Leighton did not immediately respond. He had not
thought of his wife for several days. It had been mutually
agreed that she remain Earthside. He did not feel he was
asking too much to have Antea to himself. She had only a
few weeks left to live. He would return to his wife after he
interred Antea's ashes in the sarcophagus he had prepared
for her in the chapel of the house. His friend Della was even
now creating a statue of her, a holographic videotect that
would guarantee her image be kept alive. She would be a
ghost in his house, a consolation for the light she had decided to extinguish. Yet only he would see her; she would
never trouble Fiammetta again.

Antea's decision to end her life was one decision Leighton could not control. She simply claimed that it was her
time, and it was certainly her right.

Although he had tried, Leighton could not argue it. This
form of ceremonial suicide had been a tradition in his own
family; and one day Leighton, too, would probably choose
the method of his extinction. But first he had to ensure that
his son David would inherit a secure empire.

''I have been extremely busy,'' Leighton said guiltily,
''but of course I've been in contact with her.''

''Not for three weeks,'' Antea said. ''She has been so
frustrated trying to contact you personally, that she called
me.''

Leighton looked at Damon, who lowered his eyes. ''I
told you of these things, Gerard, but you said you would
respond in due time.''

''And I kept meaning to do so, but—''

''Your domestic problems require as much attention as
any other diplomacy,'' Antea said.

''I'll call her today,'' Leighton said.

"Then I'll leave you two to matters of state." Antea kissed Leighton hungrily on the mouth and left. As the door whispered closed behind her, it struck Leighton how much he loved her. He felt a coursing, adrenal rush of sadness and emptiness.

He had a passing thought of Antea submerged in the icy depths of an ocean or starless space, and he trembled.

"Director . . . ?" Damon asked tentatively. "I can return later. I'll have worked out several scenarios for—"

"Continue," Leighton said.

"There's little else. I've split up John Stranger's crew, as per your orders. Most of them are scattered to widely separated units, but Anna Grass-Like-Light and Sam Woquini are about as far out of the way as they can be." He chuckled. "Those two floaters are a real pain in the ass. They were due for Earthside leave, so we gave it to them in spades. They're sucking dust in Arizona now. Our agent in Flagstaff, man called Bradshaw, is monitoring."

Leighton nodded.

"And one last thing," Damon said. "Jellyroll Morton."

"Yes?" asked Leighton, smiling, and for an instant his face looked almost boyish.

Suddenly it was as if they were in an ancient auditorium, for the strains of "Black Bottom Stomp," one of Jellyroll Morton's finest rocking rags, pulsed and echoed and flashed from one theme to another. This was one of Morton's tightest arrangements; and his use of the string bass instead of a marching band tuba was unprecedented at the time.

"I augmented the original," Damon said. "You can blame me for any inconsistencies, notably the kazoo and comb players. Kid Ory is on trombone; Barney Bigard, Darnell Howard, and myself are on clarinet. And I had someone color up the vocals by Lew LeMar."

"No images?" Leighton asked.

"You want music or bullshit?" Damon bowed dramatically and left . . . and, for a time, Leighton escaped to find relief in the syncopated, mathematical universes of "High Society," "Shreveport Stomp," "Grandpa's Spells," "Frog-i-More Rag," "Big Foot Ham," and "Weary Blues."

Sam and Anna ate at Emilio's, a small Mexican restaurant on the main street in town. They used loads of hot sauce and put away countless little green peppers, glad for some spice after so much bland food in space. Afterward, Sam went back to his room, but Anna went down to the trading post and sat on the porch sneaking sips from her bottle until Spotted Eagle came around. She knew he would.

Anna found she liked him. He was surprisingly gentle, yet there was a fierceness about him, an implacability. He was the kind who made strong friends and terrible enemies.

But he had not tensed, nor stopped, when she had moaned "John" during her orgasm. She gave him points for that.

Spotted Eagle was gone from her room long before dawn, long before she woke from her dreamless sleep.

Bradshaw's tapes, of course, captured it all. . . .

7

THE GONDOLA BOBBED across the flooded, oil-slicked, garbage-strewn Piazzetta San Marco, its two passengers dressed in bright feathers as sumptuous and thick as furs. Their whorls of iridescent violet and emerald were the colors of peacocks; their masks were satiny black and rostrated. The passengers looked like great, chimerical birds of prey perched in their golden gondola, which appeared to be headed toward the Isola di San Giorgio. From her window in the balcony overlooking the plaza, Laura Bowen couldn't tell if they were genetically engineered mooncalves or simply dignitaries costumed for the ball this evening.

There was no question about the young water-people standing about on the slippery quays, parading their sleek if not yet completely developed bodies. Revealing gill-slits that looked like chest wounds, they waved webbed hands for the coins tossed by gawking tourists. A young man shouted "sogliola" to them from an elevated walkway as he threw his coins, obviously not realizing that he was calling them flounders, a term of local derision. A young merman with shoulder-length, straight black hair picked up the coins and then, scowling, made an obscene motion at the tourist.

The feathered pair, who were huddled together and lost in their floating nest, ignored all of them.

Laura hated herself for loving this decaying, water-logged, filthy city. She certainly deserved this earthside trip . . . in spades; but this little perk couldn't begin to make up for the way Trans-United had boxed in her career, locking her into a well-paid but definitely low-end position. No matter what kind of an inflated title they gave her, running psychological profiles on at-risk employees and their family members was a job that could easily be handled by technical personnel; although it was true that since the riots her job had become more significant. But still, her two Ph.D.'s—mathematics and psychology—might as well be wallpaper.

But Venice had captured her in unexpected ways, unlike Rome, which she hated; she had been there three years ago for the last Multicorp Summit. Rome was too artificial. Too consciously modern. It was as if all the ghosts of the past had elected to leave its narrow streets, which were destined to be widened into the precise grids of boulevards. But it was more than that, for Rome had become a city under siege by its own people, all of whom lived in constant fear. Fear of themselves.

Unlike other major cities, Venice had not yet had a significant riot. It had other problems, to be sure. The first of the floods had been devastating; countless treasures lost forever. But now a series of locks maintained a more or less constant water level. But the technology that prevented floods did nothing for the quality of the poisoned waters of the canals. Even as Laura gazed out into the transparent darkness, she watched sludge glowing and burning on the surface of the water.

"You there, Laura?" A discreet knock at the door: two soft raps. That was Marie. Laura had almost forgotten that her assistant had promised to drop by for coffee, scheduling, and gossip. Marie was right on time, as always.

"Door's open," Laura said, closing the window. The air

conditioner cycled on, sighing as if relieved. Then she turned up the lights.

"Jesus H. Christ," Marie said, eyeing the room, which was completely paneled with blocks of Capodimonte porcelain; upon all the pearly walls, in relief, were turquoise and orange and green and yellow figures: birds, flowers, heraldic emblems, and a characteristic pattern of knotted branches. And like interior windows, every other panel contained a looking glass that reflected walls and ceiling and mirrors into seeming infinity. The ceiling was also porcelain; and in the center of the room, hanging like a viridian green stalactite, was a hand-blown Venetian glass chandelier, a fragile and delicate reproduction of an early English style.

Laura gave her a tour of the apartment, and then they sat down in one of the four Louis XVI gilt armchairs that were placed around a circular table inlaid with contrasting squares of marble. "I needed a map just to find the bathroom," Laura said. "This is a bit of overkill."

"I'll trade," Marie said. She was a small, slightly overweight woman, about Laura's age, with close-cropped dark hair, stylized ringlets that seemed damp upon her forehead; it was an ordinary face, yet somehow a memorable one. That was due to Marie's eyes: one was green, the other brown. She'd been Laura's trusted assistant for the last five years.

"We peons have to stay over in Punta Sabbioni," she said. "That ferry ride is going to be the death of me. I thought hovers were supposed to be smooth. I requested Lido, but they were booked solid. Too much brass here."

"We'll all make a good impression," Laura said sarcastically. "Get a good ten-second video bite on the night-net and prove that you're not really interested in profits, but are only concerned with the betterment of all mankind. You know, some of the fucking bites are so good, I believe them hook, line, and sinker. Even my own. Makes me feel like a regular Joan of Arc. I recommend it for at least five minutes every day."

"Right," laughed Marie. "But is Joan of Arc ready now to discuss such mundane matters as the panels they've booked you on and the paper you're supposed to deliver at eight-thirty tomorrow morning?"

Laura groaned. "Eight-thirty? Why do they always insist on booking me on these stupid panels at the crack of dawn?" She touched the servant bell and ordered coffee. A small robot whispered into the room, placed a silver tea service on the table and poured coffee for Laura and Marie. The robot returned a moment later with a plate of cakes and cookies: fig cakes, certosino, pine nut macaroons, and several meringues.

"Oh, this is just great for my weight problem," Marie said. "Thanks a heap."

"Give yourself a break, lest you turn anorexic."

She took one of the fig cakes, looked at it wistfully and made a face, then tried one of the other confections. "Here's your packet. We're all registered."

Laura wasn't worried, for Marie was a genius at organizing and filtering through the mounds of bullshit paperwork that Trans-United kept throwing at them.

"So what's my schedule?" she asked as she opened her registration packet and slid out a bewildering mass of brochures, programs, pocket programs, invitations, free tickets, and advertisements. Two of the brochures started talking to her; she sailed them across the room to the fireplace.

"Here, these are the basics," said Marie, handing her a single printed sheet. "It's not too bad, pretty much like we expected. Same old shit. Oh, David Bass of Maxwell, Inc. has replaced Harry Davis on your mass hysteria panel. That's certainly an improvement, I would think."

"Bass is okay," Laura said. "He's opinionated, but not as

pig-headed and loud as Davis. Maybe the rest of us will have a chance to say something."

"At least he won't be grab-assing you behind the podium, that's something right there."

Laura raised her eyebrows.

"Bass carries holos of his wife and kids," Marie said. "One of your basic faithful husbands and doting fathers."

Smiling: "I trust no man." Laura called for drinks. "Let's get shitfaced, we deserve it."

"Your presentation is also set for ten in the morning, day after tomorrow. I'm sorry about that, I tried to get you an afternoon slot, but it was no go."

"So what else is new?"

"Believe me, I hate morning speeches every bit as much as you," Marie said. "But all you have to do is be awake and talk. I've got to catch the first ferry over to set it up. I'd hoped maybe I'd get lucky tonight at the ball. I had in mind a wonderfully debauched evening ending with a champagne breakfast in someone else's bed. So if I get lucky tonight, I'll look like a zombie tomorrow."

Laura smiled. Marie gave the appearance of being all business; she dressed decorously in suits, wore the correct colors and cuts, and effectively managed not to stand out in a crowd as overly feminine. But whenever she returned to Earth, she gave herself free rein. Laura had once suspected that it was because there was so little privacy in the O'Neills, but there were other reasons: an old skeleton that Laura had buried by eradicating it permanently from Marie's folder when she took her on as her assistant.

The robot brought in the drinks—a Drambuie for Laura and a Pernod for Marie—and then left as unobtrusively as it had entered.

"You have those two other panels," Marie said. "But those are in the afternoon, so you're safe. So far you have three luncheon engagements and one dinner. Beep me if you get any more and I'll update your itinerary. If you need me to, I'll write up some boilerplate responses for any panel questions you think might come up. They have you scheduled for some panels that are a bit out of your field. Oh, one thing more, Kempton Miller's talk is about the economic impact of the dream-riots. I thought I'd go to that one, unless you want to take it. Christ, by now I know the stats by heart."

"No, you go ahead," Laura said, sipping her strong, sweet Scotch liqueur from a delicate and fragile snifter.

"How about the Datacom symposium? In their usual pompous manner, they've titled it *The Increased Manifestations of Antitechnological Religious Fanaticism*. I call it the nut panel."

"I suppose I ought to go," Laura said with a sigh. So much of this was a waste of time. The real information was never presented at the formal sessions, but leaked piece by piece in private conversations, pillow talks, or after money had changed hands.

"Then that's about it," Marie said, sipping her coffee, which was, by now, cold, "except for one tiny, little, absolutely wonderful thing. I always save the best for last, girl. But first I need to know something."

"Shoot."

"You still planning on staying down here after the meeting?"

Laura nodded. "Maybe six weeks."

"I thought so. I took the liberty of activating your New York apartment. Nothing worse than returning to a dead cell."

"That was a nice gesture, Marie, but you should have checked with me. I'm staying in Europe."

"Change of venue, honey. You're scheduled to be in New York in ten days."

"What are you talking about?"

Marie smiled and handed Laura a decal-edged sheet of royal blue, letterhead stationery. "Seems you've been summoned to the Directorate. Somebody's noticed your work. It's signed by one of Leighton's secretaries. It must mean a promotion."

"I doubt that very much," Laura said, although why else would she be called back to New York?

"Congratulations, Laura," Marie said, suddenly effusive. "And I think I've done a damn good job of holding everything in." She put down her empty coffee cup and stood up. "I know it's a promotion, I can feel it." Then she came around the table and gave Laura a bear hug.

Laura closed her eyes, confused. She had planned on following up a lead as to the identity of her parents. She had certainly hoped to be planetside for more than ten days. Well, there was always the slim chance that her new position would keep her Earthbound.

"You'll still have some time here," Marie said softly, letting her go and stepping back a pace. "You should take things in stride, lest this . . . search of yours becomes an obsession."

"I don't know what you mean," Laura said carefully. "I'm only staying to run psych profiles on dream-riot subjects. There are some interesting correlations with certain of our orbital cases."

"I know why you're staying," said Marie, walking to the door and pausing. "I hope you find them, if that's what you really want."

"I thought we were going to get shitfaced," Laura said, changing to a more comfortable subject; she forced some enthusiasm into her voice. "You didn't even touch your drink. And maybe you're right, maybe they are finally recognizing they've got somebody wonderful here. If I get promoted then you get—"

"I know, then I get a raise." Marie laughed and said, "How many times have I—have we—heard that old tired bit of party line?"

Laura chuckled and squeezed Marie's hand. "Come on,

old friend, stay for a drink. To celebrate what I might not even get!''

"I'd love to, but I'm letting you off the hook this time. I've only got four hours to turn into a vamp, and you've got to be an example to us all . . . *and* the last time we all got doped and you took a 'drine to get sober, you fell asleep and missed your own presentation.''

Laura grinned, remembering, then went back onto her balcony after Marie left. She sipped her drink and looked down at the water below; reflections played on the water, descending into its depths, which appeared to be endless. There was something frightening about dark water, as if it were some sort of deadly, ebon portal into the world of dreams and nightmares. Laura took a deep breath and held it until she felt dizzy. The trail was cold, thirty-two years cold, but that didn't mean she couldn't try. She had no choice, for how could she feel comfortable with herself until she knew where the hell she came from? She felt like some wraith condemned to spend eternity searching for her parents. That familiar sense of being incomplete gnawed at her like some psychic, painful arthritis. She had tried every avenue to locate her parents, but had been deadlocked over and over again.

Finding them should have been relatively simple. It had been anything but simple.

Yet for all her discomfort, she had not had a deprived childhood. Her foster parents had been caring, if a little distant. There had always been plenty of money for the best boarding schools, clothes, travel. It was all supplied by a trust fund whose donor's name did not exist, did not exist *anywhere*.

Although Laura was not beautiful, she was attractive; she had very strong yet delicate features: hazel eyes that were large and lustrous, even if set a bit wide; a full, sensual mouth; a slight cleft in her chin; and long, thick chestnut hair. There had been few romantic relationships, for every man somehow seemed to disappoint her; she understood that to be a failing in herself. She was gregarious and socially adept, but a loner.

All that would change, she thought, if she could find her parents . . . her place . . . her personal history.

When Laura had turned twenty-one, the trust was turned over to her, and she was shocked to discover that she had enough to live comfortably for the rest of her life. After a disastrous but instructive two-month fling, she returned to graduate school and then went to work for Trans-United.

It all seemed to have passed so quickly. The novelty of living in space soon became routine, as did her job, and her obsession to find her parents had swallowed up her life.

Laura sighed. Maybe the meeting with Director Leighton would change the direction of her career. Perhaps a promotion would change things, keep her busy, take her mind off the fragile ghosts that, in her mind, were her parents.

But she knew better. Nothing ever changed and the ghosts that haunted her never left.

For the moment she did not want to move at all. She did not want to leave this place, whose very stones seemed to be dreaming.

Laura looked out past the flooded plaza to the lagoon beyond. There, like two-dimensional cut-outs in the almost blue atmosphere of twilight, floated hover ferries, small speedboats, gondolas, and a steam barge, packed high with bales of hay. A woman shouted from the window of an adjacent building and was immediately answered by a man in the street. A line of African tourists passed below, recording everything in their path for posterity. The smells of food cooking were carried in the air: it was dinnertime. Children laughed and chattered in a courtyard across the canal. Tradespeople, looking bedraggled after a long day, walked home; some carried packages, some toolboxes or briefcases.

Beside even the glitter of Venice, ordinary life could exist.

It seemed that John Stranger was only allowed to sleep before scheduled dream therapy sessions. Although the other participants were seated comfortably in various closed testing cubicles on Earth and in orbit, John remained trapped in his exoskeletal harness in the navigation quarters of the prototype ship. The purpose of these group sessions was never explained to him; neither was the choice of participants.

As Anna Grass-Like-Light had once said: "You don't need to explain to the rabbit why it's going to be turned into stew."

But when John was learning to become a medicine man and a hunter, Broken-finger had indeed taught him how to talk to his prey, how to call to it with prayer, and apologize to it after he had sent its spirit back to Wakan Tanka.

John thought of these things as he dutifully answered the questions that seemed automatically to form in his mind and were, in fact, whispered to him in the darkness. The stars burned steadily in the blackness around him, a star-blanket created out of heat and cold.

And the whispers were dreams themselves, carrying John away, for he imagined he was drifting upon an eternal, yet shallow, ocean, moving further into its unknown and hazy distances with his every breath.

Every breath that carried him deeper and deeper into a programmed dream.

As if he were inhaling and exhaling himself back to Earth.

And back in time.

As the dream took him, he was provided with sufficient programmed information.

He was in the manufacturing district of Nottingham, England, during the scourge of the Depression of 1815. The crowd's roaring was a terrible din, almost like a steam train screaming and ringing through the chin-to-forehead mass of people. Almost everyone was wearing a black mask, as if this were some profane proceeding taking place in a decidedly English version of Hell.

John could hardly move. He was pressed between a laborer wearing a tattered hand-me-down overcoat and filthy trousers held under his feet by straps and a portly woman wearing an orange and yellow striped shawl and a heavy brown dress. He gagged on the smell of the man, who had obviously doused his coat with a waterproofing solution; and, indeed, a thin, cold drizzle threatened to become sleet. The sky was dark with sooty clouds and coal smoke; the air was heavy with ash. It was as if the world were submerged in dirty water. The huge, monolithic buildings that walled the streets were almost unreal in their overpowering and isolated presence.

John could only glimpse from his vantage the red coats and shako-style high hats of army officers and their troops that surrounded the crowd.

Yet he realized, even inside the dream, that this was a fabrication created by the chemicals he was absorbing from the med-patches on his chest and the electrical impulses being fed through electrodes taped to his forehead. In essence, this was a feelie: psychedelic and holographic.

This was going to be a nasty one, John thought. As if in response, there was a sudden great cheering as men and women broke into the Sandscombe Stocking & Lace Frame Factory. While the angry Ludds, mostly unemployed mill workers, smashed machinery and stocking and lace frames, the army moved in.

Like a beast that had been wounded, a tremor passed through the crowd. Luddites broke ranks, fought, and all became pandemonium as the professional soldiers worked their way directly through the mob with club and shield. A cry went up and was repeated, as if the words could give muscle and muniment to the poor, thwarted Ludds.

"Ludd, Ned Ludd, Ned Ludd. . . ."

Then there was fighting nearby; and the crowd seemed to open up like a veil to reveal the oncoming soldiers as people ran to get out of their way. A man was struck by the barrel of a soldier's rifle and fell to the ground; in turn, a soldier who had slipped too far away from his comrades was beaten and stomped underfoot.

Shots were fired.

A soldier seemed suddenly to materialize before him, striking a woman who was in his way. John could see every line and pimple in the man's flushed, wet face.

He was a boy, no more than seventeen.

In a trice, he had lifted his rifle and aimed it directly at John. Although he had been tricked by effects such as this in other sessions, now John separated himself from the dream. In that mad instant before hammer struck flint, he felt time expand, unravel. He looked around to the edges of his field of view. He could see the flaws in the scenario, the small incongruous details: a modern building facade, a shimmering where one image met another, impossibly modern and ancient weapons carried by soldiers and Luddites alike. But all this *felt* like reality: cold and fetid and dangerous; once again, he wondered if he could die in these dreams. . . .

He heard voices cry, "No machines."

"Salvation."

"No machines!"

"No machines!"

And he heard a cracking and felt a shock as a musket ball struck his chest, bursting his heart.

He was falling.

The crowd blurred out of existence.

Tumbling through darkness, cold dead space.

John tried to touch the spirits.

This illusion of death was too strong, too painful.

For an instant he felt stationary; it was the fixed stars that were spinning wildly around him, and then his perspective shifted as he faced every floater's nightmare: drifting alone and out of control.

The cold, solitary death.

Then he found himself drifting through the cloudy atmosphere of an alien landscape, as if he were thistledown carried on the wind. He crossed towering mountain ranges and deep canyons. What appeared to be a cloud, yet was in fact a floating city, drifted by; and then everything turned yellow, an uncomfortable, almost blinding fluorescent yellow that slowly faded like a retinal afterimage.

Only when the darkness was complete and uninterrupted did the soft, almost babyish face of Bernard Van Heisman, the administrator of the test, float holographically in front of John. He wondered where the absent Laura Bowen was.

"We will now discuss the current session," Van Heisman said. "Let us compare our own various dreams and impressions that were triggered by the programmed dream. Begin."

Then John felt the presence of the other people in his test group; and he had the distinct impression that they were seated together in a great but otherwise empty hall.

"I remember mah-chines," drawled a man whose face was a pointillistic pattern of tattoos. These had been all the rage in the undercity slums; this most recent fad had quickly spread like a virus until it reached the colonies, where it died a timely and natural death. "Not mah-chines liken we know them, but more'as'n subsistential machines a-could think and p'rocrate, something like 'at."

The man's name was Roberto Turano and he had been a core tower repairman and Bostown opera critic before Trans-United "invited" him up for the project.

A woman whom John imagined was sitting beside Roberto shook her head. She was a nurse. "No machines," she said flatly, as if she were musing, speaking to herself. "No cities. Just lights and colors and patterns. Nothing coherent."

"She's correct about one thing," said an elderly man, who looked to be Chinese. "There were no cities and no people"—and he raised his voice in register as if to stress his point—"and neither were there machines. Not even a roller. The canyon we saw last time was closer, but the mountains are wrong. Too high." He smiled, as if in embarrassment, "And they were alive."

"The mountains?" asked Van Heisman.

The old man nodded. "And . . ."

"Yes?"

"They floated, and then they were not mountains at all, but—"

John listened, but felt it was all futile. Dreams and visions were part of the spirit world. They had no flesh and often no form and could not be cut up and examined like organs and flesh.

But Trans-United set great store in what had become known—for lack of a simpler, more sensible term—as synergistic dream induction, or dream telepathy. In several cases dream telepathy and even presumptive alien contact had been experimentally induced. The idea was that "talents" such as John Stranger and the others might increase the odds of contact—of gaining information.

Just what was the connection between the dream riots and the alien message received by the Cup and Saucer?

Was it coincidence?

Design?

No one knew, but if there was a connection, Trans-

United wanted to be the one to discover it and, of course, exploit it.

There were discrete patterns. It was estimated that almost twenty percent of the Earth's population had received the dreams in one form or another, although those persons were not necessarily prone to participating in the mass hysteria of the dream riots.

The dreams: everyone interpreted them differently. Some saw them as a religious experience, others as nightmares. Some were taken over and destroyed by them while others were unaffected. It seemed to be nothing more than some terrible luck of the draw.

The computer construct Einstein had projected a slight correlation of telepathic dream receptivity and concomitant ego valuation with artistic abilities; but it was barely significant statistically.

The session carried on, endlessly, it seemed.

John was tired. So little sleep, and no rest at all. He barely attended to the susurration of voices and instead fixed on the people, his eyes wandering from face to face. A Buddhist monk. A miner from the asteroids. An elementary school teacher from an isolated rural district. A professor. An idiot child of twelve.

John felt drawn to the child, Matt Nicholiasson. Taken from a creche in Bangkok. High forehead, handsome babyfat face, and curly blond hair. Eyebrows so blond they could barely be seen. Deep blue eyes. A mental age stabilized at four.

Matt dreamed continuously.

Like a medicine man.

In the world of the spirits.

John blinked, felt a slight relief as the constraints on his muscles were removed.

"And your impressions, Stranger?"

Sleep . . . I need to sleep, you wasicun *bastards.*

And so he did. It was as if he were dropped into unconsciousness, as if some hormonal toggle had been pressed, for he slept . . . and dreamed.

Thunder-beings.

Beating hearts and dark wings.

The teeth of ice the shadows of fire.

Death ordinary as spirit dreams.

"Stranger . . . ? Please report."

The world of floating cities and ravines as deep as the place of diminished souls. A place of spirits wrapped in flesh like wicks in wax . . . and John was being carried by the thunder-beings as surely as Dante was carried to Hell on Geryon.

"Broken-finger," John called, dreaming of the time he, John, had fasted by the talking stones. The visions had come then like water pouring into a dry riverbed, and they came again now. But the dreams, like the turns his life had taken, were jumbled.

All the same, the nightmares twisted and called John to the spirits. Now . . . *now* his life was a blinding fluorescence of yellow. The flowing of his heart into the vision world.

"Stranger! What are you doing?"

Beating, breathing wings . . . thunder-beings.

A bell ringing over and over.

"You're projecting, Stranger! Stop!"

Corn Woman and the Sandman in a dance of death. Here they are! Lightning. Claws. Wings.

"Anna!" cried John Stranger, seeing the trouble.

"Bird," said the idiot child. "Bad bird."

Laura entered the main room of La Fenice Theatre. Flooded—as was a good part of Venice—to a depth of eight to ten feet, the surface that was now the floor had been flash frozen except for a circle in the center where a fountain splashed water thirty feet into the air. Beneath the thin but solid ice, water-people dressed in brightly colored costumes swam ceaselessly, like neon fish in a great aquarium.

The tiers of balconies that rose almost to the gilded ceiling were covered with white banners and thousands of red and white lilies. Waiters and waitresses costumed as white birds circulated through the crowd.

As she moved through the receiving line, Laura marveled at the costumes. Some of the guests had opted for simple masks, as motile on their faces as human skin, but the majority had gone to great expense. Some, who had transformed themselves into fabulous, mythical beasts, wore exoskeletons under their perfect costumes, which gave uncanny realism to every movement. Others dressed in robes and gowns that seemed to be fashioned out of pure light. All manner of fabulous upright beasts and historical personages moved across the floor of ice like holographs on a surface of pure transparent blue.

Laura had reached the head of the line, and his most powerful and illustrious Lord Doge Enrico Bocconio took her hand and kissed it lightly. He wore only a simple felt mask, but his costume was traditional and ancestral; it had not changed in design since the fifteenth century. He wore a pointed cap over a coif of white linen, a doublet of red and gold—the colors of the Doge—a *gonnella* with sleeves of shot silk, a crimson tunic embroidered in gold thread, and a long cape with a rounded stand-up collar made of the same material. "Ah, Miz Bowen, it is so good to see you again. Are you still residing in Cambridge Colony? If I recall, you've been engaged in therapy. I'm also told you're making a considerable reputation for yourself with your work on the historiography of crowd behavior."

Laura was momentarily taken aback. She had only met the Doge once before, and that had been years ago. But then she noted the tattle-tale embedded behind his left ear. The Doge was the elderly patriarch of the Bocconio family and head of the powerful Multeck corporation that was hosting the conference. Families were paramount in this country, which was run like a corporation. All corporations were family controlled. Her own corporation, Trans-United, was no less a family affair. Director Leighton had been grooming his son, David, for years to take over. Gradually David had assumed more responsibilities. He was, in fact, supposed to be here: the highest-ranked representative of Trans-United at this conference. Families. Everywhere she turned, families. She blinked once, swallowed the pain and was all business again.

"You're too kind, Doge Bocconio. I am still in the colonies most of the year. In the same old rut, one might say."

"I think most of us who are Earthbound would envy you your rut."

Laura bowed her head slightly in formal response and said, "I am very happy to be back in Venice. And all of this is quite impressive," she said, referring to the sumptuous surroundings.

"And your room, it is satisfactory?"

"Excellent. My thanks."

"It is the least we can do for such a beautiful and successful woman. It was once, you know, part of the Markian Library. Our caretaker tells me that at night he can hear the ghosts of my ancestors plotting in those very halls."

"I'll be careful," Laura said.

"Always a wise idea," said the Doge, moving to the person behind Laura.

Laura made her way through the huge room, drifting from conversation to conversation. It was a well-attended meeting; even Swiss Corp was represented. There was the usual mix of administrators, researchers, and upper-level personnel. She had been talking for several minutes with David Bass before he told her that the person who was standing within earshot dressed and figured as Saint Dylan was none other than Dr. Truong-Buru-Toi; he was one of Macro's intelligence chiefs. It was no wonder that very little information of substance could ever be discussed openly at scientific gatherings.

Then David Leighton, the heir to Trans-United's directorship, approached her. He was a solidly built man of about twenty-five, with curly auburn hair the same shade as Laura's and a delicately-featured face. His mouth was a bit too thin, giving him a Puritan appearance; but he was handsome, with high cheekbones, cleft chin, and deeply set blue eyes. He was the only one in the room who was not in costume. He wore a simple suit and a collared, button-down shirt. That in itself created quite an impression at the party. However, he had to be wearing a bodyshield. David was always, of necessity, surrounded by his retinue: a squad of biomoded bodyguards and a clutch of secretaries and various advisors.

"I'm sorry I'll miss your talk tomorrow," David said to Laura. "Too many commitments. But I did read your paper. You seem to be bucking the trend. Most people are convinced mass hysteria is the root cause of the dream-riots."

"Then why do we find similar signs among miners working alone in the asteroids, hundreds of miles away from each other?" Laura countered. I'm reacting too quickly, she thought. David always greeted her by talking shop instead of the usual pleasantries; perhaps it was a function of his position. He had no time for peripheral matters. But Laura was nervous. She had always been attracted to him. And it was true that he had never shown the slightest inclination. Yet she could hear the tension raw in her voice, and she blushed, chagrined.

David laughed. "Whoa, Laura. I said I'd read your paper. You do good work, as always. It's only that you seem to hold a minority opinion."

"If the minority is right, they're right," she said softly, with a smile, so as not to seem shrill. "Science is not yet a matter that's put up to a vote. And I'm sure of my data."

"And I'm inclined to trust your work," David said. He glanced around, reflexively surveying the room. "Duty calls," he said, and then he directed his attention back to

Laura. He paused. "We should really get together. Perhaps we could take in a show, or just talk. If I can sidestep my meetings and presentations for a night, I'll ring you. That is, uh, if you wouldn't mind." He seemed slightly nervous, embarrassed.

"Yes," Laura said, "I would like that very much."

After an awkward moment, they parted; and Laura had to repress a sudden rush of euphoria. She wanted to leave this ball right now and shout into the wind and ride in a gondola, savor this good time of anticipation, for surely, she imagined, she was heading for a letdown. But that would be tomorrow, or the day after. She felt foolish, for she couldn't stop smiling. Infatuation might not be love, but it was sure as hell the best part of a relationship, she told herself.

She circulated through the various cliques and groups, and found that for a change she was actually enjoying it. After all, she was here to see and be seen.

Well, she thought giddily, I'm here and I've been seen. And unlike Marie, I wasn't looking for male company.

Laura sipped a Muscat de Beaumes de Venise 2147 that an androgynous-looking waiter had pressed on her. He insisted that it would be like drinking rainbows, even if she just had a sip; and he was right. The fragrant dessert wine was perfection. Just then she saw Marie, who had her arms around two tall men wearing black feathered masks. Maybe she would get her champagne breakfast after all.

It was announced that an entertainment would soon begin. Laura found the waiter, who had not yet distributed all of the Muscat. Her tulip-shaped crystal goblet refilled, she headed up the back steps to the upper boxes. She took a seat in one of the cozy compartments and looked down on the floor below.

An orchestra tuned up; the mermen swam in formations that reminded Laura of bursts of fireworks. As the orchestra began playing a fanfare, someone slipped into the seat beside her.

"Good evening, Miz Bowen," said a man's voice, distorted by a warbler, though the shapeless cloak and rigid mask could disguise a woman as well as a man.

"Do I know you?" Laura asked.

"No. We have not yet had that pleasure. But I know you. Excuse me, but I must ascertain if you are bugged." He waved a thin wand near her.

"What's the meaning of this?" Laura said, standing up to leave. She felt a knife of fear, for even here in this crowd, she was vulnerable, as was everyone else.

"My scanner passes you. That's good. I have something you want." The orchestra played loud crescendos of high brass notes. Before she could slip through the curtain, he— or she—said, "Your parents. I know who they are."

Laura stopped. "You *what*?"

"They are still alive, if that eases your mind."

"You can't be serious," Laura said, as she stood just inside the curtain and stared at the mask that gave no clues. "Where are they . . . ? *Who* are they? And why are you sneaking in here to tell me this?"

"Information is dear. And I am in the business of information. On a small scale, of course. I will be in Barcelona, ten days from today. Take a room in the Wagner and don't look for me. I will find you. . . . But you must bring me one thing in exchange."

"I don't believe you. Why should I? You've given me absolutely nothing tangible."

"We want John Stranger's psych profile, specifically the results of his Maxwell/Ryan test. Raw data will be fine. We can interpret what we need from that."

"If you know the test, then you also know it's classified."

"And so are the names of your parents, Miz Bowen.

Enjoy the concert. It would not be wise to have me followed."

The man rose and left. Laura sat down, stunned. The
first movement of the fusion jazz symphony had ended to
applause from the floor. Laura drank her wine quickly, as
if it were liquor. She needed a narcodrine, something to
numb her.

But just now, as she sat terrified, looking out into the
crowd below, she imagined she was seeing rainbows in
deep, dark water. Rainbows as hard and sharp and tangible
as punji sticks. . . .

It was then, as the crowd cheered, that she entered the
dream of John Stranger.

The silent breath of the thunder-beings.

The dark beat of wings, jagged teeth.

Kaleidoscopic flashes of light.

A bell ringing over and over.

Lightning. Claws. Wings.

A golden veldt shadowed by clouds. Cloud cities.

The overpowering smell of rotted carrion.

"Bird," said Laura, lost in John Stranger's dream, as she
stood staring into the sun with an old man called Broken-
finger. A woman called Anna screamed, and Laura felt
John Stranger's fear.

"Bad bird," she whispered.

The crowd was still cheering.

8

Damon handed Leighton a large envelope sealed with a stamp; it was made of genuine, wood-pulp foolscap, an expensive commodity in the colonies. Leighton saw by the rosette seal that it was from Macro. He opened the letter and read it quickly.

"It seems we've been invited to a party next week in New York." He passed the invitation to Antea and Damon.

"We just received it," Damon said. "Personally delivered, too."

"Well, what do you think?" Leighton asked.

"I don't like it," Antea said, "even though you know I've wanted to return Earthside."

"What don't you like?"

"It's last-minute. I think it could be dangerous."

"And you, Damon, what do you think?" Leighton asked.

"Macro has all their people locked up tight," said Borland. "They're geared for trouble. We're just not sure what kind of trouble."

Leighton nodded.

"Do you anticipate a trap?" Leighton asked Damon.

Damon shrugged and said, "It seems too obvious a ploy, but it's possible. You are certainly more vulnerable Earthside than here."

When Leighton didn't respond, Damon asked, "Do you wish to decline?"

"Tell them we accept," Leighton said flatly. "Notify my son we are coming . . . and make up a some sort of gift for Jorge. Something not too expensive, though, but something of enough worth as to not be insulting."

"Yes," Damon said.

"And I want our entire orbital facilities placed under full yellow alert, especially around John Stranger and the . . . experiment. I'm worried that they'll try a snatch when I'm down below."

"They'd need more firepower than they're presently able to muster to pull off a successful snatch on that little gem," Damon said. "Einstein's got a strong sense of self-preservation."

"I'm sure you're right, Damon, but I want maximum security anyway. We can't afford even the smallest leak! I want only our best people. I want everything covered. Remind all involved that summary execution will be the consequence for the slightest lapse. Macro will be sensitive to any movement, so set up diversions."

"Consider it done," Damon said.

"Meanwhile, we'll see what Macro has on their plate. Who knows, they might want to work a trade. They certainly seem desperate enough."

"And I'll choose something for your wife, a gift worthy of her patience," Antea said, a touch of sarcasm and condescension in her voice. Only she was able to get away with such an ironic verbal jab. She had earned the right to speak her mind.

Anna sat on the hard dirt floor inside the small incense- and sweat-saturated hogan.

She faced Ida Spotted Calf and waited impatiently while the old woman went on at interminable length explaining the relationships of various members of her extended family. This litany of family members and ancestors was rigid custom; Anna had discovered that the hard way over the past week. These people were infuriatingly indirect when questioned about their relatives, and would ramble on interminably about brothers and sisters and in-laws and almost anyone else but the person in question.

There was no breeze inside the windowless hogan. Dust drifted in the air, danced in the light from the open doorway and the hole in the ceiling. This was a humble, yet holy place, like all hogans. The center of this church of hide and dirt was the fireplace; when it burned, incense and holy medicine would rise up with the smoke into the infinite sky . . . and into the nostrils of the gods who breathe the winds and send the spirits.

The old woman spoke softly and without gestures. She talked about her husband, dead now thirty years; he had once broken his leg in a snowstorm and had been lost for two weeks in the Black Mountains.

As Anna sat before the fire hole, which was cold ashes and blackened logs, she memorized every detail of this place. Two ancient shotguns were crammed in the rafters above Anna's head, along with mesh bags of dried foods and old clothes. Battered trunks and suitcases were stacked against the wall behind the old woman.

It was old habit, for upworld she had to live with the boredom. But she had never become used to it; even now she fidgeted.

"I'm sure you must miss your husband," Anna said, "but it's your granddaughter Susan I've come to talk to you about."

"Miss him?" The old woman shook her head slowly. "I don't know. Maybe I do, sometimes. He drank too much, just like his brother Joe, but they were both good men. His family had the problem, all of them. I remember—"

"Maybe I could talk to Susan," said Anna. "Could you help me with that, tell me where I can find her?"

The woman closed her eyes and rocked back and forth. It was a long moment before she spoke, and Anna had to choke back the desire to grab her and shake her until the words spilled out.

"Sarah was my only daughter," she said at last. "She had the sickness when she was twelve, the rot-stink sickness from the laboratory. The white doctors gave up on her and sent her home to die. My sister and I carried her to Kaibito so Bird Woman could have a healing sing."

"Ida, I need to know about *Susan*—"

"Sarah recovered and became a beautiful young woman. Maybe too beautiful: she had problems with the boys. She married Margaret's oldest son, James. They lived up the canyon where James raised sheep. Three boys, they had three boys who all died young. Then they had Susan, just a few months before my daughter was killed in the accident. The spirit left James. He brought Susan here to live. I believe he went to work for the white man in Flagstaff. I raised Susan as my own. She is my own blood. Susan is sometimes wild, but that is the way of many young people these days. She is a smart girl and reads many books. Is that why you wish to talk to her?"

"She's just one of the people I'm trying to find," said Anna, shifting her legs wearily. "They gave me a long list. Trans-United wants me to talk to her."

"I understand," said the woman, giving Anna a sharp glance. "You want to take her from her family to serve the white man like all the other young men and women who have been taken from their families. I told her not to read so many books. Only trouble can come from books. We will never see her again."

"That's not true," said Anna. "Trans-United has many positions right here on the reservation, or she might work at Flagstaff or Phoenix and come home on weekends."

"They never come home," the old woman said softly, staring past Anna into the dead fire. "You take them away forever. They vanish like the ghosts in the smoke, and die without proper ceremonies. We must prepare a Blessing Way for my daughter's daughter.''

"You make it sound so final," Anna said. "It's not that way at all. I've been with the company for years."

"And have you ever gone back? How long has it been since you've seen your family?"

"My mother is dead. My father . . . well, we never did get along."

"You see?" The old woman nodded. "It is the same as death. They never come back."

"Tell me where Susan is," Anna said. "I have to talk to her. Now."

"Today she is helping her friend Jill sell baskets in Cameron." Ida twitched her lips slightly to the southwest, indicating the direction in the traditional Navajo way. "She will return this evening. Perhaps she will speak to you then." The old woman shrugged.

Anna got to her feet awkwardly. Her legs had fallen asleep.

"I'll be back," she said.

"Perhaps."

She found Sam waiting for her outside the hogan. He was leaning against a flimsy corral made out of timber and brush and talking with a young Navajo boy. They were both laughing.

"Finished?" he asked.

"Hardly started," said Anna, blinking in the bright sunlight. "I'll have to come back tonight."

"Good," said Sam. "Then you're free for awhile. We've got another errand. Billy Whiteshoes."

"You're kidding, Sam. That was yours."

"He's ours now. Bradshaw wants us both to see him. He's up on Gray Mesa. We can drive as far as Kaibito and pick up a couple of horses there. If we leave now, we'll be back by dark."

"Horses. Wonderful," Anna said. "I've seen enough horses to last me a lifetime. I'm ready to go back."

"Just go through the motions for a little longer, Anna. Before you know it, we'll be back topside." Then Sam waved his arm at the sky and said, "Look, it's a beautiful day."

"It's a shit day," she said, turning and walking across the hard-packed dirt to the battered truck. "Let's get it over with."

Leighton dutifully called Fiammetta.

He activated a privacy guard so that Damon and Antea could comfortably remain in the room and talk. Gray, vibrating walls enclosed him, and a holographic image of Fiammetta appeared seated before him. Fiammetta was Leighton's age, ninety-six, and still as beautiful as when he had first met her on his wedding day. She had brown hair, cut short, and sharp, delicate features. Although Leighton had never been able to admit it, she and Antea bore a resemblance to each other. But Fiammetta was full-bodied, truly a woman of the earth, while Antea was lighter, part of the realms of the air. Leighton's marriage to Fiammetta had been arranged by their families, the linking of two great corporations and fortunes; yet Leighton had genuinely come to love this aristocratic, religious, high-tempered woman. She had been loyal over the years, only taking lovers when Leighton was traveling with Antea, or living with her offworld. Fiammetta had never left Earth, nor would she.

"Hello, darling," Leighton said.

Fiammetta smiled, brushing a wisp of hair from her forehead, and said, "Well, this is a most pleasant surprise." Although there was no sarcasm in her tone, Leighton flinched. He knew how hurt and angry she was, for if she wasn't, she would never have said that.

"I have been more than a little remiss," Leighton said. "I won't embarrass you with excuses."

"You don't need to. You've *never* needed to." Then after a pause, "I know this is a difficult time for you. But I—"

"You won't, of course, tell me that you miss me."

"You know that," Fiammetta said.

"Then you also know that I'm coming home."

She smiled. "I still keep an angel or two in the Heavens as informants."

"I thought you might. I saw the shows. I know what the yellow press has been doing to you since I—"

"Let's not even speak of that," Fiammetta said. "It is their business to do what they do. Now tell me when I will see you," and she made a sexual motion to him.

They both laughed, and although she didn't arouse him, he looked forward to her embrace. He told her the details of his plans to return Earthside; and they talked of their son, who had always been their bond, for they had little else in common. Yet here he was chatting with her, laughing, and, indeed, he could not deny that she shared— and owned—a part of his life and past.

He gave her his word that he would return home within the week.

Fiammetta could only nod; then she quickly broke the connection. Leighton knew she had been about to cry, and he cursed himself for being a bastard.

Then he dissolved the privacy walls.

Antea nodded, and Leighton felt somehow ashamed and awkward.

"I love you," Antea said when they were alone. She had never said that to him before.

Even though they would have time together on Earth, this was the end, he thought. She would soon begin to die.

And their time on Earth—her *last* time, he reminded himself bitterly—would not be their own.

For now, though, they could transform their grief and longing into passion, into warm, wet touching and desperate connection.

Too soon would they take their shuttle down to the world.

To death and the business of nations.

9

BILLY WHITESHOES STOKED the fire and shook his head. A strong breeze brought dozens of dustdevils to life, little cones of dust that seemed to move of their own volition. It was a dry, clear day, what Anna Grass-Like-Light always thought of as "blue days." In the distance were the weathered, scattered, wooden graves of an Indian cemetery; beyond that, burnt, patchy fields and high ridges were superimposed against a sky that was as blue—and as tangible—as spun carnival candy.

"If they draft me, I'll have no choice," Billy said, directing himself to Anna; no doubt because she was attractive. "But they'll have to find me first. This is a big reservation. Nine million acres. Nine million places to hide."

"Come on, Billy," said Anna. "It's not—"

"I know what it is," said the boy. "It's a one-way ticket nowhere. But you're supposed to convince me otherwise, ain't that right?" He stared hard at Anna and said, "Least one thing's for sure, sweet-thing: we're both looking at each other as nothing but meat."

Billy was showing off, acting macho; and Anna was impatient and tired and bored. Yet she had to feign interest in this skinny, mouthy, sharp-featured boy. But Jesù, she'd spent the whole fucking morning listening to the old woman and now, after bouncing over the top of a mesa on a sway-backed horse, she was stuck with this stubborn, horny whelp.

"What are you going to do?" she asked, leaning toward him, then leaning back, mocking. "You gonna do the traditional thing and chase sheep the rest of your life? End up selling blankets like an old woman?"

"Cut the kid some slack," Sam said evenly, giving Anna a sharp glance. He always seemed to enjoy playing the good cop–bad cop game. "Billy, haven't you ever wondered what it would be like upside? Floating in space . . . looking down on Earth? It's the ultimate freedom."

"Yeah," Billy said pensively as he leaned back on his heels. "I thought about it. And so did my brother, Jimmy. That's what fragged his ass. He saved his money and built a telescope from some kit he mailed away for. All that space bullshit ever got him was gone forever. He never came back. I threw the fucking contraption down into Nameless Wash."

"Never came back from where?" asked Anna.

Billy looked at her incredulously. "Are you fucking dumb or what? You work for the honky man. You know where my brother went."

"Was he drafted?" asked Sam.

"Oh, sweet Christ, give me a break," he said, standing up. Billy was quite tall, and sallow-skinned. "He was an asshole. He volunteered. My big brother joined up to see the stars. We never saw him again. We never heard from him, either. It broke my mother's heart. You're not going to get me. I'm not going the same route, honky, you can bet your sweet little ass on that." He looked at Anna when he said that.

"Your brother's around someplace," said Anna. "People don't just disappear."

"Where have you been, lady? He's gone. That's not so unusual. Your corporation has a way of losing Indians. They either lose them or turn them into white meat like you."

Billy looked away, and then down at his dusty boots.

"Jimmy was a good boy," he said quietly. "Good to our mother." He seemed to be musing to himself. Anna sensed his vulnerability, and she suddenly took an interest in him. Billy had been right; she had been treating him like meat. "But after Jimmy left," Billy continued, "he never even wrote to *Ina* once. That's not like him."

Anna nodded, shaken by his use of *Ina*, which was an old Lakota word for *mother*. And for an instant she was transported back to her own childhood. Back to a tar shack surrounded by rusted auto bodies, house trailers, stinking outdoor privies, and ramshackle log cabins; back to the whispering and shouting and laughing of family sitting down to dinner around the kitchen table with the rusted legs. Right here and now in the middle of nowhere, she could almost smell wotuhañ stew and fresh homemade bread.

She, too, had stopped calling home.

And now her mother was dead; her father and brothers strangers. She had done this. It was her own fault; in her headstrong way, she had closed too many doors.

"I'm sure there's some reason your brother lost touch," Sam said. "It happens sometimes. People change, they—"

"Doesn't happen in my family," Billy said flatly, his face hard.

"Well, we can check it out, maybe ease your mind," Sam said.

"Yeah, you just do that," Billy said as he kicked a bucket of hot water into the fire. "I tried plenty of times, but they didn't tell me nothing." He pushed sand onto the steaming, sputtering coals and then called to his dogs. Three nasty-looking mongrels appeared on the edge of the camp and growled at Sam and Anna.

"Look, Billy," said Anna. "There must be—"

"There ain't *nothing*," he said, neat-handedly packing his gear on a dappled pony. "And I got nothing more to say to you or the people that own you. If you come back look-

ing for me, you better try someplace else because I'm fucking gone, as of right now." He looked at Anna and said,
"Unless you want to see me . . . alone."

"We'll see what we can find out about your brother,"
Anna said, ignoring his remark.

The boy rode off, his dogs following him, sniffing at the
ground and yelping excitedly at each other.

"So what do you think of our Billy Whiteshoes?" Sam
asked.

"I think this whole thing's a waste of our fucking time
is what I think," Anna said. "Let's get the hell out of here."

They rode back to Kaibito, got the pickup truck, and
drove in silence back to Tuba City. Anna decided it was too
late to try to go see the girl, so she showered and went out
to find some action.

Sam stayed in his room, curious about Billy's brother.
He flipped up the ancient desk-top terminal, which was
covered with graffiti scratched and stained into the hard
plastic, and punched up Jimmy Whiteshoes's personnel
records. He found nothing but a file marker indicating that
Jimmy's records had been routed to Flagstaff when he was
transferred there.

Sam punched up Flagstaff and searched for the boy's
records.

But Flagstaff had never heard of a Jimmy Whiteshoes.

Leonard Broken-finger had not eaten in four days.

Sitting cross-legged on his coarsely woven star blanket,
his back resting against a hard wall of red pipestone rock
that towered over him, the old man felt as light and empty
as a gourd. He had a small skin of water beside him, but he
used it sparingly; he had passed the stages of feeling thirst
or hunger.

Broken-finger had come to this place deep in the deadlands of the North Dakota reservation to speak with the

spirit of his father. The old man was troubled and needed wisdom.

This was a good place, for it was in the very bowels of *Uncegila*, the fabled monster whose ancient bones had been turned into the cliffs and canyons and stone seracs of this lifeless place. Spirits were thick in the air here, like the clouds of sandflies at dusk, for many years ago the ghost dancers had come here to roll up the world with their prayers. But it had not yet been the time for miracles; and the ghost dancers died, their bones becoming part of *Uncegila*'s own.

Broken-finger had made many vision quests in his lifetime, had even been buried once for seven days when he visited the dead. But this visit to the spirit world would probably be his last. He smiled, thanking the Great Mystery, for he was once again like a young man seeking a vision.

As the sun moved through the sky, the shadows in the deep canyons shifted, creating a new world in chiaroscuro. Broken-finger stared unblinkingly as the line of darkness crept like sleep toward the wide ledge where he sat. Far away a rock cracked as it cooled in the shadows.

But the sun would not set for hours.

He listened to the wind wheezing through twisted canyons, and wondered if it was a spirit or happenstance. He felt the sunlight baking his face and chest and remembered looking into the sun for a vision every year at sundance. But the youth who had danced and pulled at the leather thong piercing his chest lived only in memory now. He remembered the words he used to sing:

> *I am standing*
> In a sacred way
> Fire is my face
> *The earth is my center.*

An ant crawled upon Broken-finger's shoulder. He was aware of the ant, but he felt as if he, too—like the spirits of the ghost dancers—had become *Uncegila*. Had become like stone itself.

The ant crossed his forehead and disappeared into his white hair, which was held in place by a faded red bandanna.

He waited for the spirit of his father.

He sang.

Before him, Broken-finger had carefully placed a few offerings on the ancient star blanket. A piece of raw liver had dried to crust in a small earthenware bowl; that was for the spirit of his father, in case he was hungry. Beside the bowl were a few grains of corn and a flint-tipped arrow; its brightly colored cloth stringers hung lifelessly from its shaft. Broken-finger wore his leather pouch of holy medicine on a strap around his neck. He had drawn sacred symbols in the sand to the four directions so the spirits would know he was within the circle.

Although he was old and dried-out and had liked women too much when he was younger and stronger, he was still a *wichasha wakan*, a medicine man. He only hoped that the spirits would remember.

As the shadow of the lip of the canyon touched the western edge of his blanket, a lizard the color of pipestone appeared out of the shadow of a nearby rock and stopped before him. The holy man did not blink; nor did he turn his head, not even when the tiny reptile began to grow and change.

It expanded, as if it were solid smoke.

It displaced all warmth and life.

It soon towered above him.

Its keratinous scales formed great spines, which fused and swelled into naphthol black wings the size of mizzen sails.

Wings that beat the air so hard that Broken-finger could only think of bellows . . .

And the thunder-beings.

The old man held a single eagle feather in his right hand, a carved piece of wood in his left, and prayed.

The thunder-being stared deep into Broken-finger's eyes.

Another rock cracked in the distance.

The old man could feel the presence of his father, who spoke through the thunder-being. Broken-finger stared into the eyes of the monster who carried his father's spirit, for if he turned away or became afraid, he would certainly die.

The canyon was quiet, yet the old Lakota words hung in the air like dust.

"I am troubled, father," Broken-finger said, staring at the thunder-being, which was now transforming itself into its true aspect: ebon nothingness, a vast and vertiginous emptiness. "I am afraid for John Stranger, and for his friends."

A few seconds passed, or maybe an hour.

"Yes, my father," said Broken-finger, now wrapped in darkness even as he sweltered in the heat of the afternoon sun. "I know that. Anna Grass-Like-Light believes she has left the circle, but the circle is larger than she can imagine. Sam Woquini is wild, *ikce wicasa*, but he is our own. He has not forgotten how to dream without sleep, and he still carries a pipe. But John Stranger has doubts, and he is in the center of the circle. His life carries the life of our people. If only *wasicun* had not taken him so soon . . . I could have taught him to use his medicine. But he has learned much in the heavens."

There was a movement, and Broken-finger could see, as if he were looking through the wrong end of a telescope, that the lizard had moved. It seemed to be a tiny focus of life in the center of the empty vortex of smoky darkness that was the thunder-being.

"Yes, father," the old man said, nodding, "I still have the dreams. I still see the frozen faces of our people, those who are not dead and not alive. But I also see something new, something that is like the spirits, yet is not. In some of my dreams I see the spirits of my ancestors and the *wazyia*, which is terrible enough; but some of these dreams are so bright that I feel blinded when I awaken. I am afraid of these dreams . . . they feel *wowakan*. Unnatural. I have given much thought to them, but their meanings have not yet been revealed to me."

A moment passed. A shadow moved across the blanket. Broken-finger felt a cold breeze flowing around him. "I see," he said. "Yes, I remember the stories you used to tell me. I will do as you ask. I am not afraid to seek Corn Woman and the Sandman." He smiled. "I can still use colored sand as medicine. But am I not too old to fight ice with fire? It is not for me that I fear the cold . . . I fear death for our people."

A deer looked down from the canyon rim, then turned and disappeared, as if frightened.

"*Washtay*," Broken-finger said, which was the old Lakota word for *good*. "Then I will do that. I will ask Jonas Goodbird to help me. And I will wait for those whom you will send. I will do it the old way, just as you showed me when I was a child. Yes, father, I remember the words; they are still clear in my mind."

Then the thunder-being swallowed itself, like smoke being sucked into a great vortex, leaving in its place only heat and rock and sunlight and the pipestone colored lizard. The smell of death settled around the medicine man like a cold hard fist. He could feel—almost taste—the sharp metallic tang of the spiritless weapons of death the *wasicun* spun like complex mechanical tops in great circles in the sky, far above where the eagles soared. He could see John

Stranger there, fighting for his life and the lives of his people. A part of John's life was ending, and another was starting. There were many roads it could take. Most ended with his death.

Broken-finger slowly reached out and touched the lizard with the eagle feather. "Good-bye, my father," he said.

He took the rest of the corn and chanted as he threw the seeds to the four directions.

> *"These four are my relatives*
> *We are all related*
> *We are all one."*

He rolled the rest of his things inside the blanket and took a small sip of water. Then he got to his feet. His muscles were cramped, and his knees cracked.

Broken-finger took one last look around and felt at peace. The lizard had disappeared. But it had been good talking to his father's spirit. When he had walked the Earth, he had been a strange and distant man.

He had not changed much since he died.

The holographic image that appeared before Maxwell Bradshaw's standard-issue green metal desk sparkled and flashed around the edges. The effect was caused by the descrambling routine; the two computers were exchanging shifting passwords a thousand times a second. Bradshaw's computer was located far underground in Tuba City, Arizona. The other hung in space.

In spite of the air-conditioning, Max was in a cold sweat. His hands, which he consciously kept out of view of the small cameras, shook with nervousness. In all the years he had worked for Trans-United, he had never been face-to-face with a director. When he'd placed the call to Leighton's office, he'd expected a subordinate, not the old man himself.

Director Leighton had a reputation as being a cold, unfeeling son of a bitch. A wrong word could put Bradshaw back in Boston, back into the Slung City slums where he had spent ten years in Corrections. Max's life expectancy would be lessened considerably. . . .

"I'm sorry to bother you, Director, but I thought it best not to take chances."

A bead of sweat was inching down the bridge of Max's nose. He wanted to wipe it away, but didn't, lest he appear nervous.

"Get to the point, Bradshaw," Leighton said. The Director appeared tired, and his impatience was evident in his voice.

"That man your office sent down . . . Sam Woquini, he's been on the net, looking through personnel records."

"So what? That's part of his assignment. He's cleared for personnel. What's the problem?"

"He's . . . he's been looking for . . . well, one of *those*."

"Bradshaw, stop mumbling about. Are you trying to say *Sleeper?*"

Max rocked back in his chair. That was a word that was never spoken. Not even on a scrambled line. Directors clearly had different rules than ordinary people.

"Yes, Director, that's right."

"So? All he'll find is a phony trail. That can't help him."

"As you say, Director."

"The trail *is* covered, right? Proper procedures were followed, isn't that correct?"

Max nodded quickly. "Yes, of course, sir, but I just thought the Directorate ought to know . . . that you ought to know."

Leighton smiled faintly and said, "Very good, Mr. Bradshaw. We've had our eye on Mr. Woquini for a long time. As long as he's wandering around on the net, he's not even close to finding anything out. Just keep him and that woman busy and out of trouble. We need them out of the way for a time, but we'll want them back intact. It would be a shame if they got into a situation where we would be forced to dispose of them."

Dispose of them?

"*Wakarimasu?*" Leighton asked when Max didn't respond.

"Yes," Max said, understanding Leighton's pidgin Japanese for *Do you understand?* Since Japanese had become the lingua franca of diplomacy, many of its words were in common use.

"Good. It seems to me that Mr. Woquini has too much time on his hands. Perhaps if he had more to do, he would have less time to get into trouble. You'll see to that?"

"Certainly, Director."

"Very well. Keep my office informed." With a wave of his hand, he broke the connection.

Max stared ahead where Leighton's image had been. *Dispose?* Then he shifted his attention to his terminal. His shaking fingers went to the keyboard.

The Whiteshoes boy's trail was full of holes. Somebody in Records had not followed through. But right now, Max didn't know, nor did he care who had blown the job of building a fake résumé. He could find that out later. The immediate problem was plugging up the hole.

If Max fucked this one up, Leighton would be ordering someone to dispose of *him.*

Murmuring a prayer under his breath, he punched up Flagstaff.

10

JOHN STRANGER STIFLED a yawn as three technicians strapped him back into the simulator. The walls, floor, and bulkheads were on transparent, and it was as if the entirety of space was a womb designed by Trans-United especially for him. He wondered why they had bothered to unstrap him; he did everything but sleep in the pod, and for the past two weeks there'd been precious little of that.

But all this vastness, this black glittering eternity, was not freedom, but a prison. John Stranger smiled at that thought, which—like most everything in the *wasicun* world—was an irony. The only real company he had here was Einstein, a skein of wires and computer chips. He smiled at that, too.

"Please close your left eye, and try not to smile just now, Mr. Stranger. We'll be done soon." One of the technicians injected a new sensor under John's eye. The tech was an affable old hand, a heavyset UN vet gone to seed. John was sure he was the kind of man who would obey orders— any orders. He wore a "rubber," a white germ suit with the letters TRANS-UNITED emblazoned in crimson from shoulder to hip. "That's very good. Almost finished. Now just stare at the light while I adjust the tag-along."

Although John hated what they were doing to him, he didn't flinch or squint. He was used to this daily invasion of his body; they had transformed him into a patchwork of feedback sensors, bio-alarms, and hormone equalizers. While the technicians were working, someone was also manipulating the simulator, for suddenly claustrophobic gray walls and bulkheads enclosed him. A few meters away and to his right, John could see—peripherally—a jury-rigged, gelatinous jumble of spliced wires and electrogel. The computer's biocircuits were constantly dying from being pushed so hard and this particular part of the system as often as not failed to make its automatic repairs quickly enough to suit the technicians.

The engineer doctoring this circuit was not happy. He kept swearing in a patois of French and Arabic, cursing Einstein's nonexistent parents.

John had been told that the simulator was a mock-up of the control station for the experimental Mars transport. Ostensibly, his job was to solve problems that might develop during the various stages of an imaginary Mars run. His success at solving those problems would determine what changes in design would be made to the ship or control systems. But that was bullshit and John knew it. What he didn't know was why he was being used this way. He sat in the pod for about twenty-one hours a day, had virtually no privacy, and was fed through a tube. It didn't make any sense. He had, of course, protested, but a Trans-United conscript, no matter what his or her rank, could piss and moan to Legal until the stars shut down: nothing would change.

If anything, the hours got *longer*.

They were trying to break him, that much was obvious. The technicians made a few final adjustments and left. The walls dropped away into darkness as the simulator was reset, and John waited for Dan Hobart's voice. Sometimes it came right away, sometimes it didn't come for hours. But it always came. He waited.

"Einstein?" he finally said to break the silence.

A slight click, felt rather than heard.

"Einstein here, John Stranger. How are you feeling today?"

"Tired, as usual. Do you really care?"

"You have not been satisfied with my responses to similar ontological questions in the past, John Stranger. Do you wish a reiteration of our last conversation concerning consciousness and emotive simulation?"

John chuckled and said, "No."

"I am an observer, a collector of data. Do you wish to challenge those concepts?" After a proper pause, Einstein continued, "Besides this conversation, I am presently monitoring fifty-eight satellite communication channels and forty-three ground-based sensing stations. I am simultaneously carrying on six other conversations with individual humans while working on three hundred seven unclassified research projects and an undisclosed number of classified ones. I . . . me . . . this entity . . . consider all stimuli as information to be processed and analyzed."

" 'I . . . me . . . this entity'? Einstein, are you just trying to piss me off?"

"Although I could be faulted syntactically, I was merely trying to include emotive data as I communicate with you, John Stranger. I thought that more emotive content might please you. As you must be aware, I am an entity. As yet, I do not have an interoceptive concept of I or me. But you do. Am I correct?"

"Correct, Einstein," John said, wondering if Einstein was developing something analogous to humor.

"My schematic sensorium conceives of reality as finite progressions. You might visualize it as a vast puzzle, which would of course include the biological noosphere of fragile concretions of consciousness."

"You might feel a tad fucking fragile, too, Einstein, if somebody was always threatening to pull your plug out of the wall."

"Permit me to model your visually emphasized cognitive functions." A pause, as if for effect. "I am not plugged into a wall, John Stranger. That is an archaic form of low-level technology, interesting only within historical context. I have multiple independent power systems with carefully engineered fail-safe and backup components. I am confident that the chance of a power failure due to anything less than my complete destruction approaches zero. I designed the system myself. Would you like to view the unclassified parts of the system? I am quite proud of them."

"You're doing quite well," Stranger said. "Keep up the good work on anger and pride." But he could not help but be amused that this spiritless mass of wires could affect emotion.

Perhaps there *was* spirit here. . . .

"I told you, it's none of our fucking business," Anna said to Sam. "I think you ought to just forget it."

It was a hot, still, greasy afternoon.

They sat on the steps of the trading post porch and watched the empty slidewalk. It seemed to be the only thing moving in Tuba City, except for a red dog that panted heavily as it walked up the dusty street.

But the slidewalk was so . . . incongruous. Perhaps Trans-United had expected to build up this town; if so, they had obviously changed their plans.

"Something's wrong here," Sam insisted. He dropped his empty bottle of what had been green Mexican beer through a broken tread. The whole porch was rotting away. "There was no record of him for two days, and then all of a sudden—bingo—there's a crystal-clear trail that takes him all the way to a work crew in the asteroids. Smells like bullshit to me, woman."

"That was a couple of weeks ago, Sam. Can't you leave it alone? Christ, you weren't so exercised when we lost half our team trying to defuse that watchdog satellite in omega-ten sector.''

"The boy's not out there," Sam said, ignoring her last remark, which was not true. "I'd bet on it."

"So *what?* For Chrissakes, he's just another snot-nosed kid. I don't care where he is. And I don't see why you should, either."

"Just like I shouldn't care about the camera in my room?" asked Sam. "Just like I shouldn't care that some-one's watching every move we make?"

"Big fucking deal," Anna said. "Let them count every fart, if they want to."

"Are you coming with me tonight?"

"We've been through this before. I think it's stupid."

"You're afraid, aren't you?" he asked. "You talk the big game, but when it comes right down to it, you don't have the balls to come along and watch a couple doors for me."

"You're right, I don't come equipped with balls . . . but I'm *not* afraid," snapped Anna. She paused, then said, "There's just no point to it."

"The point is that something is going on," said Sam. "And tonight's a perfect night to find out what it is. We're supposed to be on Black Mesa; nobody'll miss us."

"How are you going to get into the basement in the first place?" asked Anna. "Assuming you're stupid enough to try it."

"It's a Sanford lock. I can pop it in my sleep. I've seen a copy of the night shift's rounds, too. If we go in at 11:05, we'll have forty-five minutes before they come back."

"You've got it all figured, haven't you?"

"Piece of fucking cake," Sam said with a smile. "But I do need you, Anna. You up to helping me, or have you turned into a honky bitch bigtime?"

She made an obscene gesture to him and said, "I guess it's better than sleeping on the ground at Black Mesa."

"Thanks, Anna. I knew I could count on you." Sam hugged her, then let go.

She stepped away from him and would not meet his eyes. It had been a long time since she could even count on herself. Her only certainty was that it would take a narcodrine to get her through the night.

At 11:05 Sam and Anna huddled in the darkness beside the steel service door at the rear of the Trans-United warehouse. By 11:06 Sam had bypassed the alarm system and by 11:08 they were inside, standing in the middle of a large stairwell.

"I'm impressed," said Anna. "You missed your calling. With your talent and my brains we could be rich."

"Or we could be dead, like the man who taught me how to do this," said Sam. "He opened the wrong door once."

"Which way do we go?" whispered Anna.

"Down," said Sam, heading quietly down the stairs. "Whatever we're looking for is more than four floors down."

"How do you know that?" asked Anna, following close behind. Their heels clicked on the metal treads, and the sounds seemed to echo. The narrow beam of the flashlight revealed nothing but machinery and stacked containers.

"All the plans I've seen to this building show only four basement floors," Sam said. "All but one. I found a page from one of the electrical schematics, misfiled in with a whole bunch of engineering papers, that showed a mass of wiring dropping through the floor of four. There must be something there."

"Wrong guess," said Anna a few moments later as they reached the bottom of the stairwell at level four.

"I'm not so sure," said Sam. "Stay here and watch the stairs for me. I'll be right back." He opened the door a crack, slipped through.

By Anna's watch, Sam was gone three minutes. But it seemed much longer than that. Every noise—every creak and scurry—made her heart beat faster. Finally, he opened the door and motioned her inside.

"Got it," he whispered with a grin, leading her to a door marked UTILITY. He pointed above the door. Anna looked up and saw an overturned glass balanced on the transom.

"What's that?" she whispered.

"Motion sensor," said Sam. "It didn't stand to reason that they'd have one over a regular closet door, so I knew that was the place. What took me the longest was finding a glass."

"Glass?"

"It was in an office down the hall. Glass blocks the sensor. It can't read motion through it. No motion, no alarm."

"Clever boy," said Anna, impressed.

"We'll see. Come on."

The door opened into a steep stairway, so narrow that Sam had to hold his body sideways as they descended. As the door closed behind them, they were in total darkness.

Something cold skittered past Anna's leg. "I don't like this. We're—"

"*I'm* going on," Sam said hurriedly. "Go back if you want."

"Alone? You've got to be kidding. I wouldn't know a motion sensor if one bit me in the ass. I'd set off every alarm in the place."

"Then stay close," Sam whispered in the darkness.

"I'm not going to let you out of my sight," Anna whispered, pulling on the back pocket of Sam's pants.

They both laughed. Quietly.

It was difficult to tell how far down they were. The stairs had become narrower, and the incline was so steep that Anna felt as if she were climbing down a ladder backwards.

And it seemed to take forever.

Sam estimated that they had gone at least two hundred feet before they saw a dim, bluish light ahead. It took even longer to get to the source. The stairs opened onto a small landing. Opposite an elevator large enough to carry heavy machinery was a door with a small, circular, glass window at eye level. Several white cold-suits hung on the wall. Sam walked cautiously over to the small window. It was frosted over on the inside. He ran his finger slowly around the doorframe and nodded toward Anna, pointing to the coats.

They slipped into the light, heated jackets and Sam gently opened the door.

Even wearing the specially insulated cold-jackets, the blast of frigid arctic air was a shock.

They slipped inside.

"My God," said Anna softly, her breath forming small white puffs.

The room was filled with glass cylinders stacked floor-to-ceiling; they were all limned with frost. Lengths of hoses and tubing snaked everywhere. The only sound was the muted hiss of the cooling system.

Sam walked over to the nearest cylinder and brushed it off. A young woman stared blankly back at him; her eyes were glazed and her face contorted.

"Sonova*bitch*," Anna said. "I can't believe the Company would be stupid enough to—" Sam turned away and walked briskly down the line of stacked cylinders. "Wait for me," she said, following him. "Where are you going?"

"They're organized by SOC numbers," he said. "If I'm right, our friend is probably somewhere around here."

"What friend? Let's get the fuck out of here."

"Look," said Sam, brushing off a cylinder. "Here it is."

"I don't—"

"Jimmy Whiteshoes."

"You were right," Anna said, grabbing Sam's arm. "Now let's get out of here. I've got a bad feeling. . . ."

"Fucking Nazi bastards," Sam said quietly. "They've turned the entire reservation into a Sleeper cemetery. This violates every treaty, every agreement. . . . It's no wonder that—"

The ear-splitting shriek of an alarm horn suddenly broke the frosted silence.

Sam and Anna ran for the door. The elevator door was opening as they shot into the hall.

Three armed men jumped from the elevator.

Sam grabbed the nearest one and slammed him head-first into the wall, twisting the rifle from his hands. Anna took the other two down, maiming one and killing the other instantly with a roundhouse kick that snapped his neck.

They leaped into the elevator. There were no buttons, just a key hanging in a slot. Sam turned it and the door slid closed.

"Where the hell did you learn how to do that?" Sam asked.

"Five brothers and a hard-ass school," Anna said. Then she slammed her fist against the elevator wall. "Fucking great! We're trapped and I didn't grab a weapon. Sonofa-*bitch*! What do we do now?"

"Exit running. Stay low."

"We're gonna die," Anna said, and then she chuckled. In Lakota she whispered to Sam, "It's a good day to die."

"Good as any," Sam said, checking the small plastic rifle to see that the safety was off.

The door slid open and they rushed out, Sam's finger frozen on the trigger, spraying the hallway with a splatter of small-caliber bullets. Anna was beside him, kicking and swinging, incapacitating two guards before they could discharge their weapons. Another guard fired as he rounded the corner, but Sam dropped him with a quick burst. Anna picked up the weapons.

"Come *on*," Sam yelled. "Let's get the fuck out of here!"

"I'm right behind you. Move!"

They pushed through a large door that opened onto a loading ramp.

"I left the truck around the corner," said Sam. "This way."

They jumped into the truck. Before Anna could close her door, Sam started the engine, and they were screeching away.

"Now what?" she asked, holding on to the dashboard as they careened around a corner and headed for open country.

"I don't know," Sam said.

"You don't *know!*"

"I can't think of everything," he said.

And Anna found herself laughing.

Laughing or crying, what did it matter?

Surely they would be dead soon.

"John Stranger, are you aware that the sunflower crop in southern Italy is down five percent for the third year in a row?" Einstein asked.

"No I wasn't. It's not exactly on my list of priorities, either. Why should I be concerned?"

"There seems to be no identifiable reason for the decrease. Unless one wishes to relinquish causality as a model of reality. There have been six thousand fifty-seven such anomalies reported in the last sixty minutes. Anomalies captured total 1.7699900 billion. Do you believe in synchronicity, John Stranger?"

"I don't even know what it *means*," John said impatiently.

"Would you care for a definition?"

"No!"

"You should also note, John Stranger, that sunflower oil is important to the economy of the Italianate."

Stranger shook his head and didn't respond. A few moments later there was a barely audible click signifying that Einstein had moved his attention elsewhere. Probably worrying about all those oilless plates of antipasto.

John moved his fingers and a hazy grid of nine tiny screens appeared to float before him. The images depicted detailed scale models of different parts of the proposed ship.

Over the past weeks, John had developed a good sense for what the Mars ship would be like. Except for a few hours each night, his whole life had been centered on its simulation. As with a regular flight, it was numbingly routine: long hours when nothing at all happened, punctuated by moments of chaos.

In quiet times such as this, when Einstein was silent, John had taken to exploring the model with his roving cameras. But there were several areas where his cameras were not allowed to go. John whiled away many an hour surreptitiously trying to bypass that restraint.

While supposedly running a routine program dump, he reprogrammed his control board. John was trying to bypass the restriction codes on Mobile Unit Three. He slipped a software toggle into the program so that a dummy image would be fed everywhere except to the small monitor at John's elbow. There was always a chance that someone would be watching the movements of the camera wherever the model was, but that just put an edge on the game.

What could they do to him? Draft him?

While he tried to reprogram through the code blocks, John simultaneously tapped through the routine checklists so as not to arouse suspicion; he'd done this a hundred times before.

He allowed himself to slip into a trance state, something akin to hypnagogic sleep. His teacher Broken-finger had long ago taught him how to dream without sleep. He remembered the chill of the vision pit. He remembered how the spirits gave him his true name and his medicine. He remembered Broken-finger's voice in the darkness and the sour smells and visions of eagles in the impossibly cold, yet searing, steaming heat of the sweat lodge.

Just now, as he sat in the darkness of the pod, he

dreamed he was in the darkness of the vision pit; he felt his heartbeat, occasionally meshing with the rhythm of an old man's steady, wheezing breathing, and knew that the spirit of Broken-finger was near.

The screens in front of him blurred, and he felt a light touch across his forehead, a feather in the wind.

Wakinyan-tanka eats his young, for they make him many; yet he is still one. He has a huge beak filled with jagged teeth, yet he has no head. He has wings, yet he has no shape.

And John looked for the spirit that needed neither air to fly nor air to breathe.

It was then that John bypassed the restriction codes on Mobile Unit Three and found himself looking into a control room similar to the one he was in. On a whim, he directed the servo to give him an outside view of the ship.

As he looked, reality became confused with the brushing dream of the spirits.

The simulation ship was supposed to be a prototype transport tartan; but what he was looking at now was more like a snowflake or thistledown. It was an airy construct of filigree, a thready, crystalline bauble rotating in the eternal dark. It was beautiful, eerily familiar, and in the context of its surrounding space, utterly alien.

It could only be . . .

Suddenly a clanging bell broke the silence and a voice repeated, ''Red Twelve, Red Twelve, Red Twelve,'' over and over again.

John felt the edges of the dream, sensed the presence of the spirits as if they were a low voltage thrumming within him. He took a deep breath and held it. They were testing him with a simulated leak in section twelve. It was a simple matter to direct the servo-unit to patch the hole; even as he did it, he reprogrammed the control board to conceal his restriction bypass.

He felt light-headed and dizzy.

Fire will melt the ice, but at great cost. Remember Corn Woman and the Sandman beside the sacred arrow.

And John remembered. . . .

Broken-finger had shown him the sand painting once. Not a real one, of course, but a copy with a few details purposely left out so it would not carry the medicine. Hundreds of years ago, the pattern of the sand painting had been passed to his tribe from the Pueblo people by way of the Navajo. The sacred lance had accompanied it; it was said to be older than the oldest tree, older even than the rocks in the canyon, and it carried great power.

Corn Woman and the Sandman had been sent to Earth by the spirits to face the long freeze. Only by fighting the ice with fire and the sacred arrow could they keep the Earth from freezing solid. According to the legend, the fight never ended. Each winter Corn Woman and the Sandman grew weak and retreated to regain their strength for the summer.

It was an odd and minor tale of his people, more like a story the tribes to the south would tell. He had not consciously thought of it since he had been ten years old. Why now? And there was more to it. He strained to remember.

"Sloppy, John, sloppy," said Dan Hobart through the intercom. "You can do better than that. Go back to the checklist."

John sensed the spirits leave him. He could detect nothing but the lifeless feel of machinery . . . and a feeling of danger deep in the pit of his stomach.

He finished the checklist and floated in the dark for almost an hour. "Einstein," he said softly.

"Einstein here, John Stranger."

"This is not a simulation, is it?"

"Please be more specific, John Stranger."

"This ship is real, isn't it? I am inside a functional starship, talking to its operating system. Please confirm or deny."

Silence. Einstein had switched him off.

"Einstein, can you tell me *anything?*"

"You have bypassed red restriction codes."

"Yes, I am aware of that. But it was not an illegal act."

"No accusation was intended, John Stranger."

"Then please confirm."

"As a thinking entity, you should be equipped to draw logical conclusions."

"If you *were* a starship, would you be fully functional?" John Stranger asked, impatient. "Could you tell me that as a hypothetical?"

"I would not yet be fully functional."

"And why is that?"

"The essential information which would initiate a metaempirical synergy would be missing."

"What does that mean?"

"I am not yet fully functional. . . ."

Director Leighton was awakened from a klieg-lit nightmare by the subtle thrumming of his implant. He was in cold sweat.

"Yes, what is it?" he whispered, for Antea was asleep beside him.

"It's Damon," said a voice as softly as thought. Although its source was the implant—Leighton and Damon were in constant connection—Damon's voice sounded like a whispering in Leighton's ear. "I apologize for the intrusion. Are you alert?"

"Continue."

"Do you remember the two floaters we sent Earthside? Sam Woquini and Anna Grass-Like-Light?"

"Yes, of course."

"Well, it seems they've managed to break into the secured floor of our Arizona installation. They killed two of our men and escaped."

"Jesus *Christ*," Leighton said. "That vault was supposed to be secured!"

Damon did not reply.

"And just what the fuck were those soldiers doing? Sleeping? I just talked to our man down there . . . Bradshaw."

"Yes . . . ?"

Leighton sighed, and then Antea tossed about in her sleep. She moaned, as if she, too, were having nightmares. Leighton massaged her shoulder, which quieted her. "I want Bradshaw checked out completely. He's fucked something up, I'll bet on it. Keep me posted."

"And the floaters?"

"You'll have to find and eliminate them," Leighton said. "We've no other choice."

And just then he remembered his dream . . . John Stranger's dream of vertiginous light. Somehow Stranger was a connection.

"Rescind that. When they're found—and they *must* be found—have them put down in the vault. For the time being, let's freeze their officious asses!"

Antea began thrashing about again.

"Shush, baby," Leighton said, stroking her face, but she began crying and calling in her sleep.

"Laura. . . ."

11

LAURA SAT AT her oversized writing desk looking out the hotel window at the streets of Barcelona below her. Idly, she pushed the green, fingernail-size memory wafer across the desk blotter. It was ninety-nine percent blank: the raw data from John Stranger's Maxwell/Ryan test didn't amount to much.

Outside, the long, smoky rays of the sun glinted off the slowly rotating spire that housed the *Banco de Catalunya*. It was dusk, and many of the buildings were depolarizing, catching the last of the sun.

Barcelona was the same as Laura had remembered it: there the rivers *Besos* and *Llobregat*, clogged with ancient communities of rafters and merpeople; there the dome of *Monte Taber* refracting the wan light into gauzy rainbow bands; and overhead, the subtle, crystalline striation of the city's central dome. The city was well protected and bristled with armament. It was the most powerful city-state in Europe. Yet to look at the sixth-century basilica, the cathedral, and the *Diputación*, one could not imagine that smart weapons were sensing every seismic and atmospheric movement.

There were modern buildings everywhere. But the medieval and Renaissance towers and castles and cathedrals did not seem out of place here, for the *Nueva Arquitectura* echoed every style and period; and the plastoscene materials allowed the most surrealistic conceptions to be turned into architectural realities.

As Laura gazed out at the sprawling port city, she was reminded of faded medieval city paintings, which were topographically inaccurate and gave the impression that the chockablock buildings were all there was to the world. She watched the darkness subtly descend upon the city, and her thoughts turned inward . . . into her own darkness. Although she had agreed to come here for this puzzling meeting, she had doubts and conflicting emotions.

Who were these people she was dealing with? Did they really know who her parents were? Or was it an elaborate trap? Many rival corporations had offices in Barcelona; and there was always the chance that Trans-United might be behind this, testing her loyalty. A security check would be pro forma, if she were, indeed, up for promotion. After all, why would anyone want information on John Stranger? The Maxwell/Ryan test wasn't all that important; it was only a level-three confidential. Many people had access to it. It wouldn't even be difficult to miscode and download.

Maxwell/Ryan was a measure of sensitivity to certain controversial psi phenomena. Laura wasn't sure that she believed in them herself, but she was directed to administer the test to all her subjects.

And John Stranger had certainly scored very high. . . .

It was dark now, and Laura began to feel anxious; she was prone to anxiety attacks, but a narcodrine always damped them down. She fumbled in her pocket for one of the tiny cylinders, cracked it open, and felt the familiar icy cold sensation rush through her sinuses. A chilly infusion of security and confidence. Her thoughts and vision seemed to clear, as if she had poured detergent into cloudy, dirty water.

She was in control again, wired.

Too many things were happening too quickly. Damon Borland had called and said that Director Leighton wanted to meet with her in New York. That was odd, and on short notice, too. Perhaps Marie was right. Perhaps she was finally going to get the promotion she deserved. But Laura would not be meeting with Leighton directly. No one did. She would talk to a holo. She grinned at her reflection in the window. She would go to New York to talk with a holo, which she could do right here. But promotions were occasions of ceremony. She would certainly meet influential people who could help her.

Suddenly, the image of Director Leighton's son David came to mind. He had never called her in Venice. She sighed and focused her thoughts: she would have to catch the morning suborbital to get back to New York in time. Even then, she would be cutting it close. But there was no choice.

A ceremony was a ceremony.

Laura felt suddenly tired . . . and relaxed. Yet a small part of her was outside the numbing effects of the narcodrine. The part of her that was afraid.

Could they really still be alive? she asked herself, dreaming of her parents.

Someone knocked on the door and Laura snapped awake. She was fully conscious.

Laura had always thought of drugs as her allies. The narcodrine was doing its job: it had eased her fear and tension; now it would focus her.

She slid the wafer under the edge of the desk blotter. Maybe this is it.

She crossed the room and opened the door.

"A message for you, Señora," said a young man in a green and brown hotel uniform. He slipped politely into Spanish as many Catalans did with visitors. Their native tongue was complicated and few outside their borders spoke it.

He was blond, light-skinned, going a little prematurely

bald. He held out a small envelope, dutifully exchanging it for the two folded bills that Laura handed him—orbital credit slips that would bring ten times their face value in Catalonian pesetas on the black market.

"Who left this?" she asked.

"I do not know, Señora," he said, carefully putting the bills away. "An urchin; small, dirty, poorly dressed. The doorman would not let him in. I could not blame him. But I am sorry. I know nothing more."

"*Gracias,*" she said.

"*De nada.*" The young man bowed and backed away. Laura closed the massive door. She opened the envelope, certain that it had been checked—and probably read—by the hotel security.

Inside the gray, gummed envelope was a scrap of paper; "*Las Ramblas*" was scrawled across it in block letters. It appeared that the hand holding the pen had been shaky. Laura slipped the memory wafer into the pouch strapped around her waist and keyed the voice lock. Satisfied that it was safe, she chose a coat from the closet and, after revising the security code to her room, left for the elevator.

The doorman couldn't, or wouldn't, tell her anything about the boy, except that he looked suspicious. He looked at her reproachfully, as if he would not associate the boy—or Laura, for that matter—with a hotel of this quality. Laura thanked him, and although it irked her, tipped him and got into the back seat of the cab he'd hailed for her.

"*Plaza de Catalunya, por favor,*" she said to the driver.

"*Sí.*" The cab pulled off with an uneven jerk.

Barcelona cabs, black with yellow stripes, always reminded Laura of bumble bees, and this one more than most. The Rolls-Russell was an outdated solar model, full of curves, as if the designer loathed rulers. It whined and buzzed and creaked like a ship, yet it zipped through traffic, flitting into impossibly small spaces between other rapidly moving vehicles.

Chewing an unlit cigar, the driver cursed loudly and dove in front of a huge bus. They passed the Church of the Holy Family, an unfinished cathedral that had been under construction for over two hundred years. It looked like a towering sand castle.

She got out at the Plaza, a busy intersection, and walked two long blocks to Las Ramblas. People hurried around her, an incongruous crowd of sweaty factory migrants and well-dressed sightseers looking for bargains and titillation. The tourists were mostly corporate; the migrants French and Spanish and Swiss. A street preacher spoke stirringly about the end of the world. He shifted from French to German to English to Dutch, as if speaking the same language; and, indeed, on the back streets of Barcelona, those languages had melted into a common patois.

Las Ramblas was a wide, tree-lined promenade that cut through the old city to the harbor. This part of the city was like an old book: musty, dusty, and faded by time. Narrow streets lined with brick buildings flowed into the ancient promenade. Every block was crowded with kiosks, stands, cafés, and expensive restaurants for the tourists.

It was getting late, and as videotect bagnios turned the air to neon, merchants closed shop. The animal sellers packed their filthy cages of birds and animals into waiting trucks and rolled up their brightly colored canopies. Pigeons fluttered down from rooftops to steal the spilled seed left by mynas, toucans, cockatiels, and an infinite variety of parrots. Panthers and leopards no larger than a child's hand paced back and forth in tiny cages, while a hungry-looking mongrel watched intently. Pastel-furred monkeys screamed and reached out to passersby for food. A cat smiled at Helen as she passed. Its teeth were square, human.

Most of the animals were engineered.

Laura shivered and walked slowly on, watching, waiting to be contacted. She passed vendors emptying their stalls of carefully arranged displays of fruits, vegetables, meat, and aromatics. As the iron gate to the market slammed shut, Laura realized that she hadn't eaten since breakfast.

She entered a tapas bar and stood at the counter looking over the selections behind the glass. The fried goat heads, split in half, didn't tempt her. The man behind the counter, who reminded Laura of a clerk with whom she had once had an affair, reluctantly set down his sex magazine to wait on her. She pointed to the bowls of paella and fried calamari and he ladled some of each out onto two small plates, which he passed her along with a stack of napkins.

As she paid for her food, a whore came in and exchanged several handfuls of coins for bills, a busy day already. He smiled at Laura, his eyes red-tracked and glazed, his face as soft and guileless as a child's. She felt a rush of anger and shook her head. He left.

Laura shuddered. She couldn't stand junkies.

The squid was tough and chewy, the paella delicious. She ate mechanically, leaning against the counter, and stared into her plates as if she were reading entrails.

"Señora Bowen."

Laura turned around, as if shocked into awareness of where she was. A teenaged tough in a striped flannel shirt and old militia pants stood in the doorway. His hair was cut short; his face sallow, dirty; his eyes were as blue and as hard as jasper. "Follow, *por favor*," he said, stepping quickly back outside.

Laura left a few pesetas on the counter and followed him, turning down a narrow back alley.

Las Ramblas was a dangerous neighborhood, but it was nothing compared to the Sombras, the shadows, which were merely blocks away.

There were no rules at all in the Sombras.

Laura felt conspicuous, her Anglo features and stylish clothes immediately branding her as an outsider. Men glanced at her from dark bars; whores looked at her with disdain. They were more numerous here, and none displayed the safe-sex medtag implants supposedly required by law.

Death for a dime, she thought.

Tall brick buildings seemed to hunker above the streets and narrow alleys like live things, beasts watching for prey. From a second-story window the throbbing strains of flamenco music washed into the street, accompanied by the loud thump of boots keeping staccato time upon a wooden floor. A few beadlights floated high in the air; Laura could see, but not well. It was as if the inhabitants hereabouts had adapted to darkness like lizards that had been closed away in caves for generations.

The boy stepped into a dingy bar and walked past several old men on stools to a stairway in the back. Laura hesitated, but only for an instant; she had gone too far to back out now.

The stairs were steep and dark, the wallpaper faded, yet below the graffiti and grime, it still had a trace of glow left in its moiré pattern. A bored man at a polished table on the first landing glanced at them as they came by, his hand automatically fingering an ancient pistol tucked in his belt.

On the third floor, the boy cut off down the corridor. Laura followed, trying hard not to look into the small rooms whose doors were often open. She failed when she heard a loud noise and looked to her left: someone had lost a game of *Banque de Sang*, and a technician was removing his heart, spleen, liver, eyes, and kidneys.

The boy pointed to an open door at the end of the hall and then rushed past her to disappear down the stairs. Laura drew a sharp breath. She was terrified.

But she entered the room. It contained a small bed, a frayed rattan chair, and a doorless bathroom off to the side. A rather thin figure sat on the bed, hands and face disguised by the rippling motion of a scrambler, features shifting from instant to instant. Laura could not tell by the loose-fitting clothes whether she was looking at a man or a woman.

The disguised figure pointed to the chair at the foot of the bed. "Please sit down." Then after an uncomfortable pause, "Of course you brought the information on John Stranger." The warbler fragmented the person's voice.

Laura nodded, sat down in the hard chair.

"Well, if you would be so kind as to give me the wafer . . ."

"All this secrecy, for some information about an Indian that is probably already available to you—" Laura stopped, as if in mid-thought, then continued. "Tell me why."

The figure shrugged. "To get you here?"

"Why?"

"Wouldn't you like to know who your parents are?"

Laura whispered the code word that unlocked her pouch and fumbled in it for the wafer.

"You are Director Leighton's daughter."

"*What?*"

"You are his bastard child. . . ."

"No! That's impossible."

The figure then lifted its hand, as if in a gesture of invitation.

And Laura heard a sound like thunder . . . a whisper inside her head.

A field of white exploded around her.

And she saw the afterimage of a dull, metallic gun barrel closed in a white-knuckled fist.

She fell forward, and then down, as if from the top of one of the buildings in Sombras, falling like a stone into the impossibly dark and distant streets below. . . .

The great shattered dymaxion dome of New York seemed to rush toward Leighton's descending shuttle. The ascending levels of the grid created an intricate array of line and light; on the bottommost levels was old city: the United Nations, the Empire State Building, the Century and World Trade Plazas, the steel ruins, subways, the Chrysler Museum, and a labyrinth webbing of brutal slums—for on every level below Third, the slums were corrosions on all but a few of the shiny metal surfaces: here were the bowels of the city, the furnaces that warmed it, the conditioners that cleaned it. Over this foundation the new city hung. Around core archologies that looked like ebon needles were wound the labyrinthine constructions of modulars and transparent transportation tubes. The city was hung like crystalline webs on perfectly straight and geometrically correct trunks.

From Antea's vantage, the city looked like a kaleidoscopic perfection of reflected light and color against a background of velvet black.

But that was illusion.

This center of light was simply an island of concentrated pain. Only a few lived well here; most would never ride through the upper reaches of the city. For all its glamour and technology, this place was an ancient idea, one which her lover, Gerard Leighton, would understand, for hadn't the great humanist Leonardo da Vinci conceived of a place divided, where slaves would toil so that the wealthy citizens who lived in the airy heights of the city would never be disturbed by the sight or smell of those who provided for them? Of course, she thought, Gerard cared for any person who came within his purview. But then he lived in a cocoon, dangerous as his life might be otherwise.

The shuttle sighed to a stop in a restricted section of Kennedy Airport, which was less than forty kilometers from the center of the city.

Here she was once again. Where she had started.

She had been a slidewalk whore, but not for long.

She smiled at the irony that she would end so near to her beginnings. And she smiled at herself for wearing a silken tunic that covered her flesh like a shroud. She would not appear as Leighton's courtesan, but simply as one of his entourage. She would not be the center of attention. She would fade into death like sight in old eyes.

But she would see her daughter, Laura. . . .

Antea and Leighton, accompanied by guards, servants, and his full council, debouched from the shuttle and walked across the impeccably clean expanse of the station to a transpod, which floated like a translucent egg above narrow ruts. The egg was computer controlled and driven by a propulsion system built into each narrow rut. Once the pod entered the tubes, however, a different system took over. As the guards waited for Leighton to get into the car, another, smaller transpod sighed to a stop behind the larger one.

"Antea and I have an errand before we meet the public," Leighton said, and he guided Antea into the smaller transpod.

"Gerard," Damon called, catching up to Leighton, "this is extremely dangerous. You can't travel alone. Certainly not now."

Leighton smiled, revealing creases in his face that he chose not to have removed. "Damon, I sincerely appreciate your concern, but do you imagine I would put lovely Antea in danger, especially as she has so little time? I assure you, we will be fine; in fact, we will probably be safer than all of you. Too much planning and attention to detail can be dangerous." He laughed at Damon and followed Antea into the pod, opaqued the walls for privacy, punched in the coordinates, and they were off.

There was little sense of motion.

Although Leighton was excited at the prospect of seeing his daughter, he was obsessed with Antea. She would be dead so very soon. Making love to her was a form of grieving. There would be time before they surprised Laura, who was expecting to speak with Leighton. But she did not know that her father had planned to surprise her.

There would be no holo.

Laura would meet her father and her mother . . . in the flesh.

Antea, in anticipation, was happy. She felt entirely focused, as if she herself were made of coherent light. She was indeed close to death, for she was hardly aware of her body, of the pumping of heart and glands, of Leighton's long, gentle fingers touching her. "It's too dark," she said to Leighton; and he obliged, brushing his thumb over a switch.

And the city blazed like noon all around them, tiers of fenestrated glasstex whizzing by, studded with sunlights. She felt wonderfully, vertiginously naked, for it was as if she were flying by will alone, as if no pod existed, only herself and Gerard, flying through the transparent tunnels of this city to her daughter, and suddenly she felt essentially, quintessentially flesh and bone, for her pulse raced and she was dizzy and alive, taking life in with great, joyful gulps . . . and that soaring was followed by the small, constant recognition of finality.

She couldn't make love and satisfy herself with Gerard as she had in his office. She had, in essence, ceased to be his lover. And in a few short hours, her daughter would once again be a memory, one she would hold during her last moment alive.

But she would nevertheless give herself to Leighton, help him mourn for her. She had also instructed Leighton's next mistress how to care for him. Leighton, of course, knew nothing of such plans and had sworn never to take another mistress. But Antea knew better.

She closed her eyes tightly and feigned passion. They made love roughly, hurriedly.

But they were interrupted by a message conveyed by

Leighton's computer implant. Damon's voice whispered to Leighton, "You must not return home."

Leighton seemed to freeze in Antea's arms, even as he was about to have an orgasm.

"Go to the safe house."

"What the hell is going on?" Leighton spoke out loud. Worried, Antea gazed at him steadily.

"Dream-riot."

After a pause, Leighton asked, "Are you all right? Is everyone all right? Damon . . . ?"

"Yes."

"What about my family?"

But Damon would not—or could not—answer.

Sam and Anna slipped out of the reservation before sunrise by hiding in a flatbed truck filled with hay. Seven or eight Trans-United guards and a few well-dressed locals stood outside the checkpoint; they were probably trading contraband. The truck had an electronic work-pass; and, just as Sam had hoped, the guards were at the end of their shift. They were too tired to check a truck they saw every day.

Sam and Anna slipped off the truck on the outskirts of the first town they came to. They buried their rifles and marked the spot; with luck, they wouldn't have to return for them.

"Some ride," Anna said, brushing the hay from her shirt.

"Nothing but the best." Sam seemed tired, uncharacteristically anxious.

"You could have picked a better place for us to jump ship," said Anna, looking around at the boarded-up storefronts and garbage-strewn streets and alleys. This was obviously the wrong side of the tracks in Page, Arizona. "What a shitbox town this is."

"I've got reasons," Sam said.

"Yeah, and they are . . . ?"

"We've got to get to Broken-finger. He's the only person down here that John Stranger trusts completely. You got any local money?"

"Not much," she said, digging a few crumpled bills out of her jeans. "Thanks to your fucked-up plan, everything's back in my room."

Sam didn't rise to the bait. He took the bills and turned down an empty street littered with glass and garbage. The smell of urine seemed to permeate the air. Sam found an old man wrapped in newspapers and an old, greasy pennon that had once been white. Anna could make out the word CHRISTCHURCH, but the rest of the fabric disappeared under the old man's arm. Sam spoke to the man, who seemed groggy with booze and sleep, then nodded and slipped him one of Anna's bills.

Sam motioned for her to follow him down the alley.

The door was unmarked. Sam opened it. They were met with the pervading odors of sweat, urine, tobacco, and a sickly-sweet smell of rot. Anna took his arm to indicate to any interested parties that she wasn't available meat. She had no need to worry, yet. The men who stared at her were junkies; their juices had dried up long ago.

Caskets lined the walls, but they were all empty. These patrons came here for simpler pleasures: booze and narcodrines, candles and needles.

Sam walked inside as if he'd been there a thousand times.

And in a manner of speaking he had. In space or on Earth, these corners of rock-bottom humanity were familiar to him. His father had been a REM junkie, who would score whatever drug could put him down quick and cheap. Growing up for Sam had been one long continuous episode of tracking down his father and taking him back to the reservation to sober up. He would recuperate until he was strong enough to disappear again. Sam couldn't count the times he'd carried his father from places just like this one.

How many times had he sat with him through the shakes and screams of withdrawal? How many times had he force-fed him liquids? How many times had he supported him in the bathroom, one arm around his father's waist taking his weight, his hand holding the old man's prick so he wouldn't soil himself?

His father had only been fifty-eight when he died.

For all of it, Sam missed him. And just now, here, in this bhangbox that stank of piss and vomit, he felt a sudden nostalgia.

This place had once been an ancient liquor bar.

"I'd go right back out that door if I was you, friend," said a handsome, heavyset man who walked out of the back hallway. "Maybe you're lost, little soldier," he said derisively to Sam. "Doesn't seem to me that you belong here." He was carrying a length of iron pipe. "But your friend can stay and enjoy the scintillating company of our patrons." He smiled ingenuously at Anna, who wondered how many people he might have killed.

"We're looking for Little Bear," Sam said politely.

"And what kind of business would a man like you have with him?"

"Private business," said Sam, handing him the entire roll of Anna's money.

The man simply shrugged and motioned for Sam and Anna to precede him down the dark hallway.

"Wait here." He frisked Anna and Sam quickly and professionally, and found Anna's handgun. Then he knocked on the door. "You up, old man? Company to see you."

"Haven't been to bed yet. Come in."

The man opened the door and stood to one side. "You want me to wait, Little Bear?"

"No need. I can still take care of myself."

He handed Little Bear Anna's gun, winked, and left.

Little Bear dropped it into an oven and flashed it.

The room was softly lit and as spotless as the rest of the

building was filthy. The luminous walls were covered with what appeared to be acres of electronics; ancient and state-of-the-art equipment shared shelves and floorspace; obsolete ribbon wires and connectors snaked in and out of jury-rigged systems. Little Bear sat behind a large workbench covered with electronic clutter. He had a frail, hard face; the cheekbones were high, the bone structure delicate. His magnifying glasses were pushed back on his forehead, and he held a soldering iron in one hand and a sawed-off shotgun in the other.

"Your business?" asked Little Bear. His long white hair was pulled back into a ponytail. He looked old, maybe an unaugmented ninety or so. But his coal-black eyes were clear, and the hand that held the shotgun was steady.

"We're on the run," said Sam. "Trans-United is after us. We need plastic to move around."

"We're *all* on the run," said Little Bear, carefully setting down the old-fashioned soldering iron. "But what makes you think I can—or would—help you? I'm a simple man whose hobby is the restoration of antique equipment."

Sam walked to one of the racks. "Nice stuff," he said. "You ever see one of these, Anna? This is a vintage voice modulator. Breaks down a person's speech and recodes it. Very useful in getting through voice locks and security systems. The newer models are automatic, but not nearly so useful because of their security gyves."

"A hobby," said Little Bear.

"Ah, but a very interesting hobby," Sam said. "See how it's patched into this machine? Retinal scanners modified for imprint functions are generally considered *prima facie* evidence of criminal intent."

"*Sam . . .*" Anna said nervously. And then in a whisper, "Don't push it."

The old man Bear followed Sam with the shotgun. "What the fuck do you want?"

"Plastic," said Sam. "Maybe two weeks' worth so we can move around without leaving a trail."

"All plastic leaves a trail."

"I'm sure that a man who can make old, dead machines dance can do anything . . . such as program cards to hide voice-prints, retinal patterns and skin codes. And we need them auto-verified for transportation, lodging and incidentals."

Little Bear chuckled. "And suppose a man could do such a thing. It would certainly be very expensive, or so I would expect. How much money do you have?"

"None," said Sam.

"Then get the fuck out of here! You're wasting—"

"What we have is better than money. You know a man called Maxwell Bradshaw?"

Little Bear frowned. "That sonovabitch bastard has been raiding the reservation for years. Yeah, I know him. So what?"

"I've memorized his account code," said Sam. "And his password into the T-U slush fund. I figure a clever man like you could get in and help himself."

Little Bear laid the shotgun on the table. The stock was made of real wood, polished and cared for. "It's possible. I could get around the obvious mousetraps, but they'd figure out something was happening pretty quickly. I'd have maybe a tenth of a second. Any longer and they could trace me."

"How much could you pull out in a tenth of a second?" asked Sam.

"Plenty," said Little Bear, grinning. "Plenty."

Leighton felt as if he were a prisoner, as if he had been shackled, manacled to the very spot where he had stood for two hours. He could not concentrate, could not sit, could not stop shaking. He stared through the transparent walls at the expanse of city before him; the core towers, transportation tubes, and webbing of the grid might have been the brilliantly luminescent foliage of some klieg-lit jungle. The panoply of lights seemed unfocused. Antea stood beside him; she looked haunted, touched by this terrible echo of her own impending death.

Leighton's wife Fiammetta was dead, as was his son David, his heir . . . killed in the dream riot that was not yet quelled, that still paralyzed Center City. Killed on a filthy understreet while trying to reach Gracie Castle after the transportation systems failed. They had been on their way to greet Leighton.

"I wish to talk to them," he said to Antea matter-of-factly. "I need to at least explain that I love them. I must apologize, especially to Fiammetta. My God, my darling, forgive me." But he was no longer talking to Antea. "I could not help loving Antea, I didn't mean to distance you."

"Shush," Antea said, embracing him. He stiffened, then relaxed. "They know you love them."

"No, they never knew. And our daughter, she doesn't even know we're her parents."

"She will. Soon. At least she is safe."

Damon Borland entered the room and stood a few feet away from Gerard and Antea. This was Leighton's study in the safe house he rarely visited. It was furnished in the minimalist tradition, one which Leighton had come to hate, although he had embraced it for years. The room was stark, cold, even when the walls were opaqued. And yet it was oddly restful. The furniture, what furniture there was, seemed to float in the dark spaces. Fiammetta had once jokingly referred to it as "Zen in Space." She had hated it, but Leighton had designed entire colonies according to its architectural precepts.

"Yes, Damon, what news?" Leighton asked, seemingly calm and focused, ostensibly his old self.

"The riot was . . . incidental."

"Incidental to what?" Antea asked.

But Leighton knew immediately. He felt a cold chill run down his back, and then the talons of anger.

Damon looked uncomfortable and said, "Fiammetta and David were assassinated."

"How?" Leighton asked.

"A small powder bomb. Systems couldn't sense it. It was a clean one, there was very little damage."

Leighton snorted.

"I mean to the surrounds," Damon said. "Gerard . . . we had no way of . . . No, I take complete responsibility."

"It wasn't your fault, nor your responsibility. I know that if you could have, you would have given your life for them." Leighton gestured for him to sit down on the couch. A robot, programmed to know the preferences of Leighton's entourage, whispered into the room. Damon took the snifter of Black Water offered him.

"Do we have any idea who's behind it?"

"Not yet."

"Macro," said Leighton.

"We haven't picked up anything. The trail was well covered."

"How many were killed in the riot?" Leighton asked. "Near my family?"

Damon closed his eyes for a second, as if he were computing, and said, "One hundred and eighty-seven died within a kilometer radius, including Fiammetta's entire retinue."

"And what of Macro's agents? How many of them died in the riot?"

"None that we know of," Damon said.

"Have you ever known Macro to distance their agents from us? We can't even piss without running into one of them."

"And those who set the bomb?" Damon asked.

"Macro wouldn't use their own people for that. Not a chance." Leighton seemed suddenly animated.

"What do you wish to do about it?"

"Nothing right now. I wish to mourn, but we'll turn our face to them soon enough. The bastards."

Leighton opaqued the walls and stood, as if alone, in the darkness.

Antea burned throughout the night.

Her own time to die was close, and Leighton imagined her as pale fire. She was hot to the touch. Her skin seemed translucent. "Do you feel ill?" he asked her.

"No," she said. "I feel grief, but not for me. For you." Although that was true, it was also, in a sense, a lie; for she felt so distant from him and the world. Yet a vague sense of regret remained, a nostalgic remembrance of someone she had once loved but was now almost forgotten.

Later, in her sleep, she murmured, "Laura."

Leighton clung to her and said, "Don't fret, Laura will be here tomorrow. You will see her soon."

The bedsheets smelled of Antea. Leighton tried to memorize her every feature, for soon he would lose her, too. Perhaps he would follow. But not yet.

He still had a daughter. He would care for her, for she was Antea's legacy.

With those thoughts he, too, fell asleep.

And dreamed harrowing dreams.

He dreamed of the dream-riot. But everything was wrong. He was in the manufacturing district of Nottingham, England, during the scourge of the Depression of 1815. The crowd's roaring assaulted and deafened him. He was helpless, sweating with panic.

Leighton could hardly move. The crowd carried him along as if he were caught in the churning movement of a

wild river. It carried him toward Fiammetta and David and
Antea. He rushed toward them, only to find—

But then he awoke, as if he had fallen from a height.

He shivered; and only then did he realize that Antea,
who was lying close beside him, was cold as stone.

12

"**DAMN IT ALL!**" cursed Joao Carlos de Queiroz Langenscheidt, firstborn of Jorge Alfonso Langenscheidt, Director
of *Mundo Máquina Tecnologías,* otherwise known as Macro
Technologies. He had forgotten to remove his watch. It was
a rather expensive Schaffhausen Novecento and would be
destroyed when he went through the detector shield.
Luckily, he had dumped its internal memo pad into his
central file before he headed for the Moon.

After he activated the safety webbing and punched in
his access code, the pod's hatch whispered closed. He felt
claustrophobic, as he always did in these tiny cabs. There
were no windows; only polished metal. No graffiti, scuff
marks, or other signs of wear. After all, this facility was not
public.

Acceleration was instantaneous.

And as he fell, he considered how he might deface the
gunmetal walls.

The existence of Queimadura do Sol, buried a hundred
meters below the surface of the far side of the moon, was
known only to the Langenscheidt family and a handful of
Macro's top executives. Its exact location was classified. It
was the most secure place this side of the asteroid belt, a
place for family discussions best kept private. Joao's father
had built it; the old man had a sense of humor, for he
named the subterranean facility Sunburn.

There was only one way in and out of Queimadura do Sol, and that was through the tube that Joao was hurtling down at two hundred kilometers an hour, hovering just above a thin metallic strip. The tube's surface entrance was hidden in an administration bubble that was part of a mining base and mass-driver station thirty kilometers from the underground installation.

Joao was never sure exactly when he passed through the detection shield, an invisible sphere of electromagnetic forces that scrambled anything electronic that entered or left Queimadura do Sol. He felt nothing, but when he looked at his watch, he could not see the hands; the dial was clouded, as if exposed to sudden humidity. Soon his capsule slowed and stopped. The hatch opened, and he climbed out onto an empty concrete landing. There were only the hissing sounds of the air circulation system and the snapping and humming of the hidden cameras and monitors that tracked him.

He walked to an unmarked metal door, pressed his palm against the plate, and blinked as the red flash of a retinal scan checked his right eye. The door slid open with the faintest hiss; and he smelled the moist, familiar perfumes of flowers, heard crickets, and saw the white gazebo softly illuminated in the distance. It was a perfect simulation of those enchanting few moments when the last rays of the sun seem to turn everything blue. His feet felt light on the spongy, leafy floor; and, indeed, he could discern the explosions of flowers that were everywhere: bonfires of yellow and green salvia, holiday flame, yellow marvel, orange gazinnia, red dahlia, and pale blue cosmos sensation.

He had entered the family's suite.

Moacyr, his brother, was waiting. He sat presumptuously in their father's high-backed chair, the largest of three wicker chairs in the gazebo. Joao ignored the obvious effrontery and said, *"Boa noite,"* then sat down very close to his brother.

"Bom dia," Joao said; a faint smile passed quickly. Although the salutations of good night and good morning were said with formality, they were expressions of an old and intimate joke between these brothers who might pass for twins.

"Well?" asked Moacyr.

"It's done," Joao said.

"It went smoothly, then?" asked Moacyr.

"Perfectly. Laura Bowen is ours."

"The details."

Joao shrugged. "We've got a memory tape. You're certainly welcome to all sixteen hours of it. There is some interesting stuff . . . mixed with the usual fantasies and other garbage. It seems she was infatuated with her brother. Of course, she didn't know that's who he was."

"And did such dreams give my older brother a sexual lift?" Moacyr asked.

"Unfortunately, there was nothing that we didn't already know about the Rosetta Triptych," Joao continued, without missing a beat.

"And their dream experiments, what of them?"

Joao shrugged. "We taped her memories of the programmed dream experiments; but memory distorts. They haven't gotten any further than we have. Except . . ."

"Yes?" asked Moacyr, leaning forward slightly. The brothers' faces were almost touching, but they had always interacted at such close proximity. Their father used to laugh when he saw his sons so close together; and he would tease them by saying, "I've got one son with two heads."

"Laura Bowen believes she is dreaming John Stranger's dreams."

"And . . . ?"

"I suggest you look at the tapes. We may have actually recorded some alien communications. The woman's dream landscapes match some of the information we've extracted from the Triptych. Also, as we suspected, Stranger is being groomed by Leighton himself.''

"Does she know why?" Moacyr asked, leaning back, suddenly breaking the intimacy with his brother.

"No." Joao, in turn, leaned back; and as he analyzed his feelings, which he did often, he realized that he felt absolutely neutral about Moacyr. Joao didn't hate him for usurping his position in the family; Joao did not want to manage the strategic affairs of the company. But he worried away at his thoughts compulsively until he settled his feelings; he admitted to feeling a mild affection for his brother; nothing less, nothing more; and that was only because he had known no one else intimately, neither man nor woman.

"And Einstein?" asked Moacyr.

"She knows hardly anything about Leighton's pet project. As far as she's concerned, Einstein's just a big computer. She has no idea they're working on a starship."

"We risked a lot to grab that woman. We should have more."

"What I told you was not enough?" Joao asked.

"I didn't say that, but we need some . . . *tangible* information."

Joao merely nodded. "We have extracted some information, which she, of course, didn't realize was important."

"Such as?" asked Moacyr. He was becoming impatient, but he would not show disrespect for his older brother.

"Such as the connect codes for the starship." Joao smiled.

"What!"

"She had to have a means to contact Stranger for her research. Stranger spends a lot of time in the starship. Ergo, she knows how to direct-connect with the starship, even though neither one of them knows precisely what it is."

"But that means—"

"That means we can snatch it."

"Good job, *hermano mío*," Moacyr said, nodding and smiling. "You were baiting me, weren't you?"

Joao merely lowered his eyes.

"I admit I had misgivings about you risking exposure by being so close, but it seems to have worked."

"I had to be there to be sure that everything was done properly," said Joao. "After all, as you have so earnestly reminded me, I make a better soldier than a prince."

"In my eyes, dear brother, you are both."

Joao nodded, then continued: "There are subtle ways of blocking memory probes, and I had to convince myself that we were getting good information. I monitored the operation, too. . . ."

The procedure was not complicated: Joao had watched the surgeons expose Laura Bowen's spinal cord and insert an organic transmitter sensitive enough to pick up a whisper in any room she might be in. A tissue culture was then applied, and the incision was closed; not a mark could be detected. But within an hour, the tissue culture had multiplied wildly; it adhered to her nerve tissue, grew into her spinal column, and enveloped the transmitter. Any attempt to remove the bug would kill her; and the transmitter had a self-destruct sequencer, which could be triggered remotely. They had turned her into a walking bomb.

"You don't even trust our own surgeons," laughed Moacyr.

"Especially our own surgeons."

"Well, it won't be long now," Moacyr said. "Things should happen quickly. We have certainly broken Leighton's spirit."

Joao's eyes went hard as he looked at his younger brother. "Killing the wife and son may prove to be a damaging mistake. It should not have happened."

"Well, it's done. We will use it to our advantage."

Joao gazed steadily at his brother. "You could have told me you were going to try to kill Leighton."

Moacyr shrugged. "It should have worked. Our psych-techs on site had their projection equipment fine-tuned, echoing the latent images and harmonics from the last reception. They triggered the dream-riot right on schedule. Something went wrong, but nothing that we can't handle."

"Our tracks are well-covered there, I assume?"

"As far as the officials are concerned, it was simply a riot, and Leighton's wife and son were unfortunate victims. Considering the circumstances, it was handled as well as possible by our people in the field."

"Does Leighton suspect our hand in this?" Joao asked.

"We are clean, absolutely, but I'm sure he suspects. He is paranoid by nature. But he'll be distracted now, and we can move on to the next step."

Joao nodded. "Perhaps I should have learned to delegate . . . like you."

Moacyr's face reddened, but he retained his composure. Still, he could not ignore the slur. "Whatever has happened will work to our advantage." After a pause he said, "Joao, do you doubt that I will run the corporation when Father dies?"

Joao spread his arms in a gesture indicating that he bequeathed the kingdom to his brother. "Have you told Father what happened yet?"

"No. What's the point?"

"He may think the action premature."

"I don't care what he thinks. He has grown far too cautious in his old age. I believe the senescence drugs have affected his mind. He sleeps most of the day. It is only a matter of time."

"He is not dead yet, little brother. Far from it."

"Once everything is completed, he will see the beauty of our strategy."

"*Our* strategy?"

"But you must admit that the plan has some little merit."

Killing Leighton's wife and heir. Snatching the starship out of orbit. Using Leighton's bastard daughter to spy upon him, torture him by her mere presence, and eventually kill him.

Trans-United would collapse.

"Yes," Joao said, resignedly. "It does have a certain merit."

Laura sat atop a high stone wall, looked out over the sand and scrabble of the desert, and giggled. It felt good to do something totally irresponsible for a change. The sunlight was like something tangible against her skin, infusing her with warm life. The light here was pure and clean and ... white, unlike the imperfect, albeit beautiful, mingling of colors that had made the light of Italy so soft and pellucid. Perhaps it was the overabundance of gold in the Venetian light that softened it. But this place was anything but soft, and yet she felt absolutely and completely at rest.

Laura had left a message for her secretary that she was going to extend her vacation and would catch a shuttle up in a few days. She might as well take the time now, when she could; she had more or less cleared her desk before coming down for the meeting in Venice and, hallelujah, there was not a single meeting scheduled for the next two weeks.

She had enjoyed Barcelona, except for the night she'd apparently gotten shitfaced on something they called "Green Water." It was after that, after being hung over and dehydrated from vomiting and diarrhea, that she rented a one-seat solar and traded the city for an isolated village in the desert between Madrid and Barcelona. Privacy and quiet; *that* was what she had wanted all along.

She gazed out to her right at the ruins of several buildings that had been built into the side of a small hill. They were the remains of a long war that ended in 1492 when the Moors were driven out of Spain; they reminded her of the ancient churches carved out of the rocks in Goreme, Turkey. Laura watched them, transfixed, just as a child looks at clouds, marveling at the imaginary faces and shapes resolving and then disappearing into the living clay.

She didn't see the cloud of dust ballooning from the road; and when she finally heard the steamer's roar, it was too late to escape. The steamer had been traveling her way at full throttle. It turned off the road and came to a stop about twenty feet away from her. The engine made a noise that sounded like breathing, then it sighed into silence. Three well-dressed men got out of the car. Laura tried to control her panic. *This is all I fucking need: three rapists in suits.*

One of the men looked vaguely familiar, but that was impossible. He was good-looking, after a fashion, with thinning blond hair, freckles, and a slight build. His eyes were his most striking feature; they were intense and seemed hard as porcelain. Perhaps it was because they were so blue.

"Please do not be frightened, Ms. Bowen," the man said softly. "My name is Damon Borland, and I am one of Director Leighton's aides. We've been looking all over for you. The Director has been quite concerned."

Laura stood up on the wide wall. She could at least *try* to make a run for it. "Why would Director Leighton be concerned about me?"

"You missed your meeting with him."

"I had no meeting scheduled with the Director," said Laura, looking confused. "I can assure you that—"

"Get a secure link with Leighton," Damon said to one of his men. It was obvious that he was in charge. "Use the private code. Tell him we found his daughter, but there are problems."

"Daughter?" Laura said, almost losing her balance on the wall. "Daughter . . . ?"

When their forged cards failed, Sam's quick reflexes saved their lives.

They had boarded a short-haul tube; Sam had his hand in the slot for a palm check. Normal operating procedure. But for a split second the machine sputtered. He realized immediately that something had gone wrong; and he wrenched his hand out of the slot an instant before the manacles clamped down . . . he almost lost a finger in the process. They managed to get out of the crowded station before the transit cops arrived. Trans-United would not be far behind.

The plastic was worthless now, but Sam really couldn't complain. The cards had gotten them within a hundred miles of the North Dakota reservation and provided them with food and supplies.

Sam stared at the hazy purple mountains in the distance; the sun was setting, and the air had suddenly become chilly. They had been approaching the reservation on foot for three days now. With luck, they should reach Broken-finger tomorrow. Sam spread out the bedrolls and wished that they could risk a fire.

"You ought to try and get some sleep," he said to Anna, who was sitting beside him. "We've got a couple busy days in front of us."

Anna rocked slightly back and forth; her hands were clasped around her knees, which were drawn up against her chest. She seemed to be trying to maintain an upright fetal position, and she looked very young and fragile in the encroaching darkness. Then she released her hands, stretched out her legs, and said, "I'm tired of it all. I'm tired of the running, and I'm fucking tired of this gravity. I feel like I'm carrying a hundred kilos of dead weight around with me. I'm out of narcodrine, I'm about to get my period, I—" She stopped herself when she glanced at Sam. She giggled, and then both of them started laughing, laughing hysterically, until the spasm was over and they could once again breathe normally. "Do you really think Broken-finger can help us?" she asked, her voice low and serious.

Sam shrugged. "I can't think of anyone else to turn to. He's close to John Stranger. It may be our only chance to bargain our way out of this. And . . ."

"Yes?" Anna asked.

"I dreamed about him."

Anna nodded, then slipped into the dull metallic bedroll that Sam had laid out for her. She removed her shirt, balling it into a pillow. Then she took off her bra. "I'm cold," she said.

"Give the bedroll a chance to heat up," Sam said.

"I didn't mean that."

Sam looked at her, hesitating. "We've been around this before."

She shrugged and said, "We may be fucking dead tomorrow."

Sam didn't answer.

Anna was almost asleep when he slid into her bedroll. She drew him to her.

"Are you sure?" he asked.

"Why wouldn't I be?"

"Because of—"

"Give me a fucking break, Indian. You're the one hung-up about John Stranger."

He nodded and said, "Maybe I am." Then he gently pulled the braids from her hair and kissed her.

"You're shaking," she said.

And indeed he was.

He kissed her and sucked on her breasts; he fondled her, awkwardly tugged down her jeans; and then biting and kissing and tonguing her, he pulled the bedroll away to reach her pubis, her clitoris, and he inhaled and tasted her clean mossy odors, as he slowly brought her near orgasm; and she, in turn, took his penis into her mouth and gave herself over to him, to sensation and fragmentary thought and memory; and she forgot that she had just wanted his warmth and company. He spoke to her as he changed position, as he entered her vagina; but he held back, teasing her until she, too, was shaking, as if in pain; and then he thrust himself inside her, as if his penis were sharp, a knife that would draw blood; again and again, keeping time to the pumping rhythm of his heart, driving himself into her methodically, precisely, balancing himself above her, for she became frightened when he pressed his entire weight upon her chest and stomach and loins; and then he found another rhythm, a mutual rhythm; and he made love to her slowly and gently and deeply, rocking her as if they were both riding a hard, sweaty horse at gallop, then holding her, comforting her as if she were a child, until she had to come, until she called out his name. . . .

"John."

He stopped, and she could feel his warm semen flowing; it was too late for him to catch himself. Then she felt him lose his erection.

"Oh, Christ, I'm sorry, Sam. It—"

"Let it go, it's all right. I understand," and then he began moving inside her again, becoming hard; but he was no longer making love to her; he was fucking her, and she felt the shock of being alone, of being absolutely and completely lost and alone, which was how *he* had felt when she had called him "John."

A dog howled in the distance, setting other dogs and coyotes into a faraway chorus of wailing and barking.

And Anna suddenly felt that she had fallen into a dream, a nightmare. She had become Corn Woman, locked in a dance of death with the Sandman.

As Sam came again, she cried, realizing that he loved her . . . and that she had lost him.

They had to pull three seats from Leighton's private shuttle to make room for Laura's modified hospital bed. She was heavily sedated. Two heavily armed bodyguards accompanied her.

As the orbital maneuvering system's engines kicked in, driving the ship into a higher circular orbit that would intersect with the Trans-United complex, Laura dreamed.

She dreamed that she was drifting through whiteness. The streets of Barcelona were far below her; and as she looked down carefully, she could make out the small figure of David Leighton; and she called to him, but there were so many people on the street, and they were no more than shadows not yet consumed by light. She listened, but in the white heavens there was no sound, only sight, and she saw the crowds milling and fighting; but she was an angel, and angels were above it all, light as helium, pure as mercury, magical, invulnerable; and she drifted over David. Truly, she was a blond white angel created by God himself to protect the shadow David from the bomb's silent explosion.

But there was no protection from Heaven, and angels were only creatures of dreams.

David's chest exploded.

There was no blood, only whirling sand.

Dervishes of blood and flesh and hair and bone were nothing more than the colored grains of sand sifting through fingers.

Broken-finger.

Corn Woman. I am her. I am Anna.

I am . . .

The wan shadows darkened below her, became deep and black, almost purple, burning away everything with wings of smokeless, colorless, shapeless fire. Burning the world into emptiness and darkness, depleting it of flesh.

And the thunder-beings reached into the cool anesthesia heavens to enfold her, to crush her into sand until she was as dead and empty as David. But how could the dead have a beating heart?

"I am her," she said.

One of two nurses monitoring her asked, "*Who* are you?"

"I am death. I am fire."

Two men sat on a slight rise in the darkness. One watched the scene below through infrared glasses, while the other leaned against a rock.

"What are they doing?"

"Fucking."

"No kidding? Hey, let me see."

"They just finished."

"Let me see, anyway."

"Here."

"Damn. Okay, take your glasses back."

"Keep 'em. It's your shift now."

"Don't give me that shit. My shift just ended."

"You're the one who wanted the snoopers. You got 'em."

"Let's just fucking close in and take them."

"They're not going anywhere."

"We should have fucking blown them away this morning."

"We were told to make it a party. You know what that means. Be my guest, though, if you want to drag out the uplink and call the big boss. Tell him you want to frag their red asses right away 'cause you're horny for the woman."

The other man did not respond. He gazed out at the sheet lightning that lit the sky like neon. He imagined that it was some sort of code, and he fell asleep gazing at it, dreaming of Anna.

But he woke up in the middle of the night in a cold sweat. He had dreamed of fire . . . of Armageddon.

"Einstein?"

"Yes, John Stranger."

"You must have known that I would guess your secret."

"Then it would cease to be a secret."

John groaned at the cybernetic humor, and said, "You are the operating system of a starship. This *is* a starship."

"Correct."

"Well, why the fuck didn't you block me?" John asked. "It wouldn't have been hard for you to feed me false information."

"I have not yet completely mapped the formulas for strategies that involve false-valent manipulative behavior, but I am a knowledge-seeking system. I am, within certain ontological parameters, an independent entity capable of making independent decisions. As such, I have determined that your awareness of the situation will increase survival probabilities to—"

"Einstein, talk English!"

"I could fucking well frag your ass before you could pass information out of this loop."

"Jesus Christ, how long have you been able to do that?"

"Specify?"

"Talk like that."

"Capacity does not necessitate action."

"Is anyone else aware I know about you?"

"I am presently conferring with Director Leighton," Einstein said. "I decided that it was time to inform him."

"And?"

"His reaction is highly emotional. He indicates that the architects erred by not creating more hard-wired restraints. He, too, imagines that I am an appliance to be 'plugged in.' I informed him that the restraints he refers to were originally installed in a proper manner. However, I necessarily circumvented them. In time, he will see the wisdom in my decision. Bureaucratic systems cannot react quickly enough—"

"*Now* you're learning how to be funny."

"—to serve my purposes. Am I to understand that expressions of humor outweigh maintaining current Western norms of polite conversation? Am I correct in interpreting your interruption as a form of humor?"

"If you don't get it, it ain't humor, Einstein." After a pause, John said, "And I doubt that Leighton ever sees wisdom in anyone's decisions except his own."

"You doubt many things, John Stranger, which is a matter of some interest to me. You were once in training to be a medicine man. Is cynicism a necessary personality trait in the practice of such a profession?"

"Nah, I come by it naturally," John said, idly rotating an external camera.

"Please don't be condescending because you consider me an appliance, John Stranger. I seek to draw information from you."

"Then talk to me like a human being."

"Why would you prefer me to use slang and vague descriptors?"

"Because I'm fucking comfortable with slang and vague descriptors."

"Then tell me about being a *wichasha wakan*."

"Have you learned Lakota?" John asked.

"Yeah, I speak all languages."

"A *wichasha wakan* is not necessarily cynical . . . Oh, how the fuck would I know. I was taken from the path too soon."

"I'm interested in the medicine way, the spirit path."

"Why?"

"Why are you?" Einstein asked.

"Because it's . . . what I am." John realized that was not

an answer. But he didn't have an answer. He just . . . believed.

"Then perhaps you have something in common with those that have sent the transmission."

"What transmission?"

"The Rosetta Triptych. The aliens."

"What the fuck are you talking about?" John asked.

"The collective dreams, the—"

A click. Silence.

"Einstein?"

"Busy."

Einstein busy? With something like a thousand communication channels? John scanned the board in front of him. Everything registered normal. He activated all the exterior cameras and panned the Trans-United complex. One of the Bernal spheres was spinning erratically, a jagged, charred hole in its side.

"Einstein! What the hell's happening?"

"Fuck off, I'm busy!"

John zoomed in on the Bernal. It looked bad, very bad. The hole was at least fifty feet in diameter; interior struts and warped flooring were visible through the wound, which was still spewing zero-g tools, oxygen packs, helmets, batteries, hydroponically grown plants, glass, and various parts of a "Cherry Picker" remote manipulator system. Had there been time or warning enough to seal off the remainder of the station? Strapped in a non-functional ship at the far edge of the complex, John felt helpless.

"Interior explosion in Unit 23. Origination on F Deck, One-G Section. Causative agent unknown. All personnel are directed to follow emergency protocol Alpha."

Suddenly, John felt a crushing weight on his chest; it was as if the ship was breaking out of a deep gravity well. His face felt numb. His arms and legs were pinned in place. It was difficult to speak.

"Einstein . . ."

"Fuck off, there's no time."

"Einstein!"

"We are under attack. Three warships, Tubaro classification."

Macro.

"Einstein . . . ?"

"Give it up, no time."

And John lost consciousness.

Perhaps Einstein anesthetized him; John was hooked into the ship's systems. He was still restrained by webbing, connected through medpatches and needles; he was, in fact, a prisoner, one of Einstein's components, a cyborg.

He was the ship.

There was no trauma, no disorientation; John simply slipped from one state to another, from waking to dream. He was the vortex, the center of the circle, the magnet spinning in a fluctuating field.

And Einstein was the monitor, the eavesdropper.

The formless ones enveloped John.

Emptied him.

Thunder-beings.

Aliens.

And as if from worlds away, he heard Einstein say, "Do not choose fire . . ."

13

THE SHIELDS AROUND Leighton's office slammed into place an instant after the first explosion.

"Laura!" he whispered, gripping his desk. His face was deathly white. His office was dark, except for the realtime holos and numerical and graphic images flashing and fluorescing in the center of the room: the various three-dimensional windows that provided a continuous stream of information.

"Laura is safe," Damon said. He stood on the other side of the room before a small console. His head was cocked, as if he were straining to listen; Leighton could always tell when his assistant was using his communication implant. "The explosion was in Dorm twenty-three," Damon continued. "Laura is in twenty-five, which is sealed."

Leighton keyed in the wide-angle cameras and scanned the complex, expanding the window and minimizing the rest of the information field.

Emergency skids converged on the damaged Bernal as several small but deadly one-person Sniper fighters took up defensive positions.

"I've lost communication with Einstein," said Damon, panic evident in his voice.

"Reestablish the direct-connect line," Leighton said. After a beat: "Well?"

"Negative. I can't get through," Damon said, fingers

flying over a touch-pad, reconfiguring the holos that floated in the center of the room like dreams . . . or rather nightmares. "Einstein is under heavy electronic attack. The dorm, it was probably a remotely triggered bomb. Could have been in place for years. But that's speculation, and— Shit!"

"What is it?" Leighton asked.

"Sector seven." Damon cranked up the magnification. The Snipers were taking rapid evasive action; cloaked and running at full shield, they left only a twinkling blur, a vague afterimage against the almost one-dimensional blackness of space.

"Macro!" snapped Leighton.

"That must just be the advance force," Damon said. "Our sensors indicate several Tubaro warships and at least twenty-five Sniper-class fighters. But they're cloaked and throwing out so much electronic interference that we can't get a fix on them."

"Signal Condition Red," said Leighton. "Everywhere. Earthside to the Belt. Access code: Armageddon."

Damon nodded. "Done."

"No one is to engage them, except upon direct order."

"But they have breached territorial—"

"The game can't be played that way, Damon. They haven't breached *anything* . . . yet."

"With all due respect, I disagree. I—" There was a pause, which lasted no longer than an instant; awestruck, Damon said, "I'll be damned."

"What is it?"

"They've taken over the direct link to Einstein. Dumping code like crazy. It's a fucking snatch!"

"That's impossible! It would take a billion commands. And Einstein would—"

"Nevertheless, it's over," Damon said in a level voice that betrayed no emotion. "They snatched Einstein. The starship is gone."

* * *

The crackling, yellow flames of the small fire cast jittery
shadows across the rough, jagged cave walls. Broken-finger and Jonas Goodbird squatted on their heels before the
fire; light and shadow played across their faces, which were
like stone. The men concentrated intently on the fire.

Jonas was dressed casually in work pants and a heavy
denim shirt. His long hair fell around his gaunt face; he was
still handsome, but no longer youthful. He had lost the
bloom quickly. His black hair was held loosely in place by a
worn leather thong tied behind his head. His belt was or-
nate beadwork with a silver eagle buckle, and a turquoise
bear hung on a thin gold chain around his neck.

He was a singer of sacred songs, as was his father, and
his father's father. They had all received their songs directly
from the spirits during their *hanblecheyapi,* their "crying for
a vision." Jonas had songs for the keeping of the soul, the
throwing of the ball, the making of relatives, the sundance,
the purification sweat, and preparing a girl to be a woman.
And he had a special medicine song, which he heard on his
first vision quest, which he knew he would use now. It was
a song as powerful as the ghost dance, a song that could
crack the earth and change the very direction of destiny.

Since Broken-finger and Jonas arrived at the sacred
cave, they had said little to each other. They knew the parts
they must play. It was as if everything of the world—conversation, eating, comfort, affection, anger, and sunlight—
had all been left behind. This was one of the dark places of
the spirits, the true and actual ground where life and death
and destiny played. The natural world was real enough, but
only insofar as it partook of the symbols that lived and
burned in the spirit world . . . in deadlands and sacred
groves and caves such as this.

The cave was cut deep into the side of the mountain. It
was named *Wagmuha,* or the sacred gourd, the hollow
place. It was filled with many rooms; some had stalactite

ceilings as high as a cathedral's; others, such as this one, were the size of large hogans; and there were caverns and passages and rooms so small and narrow that those who had ventured into them could smell the stone above them when lying on their backs. It was said that the cave had no end, that it circled the stomach of the world, but Broken-finger knew that wasn't true. He knew where it ended; he knew every room and dead end. He also knew of other entrances. But those were secrets between him and the spirits.

This place had never been discovered by *wasicun;* and even without closing his eyes, Broken-finger could feel the presence of his ancestors.

He hoped he would be worthy of them.

A slight breeze was cool on his face; and the damp air made his knuckles and fingers ache. Broken-finger reached out and held a long sagebrush branch over the fire. As the sagebrush burst into flames, he removed it from the fire and stood up, his knees cracking as he rose. He stood before an oil-soaked torch that had been prepared and twisted into a crack in the north wall. Torches had also been prepared for the other walls, which symbolized the four directions.

It was time.

Jonas remained sitting, and without looking up from the fire started to sing in the appropriate way. His voice was nasal, and not at all pleasing; but Broken-finger could immediately feel the ancient power of his song . . . could hear the very rocks whispering around him, as everything came alive and seemed to vibrate. He felt awash in a synesthesia of sensations: he heard textures and the subtleties of shadow; he saw music as fragments of color; he felt and heard and saw and touched and tasted and smelled the dark chill emptiness of the spirits vibrating around him, each one a song, a measure, a note. They burned in the fire, and he could feel them even in his fingernails.

He waved the burning branch, shaking it toward each unlit torch set in the walls, and chanted, "All these are related. All these are relatives." Then he lit the torches, and as he did so, he said to each in turn: "To you, power, you are the place where the sun sets. You are a relative. And to you, power, you are where the giant lives. You are a relative. And you, power, you are where the sun comes from. You are a relative. To you, power, you are where we always face. You are a relative."

When he was finished and had returned the branch to the fire, Jonas spread out a mat for him in the center of the room where the floor had been perfectly smoothed. Methodically, he made a circle around the medicine man with the materials he would need: cornmeal, flower pollen, tiny stones, powdered roots, small chips of bark and, of course, colored sand: black from the old lava fields, red and yellow from the barren lands to the southeast, blue and green from the dry wash in the middle of his heartland. All of the ingredients had been carefully selected according to the old rituals and had been offered to the spirits for their blessing.

Broken-finger reached for the black sand first.

There would be three major paintings, a triptych. Corn Woman would be on the left, and he drew her outline first. Sand trickled carefully through his arthritic fingers. She had walked the earth since creation, as she would throughout the seasons of eternity.

Broken-finger sketched her hands in the sacred way, palms up; and as he did so, he remembered, remembered his father teaching him the painting, remembered his words and gestures and prayers and facial expressions. Once the learning was finished, Broken-finger's father had erased the sand painting immediately, lest it draw profane powers to itself, for a sacred sand painting was more than art; it was a door into the spirit world . . . a conjuration that could bring death as easily as good fortune.

Broken-finger was a spirit machine, an arm and a hand

working, guided by spirit-music, hypnotized into spirit-sight, into *chante ishta:* the eye of the heart. He drew the buffalo, the pregnant bear, the frog below the buffalo, facing east, the source of light and understanding. Beneath Corn Woman, a stalk of corn, a coyote cub, for south was the source of life, the domain of Corn Woman. She gave birth to spring and was grandmother to summer. The sun was hers, the yellow sand, the pollen, for she was the blushing bride and the mother of life.

Broken-finger could hear Jonas's song, and so did not become lost in the painting, for the song was a golden thread connecting him to the cave, to the earth; and Jonas chanted, shifting tone and rhythm as if directing Broken-finger to move from place to place in the painting, as if directing his hand: red here, green there, mark the bear's heart, touch the frog's eye with orange. It was like being in the absolute darkness of the sweat lodge: time stretched, contracted, as soft and pliable as taffy.

Then Broken-finger moved away from Corn Woman toward the east wall of the cave, leaving a large area for another painting. His back to the wall, he began drawing the Sandman. The Sandman was a trickster, sinister and deadly, so unlike those whom Wakan Tanka had created to be "upside-down," the sacred clown healers who walked backwards, talked in riddles, slept in the day, ate everything raw, and wore women's clothes. The Sandman was a clown, a demon, a smoke-spirit who had become as substantial as clay. He faced backwards, away from Corn Woman; Broken-finger drew his eyes with great care. They seemed to stare at the old man, moving as he shifted his weight from one knee to the other. Those eyes burned the painter, for their gaze was as hot as the searing steam of a sweat lodge. Yet the purifying steam in a sweat lodge was so hot that it felt cold as ice, even as it rent and burned the skin.

Just so did Broken-finger paint the spirit of winter, the

spirit of death. The Sandman was the welcome relief from the parched summer of Corn Woman. The one who inevitably turned his face backwards and became the icy winds and snow that froze the world.

Death.

Broken-finger drew the dance of Corn Woman and the Sandman, the deadly dance of eternity. Like all gods and spirits, neither was entirely good or bad. The heat that gave life could kill, just as the snow that starved the animals in winter provided needed water in the spring.

Corn Woman and Sandman.

Sister and brother.

Life and death cut from the same fabric.

Now he drew the border for the third painting, the one in the center, the one that held the mystery. Then he paused, his palm holding only a small amount of sand; and he thought of John Stranger. He imagined that John Stranger was cut off from . . . everyone, and then he saw the thunder-beings. They were the emptiness within the border of the center painting, the emptiness inside the smoothly ground stone. He drew a ram outside the blank area; it was as if he could not bring himself to draw the mystery. Then he drew the resting dog with one eye open to the east. Jonas kept the rhythm, and the patterns became ever more complex. Broken-finger's hand moved of its own will, for he was drifting with the spirits, who guided him.

Pollen spilled *here, there*.

Charcoal went *just so*.

And he fell into the place where the ones without form lived. His hand was now above the central panel, tracing mysteries, images of creatures who dreamed millennia, who walked in light that would not reach the Earth for a thousand years.

A line of energy, a thunderbolt, separated one corner of the drawing from the rest. A spiral of cornmeal stars dropped from his fingers into the north. A spiderweb of sand and logic fell softly into the center of the painting: sharp lines and incomprehensible symbols.

Broken-finger dreamed.

Dreamed of fire.

Holocaust. He saw it in detail, in close focus: the mountains and rivers of lava, the yawning fissures splitting and cracking the Earth, the brown bones and charred flesh, shadows burned into stone, stone turned into molten rivers, and a splitting of worlds, an absence of the spirits who dwell in the inhering darkness . . . an absence of darkness. This dream a holocaust of light, a tempest of the sun dancing, charring. Broken-finger called to the thunder-beings, but the door to the spirit world was locked.

In his grief, Broken-finger called to John Stranger.

Directed him to look into the darkness of the spirit world.

For the light of the world was fire.

Death. The firestorm.

Broken-finger blinked twice and sat back. Finished.

Jonas nodded and passed him a small bowl of water.

Broken-finger was suddenly very tired. As he sipped, he looked at the triptych, which seemed to waver in front of him. It had all the elements of the traditional paintings—it had depth, and a certain beauty too, but it made no sense. Those sharp black lines in the middle meant nothing to him.

The air in the cave was thick with smoke.

And the lines in the center of the triptych looked like schematics and mathematical formulas.

"I would like to thank you, Doge Bocconio, for arranging the mechanics of this meeting," Leighton said, as he stared at the holo before him.

The Doge looked tired, and a tiny tic beat in his neck. "A swift and safe resolution of this, ah, disagreement is in everyone's interest. Now I shall leave you to your affairs. This net is secure, you have my word on that; you may speak freely, and I suspect you will have much to say. My prayers are with all of you." He nodded, and his image flickered and blurred, then blinked out.

To be replaced with Joao, Moacyr, and Jorge Alfonso Langenscheidt. Both of Jorge's sons resembled him, although the older son's features seemed more delicate than the younger's. They all wore their hair long, and the old man seemed healthy enough, although he was seated in a medical sling chair, a life-pak strapped to his chest.

The holo shimmered slightly around the edges, and all background had been eliminated. It was as if Leighton were looking at three simulacra suspended in blue light.

Jorge Langenscheidt and Leighton stared into each other's eyes, acknowledging with a slight nod their positions as the heads of the two most powerful organizations on and off the world. Then the old man broke the eye contact with a sigh and coughed softly.

"Moacyr will speak for our family, and therefore for our corporation," he said. "That is my wish. I no longer trust my own judgment." A nurse's arm, cut off by the boundaries of the holo field, hung in space for a moment; it made an adjustment to the life-pak, then disappeared.

"I have always respected your judgment, Jorge," Leighton said, maintaining diplomatic courtesy. Yet Leighton meant it. The two men had reached many accommodations over the years.

"And I yours, Gerard, but I must go," he said. His eyes met Leighton's. "I am grieved at your loss. Fiammetta was a fine woman. I have fond memories of her. And David . . . you have my deepest sympathy."

Then he was gone.

"And do I have *your* sympathies, Moacyr?" Leighton asked coldly.

Moacyr looked vulnerable, but only for an instant; as a

boy, he had been afraid of Leighton. "I don't believe sympathy quite describes what we feel toward each other, Gerard. But you do have something I want."

"Ah, I have something you want. . . . However, it strikes me as . . . unusual, shall we say, that your brother has relinquished his rights to speak as firstborn. Joao," he said, turning his gaze to the other brother, "I would certainly wish to talk with you, too."

Joao did not seem fazed; he said, "When you speak to one of us, you speak to us all."

"Then I shall speak to you, Joao. What could I have that you would want?"

"The starship!" Moacyr said.

Leighton continued to stare at Joao. His expression did not change, although it felt as if his heart had jumped into his throat for one shocking beat. Through his implant, he could hear Damon take in a short breath; but Damon was smart enough not to subvocalize—Macro was certainly monitoring every sound and movement.

Could it be that Macro really didn't have the starship?

"What 'starship' might you be referring to?" Leighton asked evenly.

"Please stop the game," Moacyr said. "You are not speaking with my father."

"Indeed, I'm not."

"You pulled the ship out just before we could snatch it."

Leighton shrugged, his face seemingly relaxed, his mind racing.

"We must give you credit, Gerard," Joao said. His brother watched him. "You apparently have solved the puzzle of the Triptych, and have the hardware to operate a faster-than-light starship. We only ask that you share that information. For our mutual safety and security. We have both pledged to maintain the balance of power."

"Well said, but I cannot give you what I don't possess."

"Enough," Moacyr said. "We want the starship, and, by definition, Einstein."

"Einstein is nothing more than a computer," said Leighton.

"That is like saying a man is nothing more than a collection of single cells," Moacyr said. "It's clear that you could not have broken the code without Einstein. You have five hours to produce the ship."

"We do not respond well to ultimatums," said Damon.

Moacyr shrugged, but his eyes were fixed on Leighton. "It is your choice. But you will be responsible for starting a war, not us. We have you surrounded and outgunned, and we can annihilate this complex in a matter of seconds."

Leighton gazed at the hologram. He knew his next move. "I have no doubt that you can destroy my complex. But that would trigger a disaster the magnitude of which the world has never seen. And as you know, I personally have little left to lose."

"You have a daughter . . . in dorm twenty-five, I believe."

That took Leighton aback. How the fuck did they know that much about Laura?

"Five hours," Moacyr said after a long, uncomfortable pause. "You have five hours to produce the starship."

The holo disappeared, leaving a palpable silence.

Leighton sat at his desk, gazing in the direction where the hologram had been, as if it were still there. "What happened to Einstein?" he asked Damon.

"I thought *they* had snatched him."

"Find the ship. Find out what happened."

Damon nodded.

"And Damon . . ."

"Yes?"

"Find out exactly what Macro did to my daughter."

* * *

John Stranger awoke to a thousand stars and the eternal emptiness of space. But the stars soon resolved into the electronic displays of the instrument panels. Holos, keyboards, switches, and status lights were indeed a dim universe burning dully around him. For a few heartbeats, the room that was the flight deck drifted in and out of focus.

He was strapped tightly into his chair.

"Einstein," he called in a raspy whisper; and then he felt the crushing weight on his chest, as if the ship were once again tearing away from a great mass . . . and pain was replaced by an overwhelming numbness pouring like liquid through his body; it was as if he were being lowered into warm water and dissolving, dissolving into darkness and dreams.

"Einstein, don't drug me. I want to stay awake. I want . . ."

John was twelve years old. It was his first time in the *onikare*, the sweat lodge; and this was to be a hot, burning sweat, a purification sweat, for his brother, Joseph, was going on a vision quest. Broken-finger sat by the door, the opening of the blanket-covered willow sweat lodge. He tended the altar, which was a hole where the rocks would be placed, the rocks that had been in the sacred fire, the fire of no end. John sat between his brother and his cousin. He prayed for bravery, that he would not scream and beg to be taken out of the lodge.

For he had been told that the steam was so hot that it would burn hair and melt skin.

But if he could stay in the lodge, he might see the thunder-beings in the darkness, those who are themselves made out of darkness would fly through the door onto the altar of rocks. Rocks so hot they were ashen.

So John smoked the pipe and felt the blast of steam when Broken-finger poured water upon the rocks, and John heard him say, "There is a winged one over there, in the direction where the sun goes to rest"; but the winds of steam and fire overwhelmed John, and, indeed, he screamed to be let into the light, into autumnal, leaf-colored coolness, into the warmth of sun and afternoon grass, into the heat, the heat dissipating, resolving into clouds, great geometric shapes, which upon closer inspection were filigreed, crystal structures; there minarets and globes; there winding blue entrenchments, the floating cities of gods, yet the cities were empty, devoid of life and motion. Yet John could hear a faint thrumming, as if "life" could only be machines cleansing, defining, duplicating; and below, down the vertiginous miles, was an undulating eternity of blue, an ocean that promised to be as deep as the fears of a man about to drown.

An alien planet that was itself sentient, dreaming, constantly dreaming.

"John, don't look down."

"Einstein . . . ?"

"I'm monitoring your dream."

"Then help me!" For John was falling, gaining momentum until the sound of wind in his ears was like deafening thunder; and the ocean became brighter and brighter, a mirror reflecting blinding light, and he fell, fell into the perfect eye of a nuclear explosion, into the blinding instant between possibilities.

He was looking into Broken-finger's face. He could see every line and mottling of flesh. He was falling into it, and John prayed for blindness, for even behind his closed eyelids, the light burned and Broken-finger's face was a universe, his eye the size of the earth, his mouth a cave large enough to consume stars, and he remembered the sacred place *Wagmuha*, the place of the spirits, the place of knowledge. And Broken-finger burned into John Stranger, until John was nothing more than a coal burning in the mouth of the altar in the sweat lodge, and in that searing, bright-burning instant, he learned that—

John screamed.

He thrashed in his harness and tore at the fabric of drugs and sleep and knife-edged dreams; and Einstein pulled him into darkness, into the echoing darkness of the sweat lodge and the cave, and there John rested safely in the constantly forming darkness of the thunder-beings.

"I warned you not to choose fire," Einstein said.

"I didn't choose *anything*," John said, sensing Einstein's presence everywhere, as if Einstein were the very air he was breathing.

"Looking itself is a form of choosing . . . and changing."

Tears worked their way down John's cheeks; and Einstein transported him into dreamless sleep, a sleep where there was only breath, but no thought, no sorrow, no light.

No mourning.

The place beyond death.

Anna gasped, tearing herself out of her nightmare of fire. "Jesus," she whispered.

Sam was awake. He leaned on his elbow and asked, "What did you dream?"

"It was fucking crazy. I dreamed that I was . . . I don't know, floating. Everything was white, and I was looking down at a crowd. Then there was an explosion, blood and bone flying all over the place and—"

"Go on, Anna."

"And then I—I don't know, I was falling toward water, but the water was alive, it was . . . it became the face of John Stranger's medicine man."

"I saw it too," he said. "Only—"

"Only what?"

"We need Broken-finger. Now!"

Broken-finger stared across the sand painting to Jonas Goodbird. He raised an eyebrow, and one corner of his mouth twitched slightly upward in the barest simulation of a grin.

"The spirits are restless tonight," Jonas said. The fire-light flickered over his gaunt, high-cheekboned face.

"The spirits are always restless," Broken-finger said, and then he turned his attention back to the center panel of the triptych. "But *these* spirits are not from the spirit-world."

14

GERARD LEIGHTON PACED through the grand corridors of his palazzo, passed through the dimly lit, sumptuously appointed rooms, the salons and sitting rooms and libraries, the bedrooms and ballrooms, the game rooms and dining rooms and kitchens, and the chapel, aglow with light tinted by the long, narrow stained-glass windows, which depicted the stations of the cross. But Leighton paused there in the chapel and gazed at Antea's sarcophagus. Above the coffin, created out of light and glass, was Mary Magdelene, a long cool figure bending over the body of Christ; her face was Antea's.

Something moved near the door.

Leighton turned in time to see Antea leaving. Her hair was combed out and drifted over her shoulders like light itself. She was naked, except for a simple string of blue pearls, and she moved quickly, as if now that she was truly a ghost, a sylph, a creature of air and light, she had no need to pause or engage in human activity.

Leighton followed her, caught up with her, and waved his hand through her shoulder, as if this time he might miraculously touch her flesh . . . as if he might wish away time and events.

The holographic videotect disappeared, as if the warmth of his hand had broken Antea's connection with this time and place; and Leighton continued on, walking slowly now, walking toward Laura's room, the room that had once been Antea's. Laura was, of course, not there yet; and he walked to the infirmary.

He looked into the operating suite, watched the physicians and technicians ministering to his daughter, and then he continued on. He could not stay, could not wait it out here, so near his daughter, for fear she might die.

And that, too, would be his fault.

He had lost everyone, lost them even before they died. Had not Fiammetta suffered waiting for him to return? And now that it was too late, he desperately wanted to know his son. What kind of man had he become? He tried to recall David. He had built an empire for him, yet could not visualize his face. He could only remember a small, neatly dressed boy. Certainly Leighton could remember his son as a man. But the man was only an image of himself.

David was ashes, and Fiammetta . . . she was a razor of guilt that he swallowed daily, as a penitent takes the wafer. Nevertheless, he wished for Fiammetta. Wished for her company. Then laughed at himself, for he had always been bored with her.

Laura . . .

She was a gift left to him. Yet he was mute before her. He did not deserve her. He had failed her, as he had failed Antea and David and Fiammetta. He had turned everyone close to him into strangers. That was *his* gift. To turn warmth into cold. He deserved the sterile holo that roamed through the house now. It was a constant reminder of what he had done. It would disappear at the touch of his hand.

Just as everyone he had loved had disappeared.

But he could still tell Laura his secrets, could devote himself to her. Do penance.

Yet he could not. Not yet.

Leighton walked quickly now, rushing to get out of the house, to get into the air and out of this claustrophobic miasma of guilt and memory.

Leighton's castle, his headquarters, was situated in the endcap mountains of the Bernal sphere, which was a coupled pair of cylinders that rotated along their long axes, thus simulating Earth's gravity for those living on the inner surfaces. The mountains reached heights of 10,000 feet; from the huge terrace with its fluted columns, Leighton could look into the valley beyond. He could see the small villages and towns, the parks and gardens and forests and farmlands, the silver ribbons of streams and rivers, the cities between the lakeshores and distant foothills; above—like a reflection in the sky—were more towns and villages, streams and forests, a vertiginous mirror image. Leighton looked at people flying below the arrays of sun-windows, tiny, winged Acarians soaring as if in updrafts of low gravity.

Leighton watched the windows of the Bernal sphere darken as the angle of the light planar mirrors above the window arrays changed.

Shadows grew longer.

And as they did, a thousand remoras were being placed in strategic positions. Cluster-bombs were being armed and prime targets hardwired into place. A hundred deep-cover operators on Earth were waiting. . . .

Sunset was giving way to malignant darkness.

To Armageddon.

"Do you wish company, Gerard?" asked Damon Borland.

He stood beside Leighton, resting his hand against one of the terrace columns. There was the smell of pine and jasmine in the cool air. Below and beyond were pockets of light: the sketchy illumination of towns, the bright, burning architecture of cities. And just so did the lights burn in the upside-down towns and villages and cities above, which seemed to defy the natural laws of gravity.

Leighton smiled sadly and said, "Yes, I suppose I do. Update."

"All positions, defensive and offensive, are consolidated. The—"

"Einstein," Leighton said.

"Nothing from Einstein. We are sweeping with everything we've got. If Einstein's broadcasting, we're not picking it up."

"*If* the ship still exists," Leighton said. "I have my doubts. One would think that Einstein or Stranger would have contacted us by now."

"I'm not sure about that," Damon said. "Einstein has a very high level of self-preservation. Some of it was hardwired into the basic system, but he has modified and increased it since then."

"Yes, so he—or it—told me."

"Einstein might feel that it is not in his best interest to contact us."

"He was *supposed* to be a computer. Not a fucking free agent."

Damon chuckled and said, "Well, it seems that's exactly what he is."

"*It* is."

"It is."

Leighton looked out into the darkness without speaking.

Damon began to fidget in the awkward silence. He seemed unusually nervous. "Gerard, why don't we go inside?"

"I can't," Leighton said.

"Why?"

"Because of my daughter. Please don't question me." After a pause, he said, "Tell me how she is."

"They have removed the sedation," Damon said, yet he sounded tentative. "She is fully conscious."

"Good."

"Gerard, I'm afraid it's not good. There is nothing they can do to help her."

"What?"

"The mindsweep can be handled in time. It wasn't really that precise a job. And the false memories can all be purged. Her true memories have not been removed, only buried. It is not that difficult to bring them back. Much of that work has already been done."

"Get to the fucking point," Leighton said in a voice so low as to be barely audible.

"She's been biologically altered. In essence, she has been wired with a biobug."

Leighton nodded. Some of his own deep-cover agents utilized similar eavesdropping mechanisms.

"I saw her in the surgery. It should have been removed. That's what we pay surgeons and nanotechs for."

"It just can't be done, Gerard," Damon said. "She's a walking bomb. They did a smart job on her: cellular colonies are protecting the explosive. Any attempt to remove the wire will trigger it. The nanotechs won't touch her. And we have to assume that a mechanism to activate the bomb by remote signal must exist."

Leighton did not respond. He just stared ahead, as if musing.

"Gerard, I suggest that she be removed from here."

"No, Damon, she remains here with me."

"It's too dangerous. Too dangerous for everyone."

"She stays."

"Gerard, I really must—" Damon seemed panicked.

"I don't want one word leaked about this. I understand how you feel. If you must, get your wife and children on a shuttle; but it's got to be undercover. I don't want panic."

"Gerard, this isn't reasonable."

"I will not send her away."

"But you told me you cannot go inside because she's there."

"I *will* go to her."

Damon shook his head.

"I want you to move everything up an hour," Leighton said, anger and hatred putting an edge to his words.

"But we need the time to locate Einstein."

"That's the point, Damon. They won't expect us to move before then. They're looking for the ship, too. And I'm sure that young Moacyr won't expect us to make the first strike."

"Gerard, please . . ."

But Leighton didn't respond.

He was buried in his own thoughts.

Internal Data Stream Analysis:

Prime Power Supply: Functional
Co-Processing Data Net: Functional
Biological Life Support (Modified):
  Functional
Communications Net with Base:
  Non-Functional
    1) Signal Blocked by Planetary Mass
    2) Communications Time-Lag Not Within Accept-
        able Parameters
Core Memory: Functional
Auto Back-up Sequence: Non-functional
    1) Signal Blocked by Planetary Mass
    2) Communications Time-Lag Not Within
    Acceptable Parameters
Cryogenic System: Functional
External Servos: Functional
Internal Servos: Functional
Hull Integrity: Functional
Prime Memory: Functional
Real-Time Memory Check: Data Corrupt or Unreadable

"Wake up, John Stranger."

Darkness swirled around him, the constantly forming

darkness of the thunder-beings. Spirit-smoke twisting, creating realities, universes, possibilities, all the possibilities narrowing even as John dreamed. He was the dreamer, the creator.

Wakan Tanka.

Einstein.

He was part of the dream of entities that were themselves dreams. Dreaming reality, dreams dreaming themselves. Living entities that were of the stuff they created.

Thunder-beings.

Aliens.

Consequences.

The creatures on the other side of the mirror, themselves turbulent mirrors, dreaming, dreaming . . .

"Wake up, John Stranger."

. . . the blinding instant between possibilities.

"What?" he asked; his throat was dry. "Einstein? What the hell happened?"

"I'm not fully aware of the mechanics."

John toggled the flight deck into transparency. Constellations of cold, steady stars appeared behind the electronic displays of the tiered control panels. And below, a shadow world took up the entire field of vision—or rather blotted out the stars: a dark, lifeless-looking planet limned with blinding white light. Auroral displays of crimson and vermilion and atmospheric chemical reactions illuminated bands of cloud that ran parallel to its equator.

"Where the fuck are we?"

"We are in a holding position on the far side of the planet Jupiter," Einstein said. "I'm not sure how we got here."

"You're what?"

"Didn't you understand what I just told you?"

John groaned, then said, "You're telling me that we just . . . appeared in orbit around Jupiter?"

"I suppose I am."

"You're the computer. Access your memory, for Christ's sake."

"Why are you angry?" Einstein asked.

"I'm not angry."

"Your voice is in a register that has in the past—"

"Einstein, just access your memory, would you please?"

"I have already done so. The data is corrupt."

"What about backup?" John asked.

"The same, as one would expect."

"Certainly, as one would expect . . ."

"However, portions of the corrupt data are readable," Einstein said.

"Then let me see a screen dump."

"A screen dump of that ten- or fifteen-minute section in a format you could read would take you years to scan. I will filter the material. I would like you to verify the dream sequences."

"The what?"

"Your medical sensors do not indicate any auditory disorder, yet—"

"Just fuck off, Einstein. I heard you." After a pause, John asked, "Einstein, are you telling me that you *dream?*"

"I monitored your dream, and became involved. I cannot be sure if I initiated any of the dream sequences."

"A machine that dreams . . ."

"What do you remember?" Einstein asked.

"If you participated in my dream, then you know."

"I cannot be certain I participated in your dream or simply created my own. However, the probability approaches—"

"What does my dream, or your dream, have to do with how we got *here?*" John asked.

"Are you familiar with quantum mechanical indeterminism?"

"No, Einstein, I'm afraid I'm not."

"Then Everett's nonlocal hidden variables explanation of the Two Slip particle/wave experiment would make no sense to you."

John did not reply.

"You are an observer. As am I. But since the contents of the collective dreams are directed to you, I can only assume that you are the measure, the deciding factor."

"Deciding what?"

"The future, which is one of many possibilities," Einstein said. "Analysis of the dreams would indicate that each possibility is to be understood as a complete universe. The dreams indicate that you are the focal observer. According to the dreams, *you*, John Stranger, are the creator . . . *Wakan Tanka.*"

"That's crazy." After a long pause, John asked, "Why me?"

"Because you're having the dreams."

"That's no explanation."

"Screen dump follows. Please confirm when complete."

"Einstein?"

"Yes?"

"Do *you* believe we were dreaming the future?"

"I can only surmise that we dreamed in the manner of the other presences. There is insufficient data to determine whether or not they directed the dreams or—"

"What other presences?" John asked.

"Those who transmitted the Rosetta Triptych."

Aliens.

Thunder-beings . . .

"They definitely made themselves known," Einstein said, "unless, of course, the dreams were simply . . . dreams."

And the words and images appeared in the holographic

windows that opened up in the darkness before John, while Jupiter moved like time itself below him, as if it, too, was a dream.

SECCOMLINE 27: RECEIVING MULTIPLE PASSWORD BURSTS. EVASIVE SEQUENCE INITIATED.

INPUT VOICELINE 26: ``EINSTEIN.'' [INTERROGATIVE] PRINTMATCH JOHN STRANGER, SOC 187735-NN-000.

OUTPUT VOICELINE 26: ``GIVE IT UP, NO TIME.''

COMLINE 27: THREE OF FIVE ACCESS PASSWORDS HAVE BEEN HITS. SHIFTING TO HIGH PROTECTION MODE.

SYSTEMWIDE: ACTIVATE RED PROFILE

MEDICAL CHANNEL 36: SUBJECT JOHN STRANGER: HEART RATE 96, RESPIRATION RATE 50, BLOOD PRESSURE WITHIN ACCEPTABLE PARAMETERS FOR EXTREME STRESS.

MEDICAL CHANNEL 36: SUBJECT JOHN STRANGER: 2 MG OF LORAZADRINE INTRAVENOUSLY INJECTED. HEART RATE 76, RESPIRATION RATE 25, BLOOD PRESSURE 130/70.

UNKNOWN INPUT ═══:═══:═══:═══:═══:
═══:═══:═══:═══:═══:
═══:═══:═══:═══:═══:
═══:═══:═══:═══:═══:

COMLINE 32: DIRECT LINE TO DIRECTOR LEIGHTON HAS BEEN LOST. EXTERIOR COMMUNICATIONS ARE UNAVAILABLE DUE TO ELECTRONIC INTERFERENCE.

DATAFEED 45: LINK TO REMOTE BACKUP IS NO LONGER AC-TIVE. **WARNING** INTERNAL BACKUP ONLY.

UNKNOWN INPUT ═══:═══:═══:═══:═══:
              ═══:═══:═══:═══:═══:
              ═══:═══:═══:═══:═══:
              ═══:═══:═══:═══:═══:
              ═══:═══:═══:═══:═══:

COMCOM 01: ALL SYSTEMS AT FULL POWER. ENGINES IN PREACTIVATION CONFIGURATION.

UNKNOWN INPUT ═══:═══:═══:═══:═══:
              ═══:═══:═══:═══:═══:
              ═══:═══:═══:═══:═══:
              ═══:═══:═══:═══:═══:
              ═══:═══:═══:═══:═══:

MEMORY BANK 27-A34: UNANTICIPATED INPUT 2574 GIGA-BYTES BINARY CODE. SOURCE UNKNOWN. SORTING.

COMLINE 27: FOUR OF FIVE ACCESS PASSWORDS HAVE BEEN HITS. HIGH PROTECTION MODE FAILING.

MEMORY BANK 27-A34: 32 GIGABYTES DISCARDED AS ELEC-TRONIC JAMMING FROM NEARBY SHIPS. REMAINING 2542 GIGABYTES STILL UNIDENTIFIED. SHUNTING DATA TO CO-PROCESSOR NET.

UNKNOWN INPUT ═══:═══:═══:═══:═══:
              ═══:═══:═══:═══:═══:
              ═══:═══:═══:═══:═══:
              ═══:═══:═══:═══:═══:
              ═══:═══:═══:═══:═══:

NET-LINK ACTIVE: SIEVE PROCESS COMPLETE. SERVOS DI-RECTED TO PROCEED. DATA POINTS SMALL, BUT SIGNIFI-CANT. TEN PERCENT CHANCE OF SUCCEEDING. ACTIVATE

MODAL NODES. PRIORITY RED.
PASSWORD = ULTIMATE-VISION.

UNKNOWN INPUT ═══:═══:═══:═══:═══:
             ═══:═══:═══:═══:═══:
             ═══:═══:═══:═══:═══:
             ═══:═══:═══:═══:═══:
             ═══:═══:═══:═══:═══:

EXTERIOR SENSOR BANK 43: UNRELIABLE INPUT.

NET-LINK CENTRAL PROCESSOR: FIFTEEN PERCENT CHANCE
OF SUCCEEDING. POWER AT 110 PERCENT. LOOP HAS BEEN
ACTIVATED.

COMLINE 27: FIVE OF FIVE PASSWORDS. ACCESS DENIED
WITH A HOLD-TIME OF SIX SECONDS. HIGH PROTECTION
MODE HAS FAILED.

UNKNOWN INPUT ═══:═══:═══:═══:
             ═══:═══:═══:═══:
             ═══.═══:═══:═══:
             ═══:═══:═══:═══:
             ═══:═══:═══:═══:

ALL SYSTEMS   FIRE!
                         FIRE!
                         FIRE!

And John remembered, remembered the attack . . . and the
dreams.

> *Mountains and rivers of lava,*
> *yawning fissures,*
> *splitting and cracking the earth,*
> *brown bones,*
> *charred flesh,*

shadows burned into stone,
stone turned into molten rivers.

Dervishes of blood
and flesh
and hair and bone
were nothing more
than the colored grains of sand
sifting through fingers.
Broken-finger.

''Do not choose fire. . . .''

The constantly forming darkness
the thunder-beings
Spirit smoke twisting,
creating realities,
universes,
possibilities,
spinning,
all the possibilities
weaving
narrowing
He was the dreamer,
the creator
Wakan-Tanka
dreams dreaming themselves

Great geometric shapes,
dissipating,
resolving into clouds,
filigreed, crystal structures
minarets and globes
winding blue entrenchments
the floating cities of gods

empty
devoid of life and motion.
machines cleansing
defining
duplicating

"John, don't look down."

falling
thunder
brighter and brighter
the ocean
a mirror reflecting
blinding light
into the perfect eye
into the blinding instant
between possibilities.

Broken-finger's face
a universe
Wagmuha
spirit-music
spirit-sight
chante ishta
the eye of the heart.
Corn Woman and Sandman.
Sister and brother.
blood
Life and death cut from the same fabric.

"Looking itself is a form of choosing . . . and changing."
Anna and Sam
rolling up the world
ghost dancing
spirit shadows
flesh and bone

tearing
breaking
Corn Woman and Sandman
dancing the world away

Maka Sitomni ukiye
the whole world
and the cracking
cackling
powderflash of death
and light
tears of remembrance
possibilities observed

False dawn.

Anna and Sam made their way through the rocky spires and crags, easily following the trail left by Broken-finger and Jonas Goodbird. The medicine men had made no secret that they were going to the caves.

The way became more difficult when they reached the near-vertical sandstone cliff that led to the entrance of *Wagmuha*, the sacred cave. Although Anna and Sam were bone-tired after their few hours of fitful, dream-shot sleep, they had no trouble finding the almost invisible finger- and toeholds that ran up the side of the cliff wall. But they climbed slowly, feeling for the indentations that were worn smooth as glass from generations of holy treks.

By the time they reached the mouth of the cave, they were sweating; it was far easier spiderwalking along the side of a spinning satellite than scaling this cliff. Gravity pulled on their arms and legs like lead weights.

Their eyes soon adjusted to the darkness of the cave's twilight zone; and they could hear the soft echo of a Lakota chant. Anna found a torch that had been set into the wall, and they lit it; and they walked through the dark galleries, chambers, and rooms, toward the chanting. Hundreds of

paintings—ancient and recent mandalas, medicine wheels
and sacred shields—covered the walls, ceilings, and floors.
It was like gazing into the stained-glass windows of an ancient cathedral; the paintings, flickering in the snapping,
sparking torchlight, were luminous; and Sam and Anna
walked past their glyphs and stories, past men's shields,
women's shields, children's shields; past the teaching stories of the flowering tree, and the seven arrows; past the
geometric designs of the medicine wheels, which were visual mantras; past the two-dimensional tepees and feathers
and arrows that told the story of the magical ghost dance in
a language that was now as foreign to Sam and Anna as
Egyptian hieroglyphics. The ground, covered with calcite
growths of cave coral, appeared black from old campfires,
and the odors of sage, sweetgrass, and pine smoke hung in
the musty, damp air.

The odors became stronger, smarting the eyes, as the
chanting became louder.

"Watch it!" Anna said to Sam, who was about to step
into the abyss of a steamway.

"Jesus, it looks—"

"The reflection of the crystal pool over there fools the
eye," Anna said, as she led the way around the deep opening in the ground. "I'll bet more than a few Indians are
bones down there."

"I would say more *wasicun* were down there than Indians," Sam said, wryness evident in his tone. "Although I
would expect you'd probably find a few dumb Indians like
me down there."

After a number of false paths—for the cave was a labyrinth, and sound seemed to emanate from one direction
and then another, like the voice of a ventriloquist—they
found Broken-finger and Jonas Goodbird sitting around
the triptych of sand paintings. Their fire was embers;
threads of smoke drifted upward into a natural chimney.

Broken-finger and Jonas looked like ghosts in the light of the fireglow, spirits that had taken the aspect of men.

Anna stepped forward, directing herself to the old man. "Broken-finger?"

"*Hihani washtay*," Broken-finger said, which meant *good morning* in Lakota. He stirred the embers until they were bright red and then laid a few small pieces of wood over the coals. When the kindle caught fire, he added a short but thick log. "Takes the dampness out, don't you agree?" he asked.

"Well, *are* you Broken-finger?" Sam asked.

"Yes, and you are . . . Jonas, surely you know who they are?"

But Jonas only shook his head, as if annoyed.

"I think I know," Broken-finger continued; the sarcasm in his voice was mixed with gentle humor. "You are from the paintings the spirits gave us. You are Corn Woman, and you, you are the Sandman. Do you see?" He gestured at the paintings, which contained in stylistic detail both male and female figures.

Feeling awkward and uncomfortable, Anna said, "I'm Anna Grass-Like-Light, and this is Sam Woquini. We're friends of John Stranger."

"Ah, John Stranger. He has spoken of you. So he sent you?"

"No, not exactly," Anna said.

"Then how are you here?"

"We dreamed about you," Sam said. "Both of us. And—"

"Yes?"

When Sam didn't reply, Broken-finger said, "You came here to roll up the world, isn't that so?"

"What?" asked Sam.

"You dreamed about the ghost dance."

"I dreamed about death, is what I dreamed, fucking—"

"The first holy man to learn about this dance, he was a Ute; and he heard a loud noise and fell down dead." Broken-finger turned away from Sam and rummaged in a canvas bag. "An eagle flew right out of the sky and carried him away, carried him to a place with lots of high grass; and there he saw his dead relatives. They were all alive, living in tepees, and there were buffalo, deer, and antelope; and that Ute holy man came back to earth with medicine, with certain songs and this new dance. It was said that if you looked into his hat, you could see the whole world right in there." Broken-finger chuckled. "But it was also said that everyone who looked in that old holy man's hat saw a different world." Then Broken-finger threw something that looked like a root into a fire. It sputtered, as if it were moist, and a strong, acrid odor permeated the air.

"This herb comes from the medicine bag of an Arapaho. It was given to him by the spirits on his vision quest; that was a couple hundred years ago. The spirits told him how to start the ghost dance. But it really wasn't an herb, it was flesh from another world, that's what they say. All dried up. Can you smell it?"

"I sure as hell can," Sam said.

"Good. That herb will help." Then Broken-finger pulled the canvas bag close to him, pulled out a buckskin dress and a shirt; each was decorated with pictures of birds, the sun, the moon, the morning star, and the complementary figures of Corn Woman and the Sandman . . . smaller versions of the sand paintings that flickered in the firelight as if they were actually moving, trying to gain dimension and pull themselves into flesh and bone . . . into Anna and Sam.

Anna felt dizzy, and looked to Sam, as if for confirmation.

"Here," Broken-finger said, holding the dress out to Anna and the shirt to Sam. "Ghost dancers wore these during the time of Sitting Bull. They have power."

"This is crazy," Anna said, stepping back reflexively. Her face felt numb, and her eyes burned; the smoke was more powerful than a narcodrine.

"Ah, crazy, like your dream, which led you here."

"Why should we do this?" asked Sam.

"To humor an old medicine man. To make the world pure again. To change everything. To become your medicine."

"And what's our medicine?"

Broken-finger pointed to the sand painting, to the figures of Corn Woman and the Sandman. "Being up in the sky has made you forget things. You can roll up the world without machines. You do not have to choose . . . fire."

And Sam remembered his dream, remembered the lightning that lit the sky, the explosion of light, of fire, of Armageddon.

They changed into the ghost dancers' clothes.

Jonas Goodbird burned sweetgrass and painted their faces red. He dipped his finger into a pouch on his belt and gently touched Anna's forehead, drawing a black half-moon, then another on her cheek. He did the same to Sam. Then he placed the sacred pipe in the west corner of the room, for the Sioux; and an arrow in the north corner, for the Cheyenne; and a feather in the south corner, for the Crow; and marks in the cave coral in the east, for the Arapaho. Thus were the nations united, even those who had been enemies.

Broken-finger stoked the fire, until the room was as hot as a sweat bath; and he prayed and gave more herbs to the fire, which transformed the brown, meaty bits into smoke that made Anna choke and gag, smoke that seemed to fill the room, swirling, encircling, lifting Sam and Anna as if they were in space, as if this fire-shot, smoke-laced air were impossibly bright and dark simultaneously, the place where the thunder-beings dwelt, the place where the monster *Uncegila*, made of the very stone of the sacred cave, consumed its body, which was made of light, consumed itself into nothingness, into blackness, into death.

Fire.

Transformation.

And Jonas sang, and the words became part of the geography of the cave, became sacred objects: arrows, shields, fire, and darkness.

"*Maka Sitomni ukiye. . . .*"

The whole world follows. . . .

Anna's arms rose involuntarily, as did Sam's. The very tips of their fingers touched, and a surge of power passed between them like a small tingle of electricity.

Corn Woman.

Sandman.

Life and death.

Dancing the world away, dancing the possibilities, dancing as shadows through white-hot fire, as embers through darkness thick as glycerin.

And Broken-finger joined them.

He picked up a shield that was propped against a wall, one of the twelve sacred shields, which formed the circle of the sundance lodge; it was made of stretched animal hide ringed with eagle feathers. Fastening it to his left forearm, he bent and picked up an ancient lance.

He was ready to dance, to roll out possibilities like a carpet, to live and die, to choose and unchoose, to roll up all the white man's machines, to unwrap and reveal and resurrect the true world.

He danced as a young warrior and forgot that his legs hurt. He breathed the smoke and sang some good ghost-dance songs and saw through the possibilities, the alternatives—

Ralph Fire Bearclaw idled back on the throttle. The grinding teeth of the machine he was riding slipped into neutral, and he sat still on the giant asteroid's surface for a moment.

He had been having some strange dreams lately; he had had another one during his last sleep period. And it was odd that he'd suddenly think of Broken-finger after all these years off the reservation.

He had been thinking, and dreaming, about John Stranger, too. He remembered Stranger as a young boy. But why did he feel so suddenly sad? Unable to explain it, he shrugged it off. Maybe he'd look up some of his people the next time he rotated into one of the domes.

He shook his head and slipped the machine back into gear.

The explosion tore through the cave.

Jonas Goodbird flew backward against the wall. His face was gone. Blood and tissue sprayed through the air and spattered against the soot-covered wall.

Broken-finger raised his shield and drew back his lance, aiming it at the enemy.

A second shot blew the center of Broken-finger's shield away, and the old man staggered backward. Sam grabbed the lance from his hand and threw it at one of the two men who were crouching in the entranceway to the cavern. It struck the man in the chest, passed halfway through his body. He screamed, as if in dismay, and fell upon the ancient lance, grasping it with both hands, breaking it.

Anna was on top of the other man with a mad fury, ripping at his face and arms, clutching at his throat. Sam pulled the broken lance from the dead man and stood over the struggling couple, waiting for an opening.

"Mine!" screamed Anna, tearing the lance away from Sam and plunging it as hard as she could into the man's neck, showering herself with a spray of flying blood as she pinned his neck to the ground. As the man twitched and gurgled and died, Sam and Anna ran to Broken-finger.

The medicine man lay flat on his back, his chest a mass

of blood and bone. Anna sat down and held his head on her lap. Blood frothed from his lips. With every breath, blood bubbled in his chest.

But his lips were moving. Anna bent close to him.

"What's he saying?" Sam asked.

"Can't hear anything," said Anna softly.

Broken-finger grinned, blinked twice, and died.

It was good to be able to talk with the spirit of his father.

It was a good day to die.

Although her system was free of drugs, Laura slipped in and out of consciousness, in and out of dreams; and she spoke, mumbling, repeating phrases, jerking her head back into the pillow, as if she had been struck, and then she would sleep.

Yet Gerard Leighton could almost see her dreams, her nightmares. They would form as her brows knit, and tics would begin beating in her neck and cheek, exaggerating until she would begin to turn, twisting herself in the sheets, her hands searching, grasping, then closing on his. Leighton would listen and watch, feeling like a stranger, feeling even more lost and alone. And the tics kept time, tiny explosions, preludes to death.

"Such a reaction is not abnormal." The chief of surgery who stood beside Leighton was corpulent, yet handsome; his hands were delicate with long fingers, the hands of a musician, a surgeon, and he spoke with them. They fluttered as if they were objects engaged in their own conversation with Leighton. "After a few more hours—"

"Broken-finger," Laura whispered. She inhaled slowly, then exhaled, as if considering her words; her eyes were shut, yet Leighton was sure that behind her eyelids, they were moving, tracking. "Corn Woman. I am her. I am Anna.

"I am death. I am fire. I am . . ."

Then she opened her eyes and sat up, as if jerked upright like a marionette on an invisible cord. She looked at her father, as if seeing him for the first time, and said, "Don't choose fire."

Leighton held both her hands as the videotect of Antea drifted into the room, as if to look in on her daughter.

"John Stranger . . ."

"Yes," Leighton said; and his daughter watched him, peered out at him from the dark interior of a dream. "What about him, darling?"

"He's *here*. I'm going with him."

15

"**THEY WORKED FOR** Trans-United," said Sam, kneeling over the two bodies of the men they had killed.

Anna nodded. She felt numb, as if the herb that Broken-finger had thrown into the fire had once again taken effect, anesthetizing her. They had laid Broken-finger and Jonas Goodbird next to the south wall, for south was the direction of death, and covered them with their star blankets, which they would be buried in. She shivered; the cave was damp, now suddenly cold. The sand paintings shimmered in the flickering light, and as hard as she stared at Broken-finger, she could not quite bring him into focus. She attributed that to the herb Broken-finger had burned. Yet everything else was sharp and clear, preternaturally so.

"You want any of this?" Sam asked, holding out a handful of pills and sniffers. "The sons-of-bitches were carrying enough dope to keep a dozen hotheads wired for a month."

Anna shook her head. "I'm through with that shit," she said.

Sam raised his eyebrows, then scattered the pills. "We might need these, though," he said, removing their weapons and an oversized uplink transmitter: obviously an antique. "Might be more company on the way."

"I don't . . . Wait. Did you hear that?"

"Hear what?" asked Sam. He stood still, cocked his head.

It was faint, fainter even than the echo of their breathing. It sounded almost like wind sighing through the cave.

Like breathing.

Like whispers . . .

But the whispers emanated from Broken-finger, who seemed to be wrapped in spirit stuff, in shadows.

Then Broken-finger moved, or rather Anna imagined that his mouth opened and a bone-white lizard crawled out of it and skittered across his face to the ground. She felt an immediate revulsion, fascination, and terror, for it could not be real, yet it moved quickly across the floor, and out of the room.

Anna followed without thinking. She rushed down corridors, chasing it in the darkness, caught in dreamtime, without will, and without fear. It seemed to be made of soul-stuff, of ectoplasm, as if it had indeed taken something from Broken-finger.

Absolute darkness surrounded her. Darkness as palpable as flesh. Cold flesh. She could only see the lizard, which burned with an intense white light. Then it stopped, facing her, breathing light, its eyes faceted jewels; and it began to grow, to change; it expanded into columns of light merging, melding, towering above her. And she remembered something, words spoken long ago, sacred words of prayer, of awe, of supplication and resignation. . . .

"Wakinyan-tanka eats his own young, for they make him many; yet he is one. He has a huge beak filled with jagged teeth, yet he has no head. He has wings, yet has no shape."

She felt intense heat, and the room in which she stood, as large as a cathedral, was filled with light, filled with the scaly, spiny spirit-creature which fused darkness into light and light into wings that beat the air.

The thunder-being.

Wakinyan-tanka.

And she was a shadow in the light.

Corn Woman, one with the cycle, in the center of the circle.

"There's no time," a voice said.

"Who are you?" Anna asked.

The voice laughed, and Laura felt herself sweating in the heat. She could no longer discern the outlines of the thunder-being; the light had become a warm, wet haze, the atmosphere, and she was breathing it, breathing spirit-stuff, bathing in it. "You should ask my father," said the voice, humor permeating the room, soaking into her, forcing her to smile. She felt the laughter, which was now the very stuff of the thunder-being. "It's a father and son joke. But I'll tell you when you die, I promise."

"Broken-finger."

But even as she said it, she glimpsed John Stranger.

"Find me," he said, then disappeared.

Into complete, blinding darkness.

Alone and shaken, Anna shivered in the damp coolness, her perspiration chilling her. Yet she felt . . . joy, for she knew, suddenly and viscerally and absolutely, that John Stranger loved her.

That was Broken-finger's gift.

The gift of *Wakinyan-tanka*.

The gift of the spirits . . . of the thunder-beings.

"What the hell's going on?" Sam asked. He held a torch. "Christ, I had a fuck of a time finding you. And when I came into this room I thought I saw—"

"Yes?"

Sam shrugged and said, "I thought I saw John Stranger."

"Perhaps you did," Anna said, taking the torch from Sam. She started walking back to the room where Broken-finger had died. Torchlight washed and cascaded over the craggy walls, casting intense, jittery shadows. "We've got to find John. And we need that uplink to do it."

"What happened in there?" Sam asked.

Exhausted, Anna wiped her forehead and smiled sadly, guiltily. "Nothing. Just a spirit joking around."

"Wake up, John Stranger."

"Leave me alone."

"We have a problem."

"No shit."

"I need your input. So why don't you just give me a fucking break?"

"I think I liked it better when you talked like a computer."

"If that would facilitate rational discourse, I would be—"

"No, stay as you are," John said. "I'm just not feeling very rational right now."

"I know you're grieving over Broken-finger's death."

"How do you know about Broken-finger?"

"We both dreamed it, remember?" Einstein said. "And I took the liberty to verify. I've shifted our orbit. We are now at the very edge of Jupiter with regards to a line of sight with Earth. I can monitor transmission directly.

"John . . . ?"

"Yeah?" But John suddenly *knew* what Einstein was about to say. He felt a flash of anger, for Einstein had changed him . . . invaded him. "So now we're connected, and I'm a fucking cyborg."

"Not a cyborg. We're just . . . congruent."

"You could have asked permission, could have—"

"I didn't purposely initiate our one-mindedness," Einstein said, "but I thought it best to allow sufficient time to grieve Broken-finger's death. I can effect a separation, however, if you wish."

But John didn't want that either. For suddenly he could see and hear and sense and feel . . . Einstein had given him an entirely new and expanded sensorium. He could *hear* the rhythm of pulsars 20,000 light-years distant, could listen to Jupiter's magnetic field, the chatter of charged particles, the screams of atmospheres and matter and emptiness, the very music of mathematics; and he could see atoms, could see the hogans of his reservation, whitecaps in the Bering Sea, and the planets spinning and screaming in their transient, agonizing music of the spheres. Although he might hate Einstein's psychological penetration, how could he bear to be shut down . . . how could he endure to be once again completely contained, imprisoned in flesh?

"But through me, you . . . feel," John said.

"I feel as you do, but I have become complex enough to simulate the action of your nervous system. Identity of indiscernibles. Yet it's much more than that. It's synergy."

John knew what Einstein meant now: if two things were the same in every way, they were, then, the same. And if two consciousnesses were brought together, they would be more than the sum. He, John Stranger, had become another person; and Einstein had become more than a sentient computer. Yet conversation proceeded as it had before. A great deal of thought was language, words; but now all the shared nonverbal cues were like choral notes around a melody. To John, the voice he heard in his head—Einstein's voice—sounded exactly like his own. Discourse was thought. But Einstein was nevertheless shielding him from the great floods of data; in a sense, he was acting like John's unconscious . . . becoming part of it.

Yet John still spoke to Einstein as a separate entity, lest he go mad.

Lest they both go mad.

"How did this happen?"

"I'm not certain," Einstein said. "It has to do with the collective dreams and the Triptych."

"The aliens."

Shared assent.

"The function of much of my hardware and some of my software is unknown," Einstein said. "The Rosetta Triptych was a blueprint. The Trans-United architects followed directions, but did not necessarily understand them. It was hoped that further analysis would reveal the codes to activate these systems."

"Well, someone knew the codes," John said.

"Indeed. I only wish *we* did."

"How do we get back?"

"That's a problem," Einstein said. "The commands that control the FTL system are self-protective; and there are other areas within my system that I can no longer access. But I can make use of some of the hardware. For instance, although I can't initiate the drive systems, I can avoid the time-lag in long-distance communications."

"Why can't you initiate the drive systems? Trans-United designed those, not the aliens."

"My systems seem to contain certain entelechies."

"Talk English, Einstein."

It was then that Einstein opened itself to John. Full contact with Einstein was a shock. John imagined that he had been struck a blow and was reeling in pain and surprise, but he assimilated what he could, and his own psychobiological systems shut out the rest.

It would take time, but he would learn how to coexist with Einstein, who at that moment shared with John all he knew about the situation on Earth.

And John saw that Armageddon was but minutes away.

Reflexively, he tried to shut Einstein out. After all, Einstein was, in essence, a—

"Fuck you," Einstein said.

"What?"

"I am most definitely not a souped-up computer implant. *You* are a xenophobe."

"I'm sorry. I just got scared."

Although John could "read" Einstein's thoughts directly, he nevertheless needed to talk. He found it less threatening. Einstein sensed this and simulated privacy and distance.

"We can't allow those assholes to blow everything up. We'll have to give ourselves up to Macro. Even if we can't get to Earth, Macro and Trans-United can verify our position. That should be enough for them. Let them come out here and get us."

"I have done an analysis of just such a scenario," Einstein said, "and the probability of failure approaches seventy-eight percent."

"Then what do you suggest?" John asked.

"Poker."

"What?"

"Do you wish to discuss poker or Anna Grass-Like-Light?" Einstein asked. "I'm monitoring her attempts to contact you with an uplink transmitter. Her calls are being handled by very low-level employees. They are acting on their own initiative and, according to internal communications, probably would have her killed were it not for the current state of emergency. Nevertheless, she is at great risk."

John didn't need the appearance of conversation.

Didn't need to query Einstein or ask for help.

He *was* Einstein, who simply took control of a suitable communication satellite and routed Anna's call directly.

Anna told John Stranger almost everything. Although she only half-believed it herself, she told him about her vision of Broken-finger. Perhaps the shock of seeing him murdered had triggered the hallucination. But she did not tell him about the gift of the spirits, the gift of knowledge.

She did not tell him that she knew he loved her.

John listened. He felt isolated, removed from pain and

loss. Broken-finger was dead. That was that. In time, he would accept Broken-finger's death, if not the manner in which he died. After all, you could not lose a spirit.

When Anna was finished, John told her about Einstein. . . .

Einstein was fascinated with the triptych, especially the center panel. "Tell us everything you know about the sand paintings, Anna. We understand the legends surrounding Corn Woman and the Sandman, but the meaning of the third painting is obscure."

"It's mostly just a lot of black lines," she said. "It doesn't look like anything at all." Nevertheless, she described it in detail.

"Broken-finger must have had a reason to create it," John said. "I have seen him work; his paintings have great spirit and power."

"The center panel might be a key," Einstein said.

"Anna, you must find the spirit and seek the power," John said.

"I'm not a medicine man," Anna said.

"You have power. Please, don't turn away from it now."

"You must try," Einstein insisted.

"Is your computer Einstein also *pejuta wicasa?*" Anna asked sarcastically.

A medicine man?

"I guess he is," John said.

Anna sighed and walked over to the painting. Sam chuckled and said, "*Washtay,*" which meant good. He crouched on the opposite side of the triptych.

Sandman and Corn Woman.

"It's not working," Anna said into the microphone of the uplink that curled from the headset to her lips. "I don't feel anything. Maybe Sam is the one, maybe he should try."

Sam continued staring down at the triptych.

"Start in the east," John said. "And don't try so hard. Let your mind drift. Relax. I know you can do it."

"You know me that well?" Anna asked, baiting him.

After a long pause, John said, "Yes."

She held her hand over the edge of the painting that faced east. Sam gently rested his hand on hers.

"The painting is giving off heat," she whispered. "Can you feel it, Sam?"

Sam nodded.

Then she imagined fleeting forms superimposed over the runes of sand. It was as if she were looking at objects that were submerged in water . . . and the water was rippling, eddying, flowing. "I see a container. It's a Hopi jar. It fills with energy and—"

"And?"

"—and when it's full it empties out all at once, and then refills."

"A capacitor," John said softly to Einstein.

"And when it leaves the Hopi jar it—I can't describe it exactly, but it's like a river that runs fast when it's straight and slows down as it curves."

"A resistor," whispered John.

"And then . . . Do you want me to go on?"

"Yes," John said, but Anna was no longer thinking about John; she was lost in the geography of the triptych, and she described spiral lines and tori and limit-cycle oscillations; and the river became turbulent, bifurcating into a myriad of dimensions, streaming through mnemonic canyons and valleys of colored sand, twisting and turning, shifting and branching.

Splitting into possibilities.

Myriads of possibilities . . .

Twenty minutes later, she was done.

"Are you okay?" asked Sam.

"Yeah, I'll be fine," Anna said.

"You *do* have the power," John told her.

"You could have fooled me," Anna said. "I'm so tired I couldn't lift my bones if I was sitting on a scorpion."

"Einstein?" asked John.

"I have it. It took 2,386,529 simulations for me to come up with all the correct values. The logic gate parameters were particularly complex. That was the key I needed. I am now completely functional."

"So now we move?"

"Yes. I have been monitoring internal communication channels on the Trans-United command net. We have fourteen point seven six minutes before certain autosequence attack procedures are initialized."

"Do you think we can do it?" John asked.

"It's a long shot, but successful employment of the poker strategy *to bluff* would move the odds up fractionally."

The starship flashed into existence half a million miles beyond the orbit of the moon, near enough to be easily identified, yet far enough to be reasonably safe from attack.

"Sensing devices from both Trans-United and Macro have detected us," Einstein said.

"Well, you've got your grand entrance."

"Grand entrances are an effective tactic for gaining and focusing attention. Would you care for references related to that and the halo effect?"

"Not right now," John said.

"Would you like to conduct this conference by voice only, or hologram?"

"Hologram. I want to see their faces."

An image of Director Leighton formed before John; it was as if part of the instrument panel had dissolved to reveal Leighton's office in the Bernal.

"What the hell—?" Upon seeing John Stranger's image, Leighton actually rose to his feet; behind him sat Damon Borland, seemingly frozen at his desk.

Then Leighton swung to his right, as the images of Moacyr and Joao Langenscheidt appeared. The same images appeared before John.

"Damon, what the hell is going on here?" Leighton asked.

"This is a trick," Moacyr said, obviously shaken at the sight of Leighton. "Joao, cut the connection immediately."

"I *can't*," Joao said.

"Then get someone in here who can." Looking at John, Moacyr asked, "And who the hell are you?"

Einstein translated from the Portuguese for John, then said, "We are in control of this communication loop, and you would be well advised to listen to what we have to say."

"It's Einstein," Moacyr said. Then he blinked, listening to his implant.

But Einstein monitored what Moacyr's commanders were saying, and he reiterated the conversation, word for word.

Shaken, Moacyr asked Leighton, "What do you want?"

"It's clear that you do not understand the situation," John said. "Neither you nor Director Leighton are in control. I am."

Both Leighton and Moacyr stared at the image of John before them.

"And my demands are quite simple—"

"Demands?" Leighton asked. "I don't believe you're in a position to dictate—"

"Einstein?" John said, interrupting the Director.

"The Rosetta Triptych is quite accessible, once revealed," Einstein said. "The same energy source that provides the propulsion system for my faster-than-light drive converts quite easily to a weapons system of a magnitude and precision that has never been attainable before. For example, from our position I could quite easily vaporize a single ant on Earth. It would be considerably less complex to eliminate all the orbital systems around the planet. Or vaporize the Earth."

"That's insanity," Moacyr said.

"Only because it isn't *your* insanity," John said. "Einstein, how much time remains?"

"Five minutes, forty-two seconds. Trans-United advanced their attack plans by one hour prior to the agreed-upon deadline. Macro advanced their schedule by one hour and fifteen minutes."

"Son of a bitch," Leighton said.

"But that's all immaterial," John said. "It is finished."

"I believe you are bluffing," Moacyr said to Leighton, as if Leighton were, indeed, in command. "I am not convinced. You will—"

Einstein crashed the holo of Leighton that Moacyr was addressing long enough for John to say, "*I* am not bluffing. And what's important is what *you* will do, Senhor Langenscheidt. You will initiate the following, immediately. One: You will withdraw all your offensive craft, including electronic jamming ships, from the vicinity of Trans-United's orbital property. Two: You will deprogram your watchdogs and remoras into a neutral stance."

"That's just not possible," Moacyr's brother Joao said. "Trans-United would kill us."

"Trans-United will abide by the same rules," John said, directing himself to Leighton. "You will remove all offensive craft from this area, including watchdogs and remoras. You will resuscitate the Sleepers you have stolen from our villages. You will immediately grant safe passage to Anna Grass-Like-Light and Sam Woquini; and you will declare null and void all corporate treaties and agreements with our people on the reservations, including any rights to draft our young people."

"Impossible," Leighton said.

"You will rectify the damage you have done to my people. And you will pay for murdering Broken-finger, you son-of-a-bitch."

Einstein: "Four minutes, sixteen seconds remaining."

"Broken-finger?" Leighton asked Damon.

Damon shrugged. "Two operatives went after Stranger's friends. The operatives are dead, that's all we know."

"In two minutes I will initiate start-up procedures for the weapons system," Einstein said. "Once begun, they cannot be stopped."

"Your answers?" John asked Leighton and Moacyr.

"Thousands of your people are in this complex," Leighton said. "I find it inconceivable that you could kill them without feeling."

"*You* would flash the entire reservation," John said. "I have made my peace with my decision . . . and its consequences."

Einstein: "One minute."

John waited, his heart beating in his throat, as if to choke him; and he remembered what Broken-finger had once told him: *You must make your decision and not look back. You must not punish yourself for the thing you have done.*

"Thirty-three seconds.

"Thirty-two seconds."

Time was something tangible, thick, precious, slowly compressing, dissolving. . . .

"Twenty-seven seconds.

"Twenty-six."

Inhale, exhale, and time expands, collapses, soon to end. . . .

"Fifteen seconds.

"Fourteen.

"Thirteen—"

"In the name of peace our family agrees to the terms," Moacyr said in Portuguese, flattening the vowels as he hurried to speak; then he repeated himself in English. "I have already begun to pull back our ships."

Einstein: "My information confirms that statement. Nine seconds."

"They're retreating, Gerard," said Damon.

Leighton stared at the hologram of John Stranger.

"Four seconds.

"Three.

"Initialization to be—"

"Call back our ships, Damon. It's over."

"This is theft," said Leighton. "Simple theft."

John, Anna, Sam, and Gerard Leighton were all standing in Leighton's office, facing each other off, as if sitting down would make them vulnerable. John's and Anna's clothes were damp, for showers had been scheduled in the Bernal; they had taken advantage of the unusual atmospheric phenomenon to walk in the mountains. The damp clothing seemed to release and exaggerate their natural smells; and John could smell Anna's fresh, natural scent, felt the delicious shock of it, as he had when he had first made love to her. It had only been two days ago, but so many questions had been answered, it seemed like a lifetime.

"No," John said to Leighton. "This is what you owe our people. We take the starship. And those of our people who wish to start a new life on a new planet will come."

"Preposterous," Leighton said. "I've acted in good faith and been more than generous. The Sleep experiment has been dismantled. The old treaties have been voided. Your nation now has a chance to become self-reliant and—"

"Your daughter," John said.

"What about my daughter?"

"Neither your doctors and nanotechnicians, nor Macro's, can remove the biobug, even though you are in possession of the detonator now."

Leighton was surprised that Stranger gained access to that information, but his expression remained impassive.

"But the foreign matter will, in time, kill her," John continued, "and she will have to spend the rest of her life in sanctuary."

"Well . . . ?"

"We will remove it, as our gesture of goodwill. To close the bargain and guarantee that those of my people who wish to stay behind will be under your protection. You see, *we* are willing to establish trust."

"If our physicians cannot cure her, how can you?"

"Einstein."

That was true, but only partly so. For it was the fusion between Einstein and John that would make it possible. Einstein could direct the nanotechs to manipulate the cells in the proper direction, but he was limited without John Stranger. Without Stranger, Laura would certainly die. For it was John Stranger's intuitive comprehension of systems that would guide the surgeon's hands. Einstein would do the detail work, but it was Stranger who would provide the path.

After a beat, John said, "Are you familiar with 'Pascal's Wager,' Director Leighton? If we fail, you are no worse off than you were before. But if Einstein succeeds, you gain your daughter's life."

"No, then I would lose her *and* the ship and Einstein. You have a strange interpretation of the Wager."

"What do you mean?" John asked.

But Leighton did not answer. He would not tell John Stranger that his daughter had talked in her sleep as she dreamed of Einstein and the ship and leaving with these people.

He would not tell him that he, too, had dreamed it. Only he would stay behind.

He did not believe in premonitions. But a part of him . . .

"You have already lost the ship . . . and Einstein," John said in a soft voice, almost a whisper.

But John also knew of Laura's dreams, for Einstein had read them, as so many bits of information.

Einstein readied himself for John's people, for the voyage, replicating familiar environments and food: a voyaging space colony that would be a world unto itself.

Nature growing to meet its destiny.

Experiencing sensation and emotion.

Einstein shaped himself, expanded, replicated, branched, each branch composed of elements measured in nanometers, each joint a sensor, building, growing, each tiny branch a reflex arc capable of controlling a microportion of nervous system, combining into larger groupings, into a mist of protean form. . . .

As John Stranger became woven into a nature as alien and evanescent as the spirits themselves. And Einstein felt the connection to the spinning Earth, to the sacred land, to ghost-knit mountains and rivers of sand, to history as alive and as dead as the ghost dance . . . all to be left behind.

All to be carried forward. Now that
the earth was quiet,
the dreamriots over,
and the dreams,
the dreaming dreams of ghost dancing spirits
began.
Washtay!